The girl was human in appearance and not yet three years old

Wearing an indigo-colored one-piece suit and carrying a rag doll with red hair and a dress that matched the child's clothing exactly. The girl had snow-blond hair hanging loosely to past her shoulders, and her large, blue eyes were wide with excitement. Behind her, another figure strode at a more languid pace, shorter than a man with grayish-pink skin and a bulbous, hairless head. Two huge, upslanting eyes dominated his scrunched-up face, black watery pools like the bottom of two wells lost in shadow. Beneath these, twin nares lay flat where a man's nose would protrude, and a small slit of mouth held the faintest expression of pleasure, the corners turned up infinitesimally.

"Briggly," the little girl said, laughing as she ran up to the woman in the black leather armor.

Brigid knelt on the floor, stretching her arms wide to clasp the girl and pull her toward her.

"Welcome, Brigid Baptiste," the gray-skinned creature acknowledged from behind the little girl.

It was all so easy.

Other titles in this series:

James Axler
Outlanders®

PLANET
HATE

A GOLD EAGLE BOOK FROM
WORLDWIDE®

TORONTO • NEW YORK • LONDON
AMSTERDAM • PARIS • SYDNEY • HAMBURG
STOCKHOLM • ATHENS • TOKYO • MILAN
MADRID • WARSAW • BUDAPEST • AUCKLAND

Recycling programs
for this product may
not exist in your area.

First edition February 2012

ISBN-13: 978-0-373-63873-4

PLANET HATE

Copyright © 2012 by Worldwide Library

Special thanks to Rik Hoskin for his contribution to this work.

Printed in U.S.A.

Fire will burn itself out if it does not find anything to burn.
—Arab proverb

I have not yet begun to fight!
—John Paul Jones
1747–1792

The Road to Outlands—
From Secret Government Files to the Future

Almost two hundred years after the global holocaust, Kane, a former Magistrate of Cobaltville, often thought the world had been lucky to survive at all after a nuclear device detonated in the Russian embassy in Washington, D.C. The aftermath—forever known as skydark—reshaped continents and turned civilization into ashes.

Nearly depopulated, America became the Deathlands—poisoned by radiation, home to chaos and mutated life forms. Feudal rule reappeared in the form of baronies, while remote outposts clung to a brutish existence.

What eventually helped shape this wasteland were the redoubts, the secret preholocaust military installations with stores of weapons, and the home of gateways, the locational matter-transfer facilities. Some of the redoubts hid clues that had once fed wild theories of government cover-ups and alien visitations.

Rearmed from redoubt stockpiles, the barons consolidated their power and reclaimed technology for the villes. Their power, supported by some invisible authority, extended beyond their fortified walls to what was now called the Outlands. It was here that the rootstock of humanity survived, living with hellzones and chemical storms, hounded by Magistrates.

In the villes, rigid laws were enforced—to atone for the sins of the past and prepare the way for a better future. That was the barons' public credo and their right-to-rule.

Kane, along with friend and fellow Magistrate Grant, had upheld that claim until a fateful Outlands expedition. A displaced piece of technology…a question to a keeper of the archives…a vague clue about alien masters—and their world shifted radically. Suddenly, Brigid Baptiste, the archivist, faced summary execution, and Grant a quick termination. For Kane there was forgiveness if he pledged his unquestioning allegiance to Baron Cobalt and his unknown masters and abandoned his friends.

But that allegiance would make him support a mysterious and alien power and deny loyalty and friends. Then what else was there?

Kane had been brought up solely to serve the ville. Brigid's only link with her family was her mother's red-gold hair, green eyes and supple form. Grant's clues to his lineage were his ebony skin and powerful physique. But Domi, she of the white hair, was an Outlander pressed into sexual servitude in Cobaltville. She at least knew her roots and was a reminder to the exiles that the outcasts belonged in the human family.

Parents, friends, community—the very rootedness of humanity was denied. With no continuity, there was no forward momentum to the future. And that was the crux—when Kane began to wonder if there was a future.

For Kane, it wouldn't do. So the only way was out—way, way out.

After their escape, they found shelter at the forgotten Cerberus redoubt headed by Lakesh, a scientist, Cobaltville's head archivist, and secret opponent of the barons.

With their past turned into a lie, their future threatened, only one thing was left to give meaning to the outcasts. The hunger for freedom, the will to resist the hostile influences. And perhaps, by opposing, end them.

Prologue

Altyn Tagh region, Tibet

The redhead came to the farmhouse under the flag of truce. A Caucasian woman riding a powerful steed, she had wrapped her fur cloak tightly around her against the biting winds that cascaded down from the imposing peaks of Altyn Tagh. Svelte and beautiful, the flame-haired woman looked exhausted from her long trek through this, the most desolate part of Tibet.

Kamala watched the redhead's approach as she worked in her father's field, repairing the broken stake that held the old scarecrow in place. A willowy girl, barely thirteen summers old, Kamala had met with few strangers from outside the village, just the occasional traveling salesman and the traders on market day or the silent monks from the nearby monastery who merely nodded as they went about their business. Kamala had long dark hair and brown eyes, and her sun-bronzed limbs had become long and gangly following the first flush of puberty, yet the rest of her body bided its time, in no rush to catch up. One day, perhaps, she might be beautiful like her mother, Bayarmaz, but for now she seemed awkward, all flailing limbs and sharp elbows and knees.

Looking up as she bound the jagged struts of wood

together, Kamala had noticed the distant rider making her slow approach to their family homestead some five hundred miles north of Lhasa, the capital city of Tibet. The setting sun stretched the visitor's shadow far across the golden wheat fields, making of it a sinister, skeletal thing like the scarecrow Kamala toiled with.

She looked to the east, spying the blind eye of the moon as it nudged over the horizon to take up its vigil in the cold evening sky as the sun set in the west. When she looked back, the flame-haired rider was closer and she could make out the glinting metal of her weapons, a gun resting between her legs as the horse jostled slowly along the frost-spattered path, a metal dirk sheathed at her hip. By the time Kamala had finished her repairs, the beautiful woman had dismounted her horse, secured it outside her parents' simple lodgings and disappeared inside.

Passing the old apple tree, Kamala entered the stone cottage through the back door and walked through the kitchen, stopping to smell the soup that her mother was cooking on the range. She could hear voices: her father's and the faintly accented voice of the mysterious stranger. They were engaged in an animated discussion about the merits of the divine, and Kamala heard her father proclaiming that religion mattered little to a farmer, so long as he could work an honest day in his fields.

"But you'd be better off, you must be able to see that?" the stranger was saying, an odd edge to her tone, as Kamala slunk into the room. Though the woman spoke the language it was clear that she was unused to the Tibetan tongue, forming the words awkwardly with Western lips.

At over five and a half feet tall, the woman seemed to tower over Kamala's mother as she stood in the main room of the cottage beside Kamala's parents, and her height made the familiar room seem as if it was somehow smaller, the ceiling low in her presence as though cowering with fear. The stranger's hair was like a radiant setting sun around her head, trailing halfway down her back in a cascade of beautiful curls, and her eyes were the emerald color of the sea. The green-eyed woman waited close to the window, pulling back the curtain with grubby fingers as she watched the dirt track leading to the cottage. She wore black armor of a supple leather that clung to her curves. Its blackness made her seem to Kamala's eyes like some strange insect-turned-man, the perverted result of a sick metamorphosis. She held a glass from the sideboard filled with her father's best apple brandy, her gloved fingers long and supple around its simple lines. She stepped closer into the room then, taking up residence in father's favorite chair, her long, black-clad limbs shimmering like something liquid as she seated herself.

Kamala's mother was meticulously hanging the woman's cloak, brushing frost out of its pile as the stranger spoke angrily to her father. The dark-haired woman looked fearful, lines of worry creasing her brow as she placed the cape on one of the pegs by the low front door.

Sitting across from the red-haired woman, ousted from his favorite chair, her father looked up as he sipped at the brandy. "My daughter Kamala," he announced, a proud smile passing across his lips, the lines around his eyes creasing in time with his smile.

Kamala stood in the doorway, huddling into herself

as she looked at the beautiful stranger who had appeared in her house.

"A fine-looking girl, sir. You have my congratulations," the woman stated, holding her glass aloft in tribute before draining it and smacking her lips contentedly. Kamala saw her mother's eyes flash fearfully toward the stranger.

Before Kamala could speak—as if she had anything worth saying—her mother urged her to check the simmering soup, and the moment had passed. Kamala saw pleading in her mother's eyes. "Go," she urged, "to the kitchen."

Alone in the kitchen, Kamala lifted the lid from the pot and used the nearby ladle to stir its bubbling contents, its meaty aroma filling her nostrils. She could hear her father and the mysterious woman in the next room as they continued to talk about the world that was coming. "Ullikummis brings the love that the world will know," Kamala heard the woman say in her throaty voice, "and you will either embrace that love or you'll be swallowed by its embrace."

She thought on that for a moment as she continued idly stirring the contents of the pot. The Caucasian woman didn't seem that different from the people of the village. And yet a cloud of anger clung to her, evident in the manner in which she argued with her father, in the way that she seemed on edge. There was a drive inside the woman that made her different from the monks of the nearby monastery, a comprehension of religion that demanded victory rather than understanding, and was scared it might be challenged for something less than absolute. As she thought of the speaker and her intense anger, the conversation from the other room became louder once more, and there came a sudden shattering of glass.

Kamala flinched, turning her head to look through the open kitchen door, but she was unable to see what had happened. Then her mother rushed into the kitchen on hurried legs, the shards of one of Father's best brandy glasses held in her cupped hands, fear lining her beautiful face. Kamala could see tears forming in her mother's eyes. "What's wrong, Mama?" she asked, her voice low.

Her mother shook her head and tossed the broken glass in the bucket by the door. "It's nothing, Kamala," she said quietly. "Just…the glass dropped. It's nothing, baby."

Kamala smiled, her bright teeth shining in the dwindling sunlight that shone through the kitchen window. "We have other glasses," the girl told her mother.

The older woman laughed, just for a breath, and then she pulled Kamala close to her, her chin resting atop the girl's head. "Get out," Kamala heard her mother whisper. "Get out of here. Run away."

Kamala felt her mother's hug tighten, pulling her so close, and she began to ask what she had meant. Just then a voice came from the doorway and Kamala looked up to see the red-haired woman standing there.

"Where the hell's that glass?" she snarled.

Kamala's mother let go of her and Kamala saw tears glistening on her cheeks. The older woman apologized as she reached into one of the cupboards and produced another glass. "Please, don't use language in front of my daughter," she said quietly, not looking at the woman.

The woman's arm darted forward in a blur and suddenly she had hold of the older woman's chin. "I'll speak however the hell I please in front of your daughter," she said through gritted teeth. "Do whatever the hell I want. Your world is past. You understand that?"

Kamala felt ashamed as she watched her mother nod, chin painfully held in the woman's grip. The woman was a cloud of fury, of hate personified. Kamala couldn't know it, but the woman's name was hate, too: Brigid Haight. The girl took a step back, away from the scene, and felt the handle of the back door jab into her lower back. "Get out," her mother had said. She reached behind her, pulling the handle down.

The woman's voice barked behind Kamala as she turned to exit the house. "Where do you think you're going, little one?"

Kamala looked back, her delicate hazel eyes piercing the woman's angry gaze. "Soup won't be ready for a while," she said, keeping her voice firm. "I thought maybe I should feed your horse. She looks tired."

The redhead nodded, letting go of the older woman's chin as she did so. "You do that," she agreed slowly, resting her hand beside the blaster that was now holstered at her hip. "But don't be long," she added.

Kamala rushed from the house.

Standing under the branches of the apple tree, the girl glanced at the cottage, looked at the ground around her feet, back to the cottage, wondering what to do. There were windfalls here—maybe she could use those to feed the woman's mount. Or maybe she should run, get help from the nearby monastery. Was that what her mother had meant? She knew all the monks; they would likely be sitting down to their simple repast at this hour as the sun set behind the mountains. They would come if she asked them to, but what would she say? How would she explain it?

She untucked a corner of her shirt from her belted skirt and made a bowl of the material, which she then filled with fallen apples. Then she walked around the stone cottage to the front of the house where the filly had been tethered, all the while listening for raised voices from the house.

"Learn to embrace his love," she heard the flame-haired woman exclaim loudly, but there was no love left in her voice, only rage and hatred and spite.

Kamala stood feeding the chestnut horse windfalls for almost a minute, a hollow feeling in her stomach, wondering what to do. She had always been a shy girl, but she had never been afraid of people before, not even of strangers. But this woman, with her bubbling resentment held barely in check behind her sea-green eyes, frightened her.

She looked back at the cottage, seeing the woman standing at the window watching her, that cloud of hair like an angry, flaming halo around her face. As she watched, the woman turned away, her lips moving as she spoke to Kamala's parents. By the time the hateful woman turned back, Kamala was gone.

Kamala could run. Since she was very young, she had outpaced children of her own age, her strides somehow longer, with never a hint of the exhaustion that the other children felt. By the time she was ten years old she could outrun grown men at the nearest village, fit men made strong by working on the unforgiving land of the mountains. Her father had marveled at his daughter's speed and stamina, and her mother had described it as a special gift—not one that Kamala had chosen but one that had chosen her.

As she ran down the dirt track toward the monastery—a building made of the same gray stone as her father's house—Kamala heard shouting behind her. She flicked her head back for a moment and saw the red-haired woman come striding out of her cottage. The spite-filled woman was calling to her angrily. Kamala turned her head back into the wind and ran, pumping her arms faster and driving herself toward the lights of the distant monastery that sat lower on the mountain path.

In a moment Kamala was off her father's land and sprinting onward down the path, hurtling at breakneck speed toward the towering structure of the monastery. The monastery sat close to the farmstead of Tsakhia and his son, Sonam. Sonam was a couple of years older than Kamala, and her father said he was far too pretty to be a boy. Kamala was always shy and awkward around him without quite understanding why, and even now her heart fluttered in her chest as she got closer to the house where he lived, the room where he slept. But as she got closer to the farm she saw the trails of dark smoke billowing into the sky, hidden before by the darkness of the shadows cast by the mountains that overlooked them. Then Kamala saw more smoke, thick and black, spuming from the monastery that nuzzled at the mountain's edge. The building was simple but beautiful, old beyond measure, its lines rough yet somehow perfect, an expression of simplicity. The nukecaust that had destroyed so much of the Western world had largely ignored Tibet, and life here had continued as it always had, the so-called Fall of Civilization mattering nothing to a people who cared little for technological advance.

Kamala stopped, her feet sliding a moment on the rough, frost-dappled path. The door to the monastery had been nailed closed, and the nails glowed like fireflies as the flames licked the walls within. Someone had set light to the monastery. Not just "someone," Kamala realized—that woman, the one filled with hate. Who else could it be?

The monks had taken in visitors before, feeding them and sheltering them from the harsh winds and cold nights that swept across the mountains of Altyn Tagh. Kamala had no doubt that they would have welcomed the redheaded stranger, patiently listened to her as she told them of this Ullikummis deity, this promise of a new and better world. Then they would have smiled and shaken their shaven heads, invited her to stay or to leave as her whim chose. And in return the woman had set light to their home, locking them inside as the structure burned.

This close, the stones that made up the monastery radiated a punishing heat, and Kamala could go no closer for fear of having her own flesh blister and spoil like a rotten fruit. Behind the monastery, Tsakhia's farmhouse was a burned-out ruin, the black smoke billowing from it like a flock of angry crows, dancing in the sky in their sick Terpsichore.

Kamala turned, heart sinking in her chest as she looked back to where her father's house stood higher along the simple track that led into the range known as Altyn Tagh. Already she could see the dark smoke pluming into the sky, the mark of hate as the woman destroyed those she could not convert to her god.

Kamala knew nothing of the woman or of her history or destiny. All she could do was hide as the redhead preached from her gospel of hate.

Chapter 1

"That's our point of entry, all right," Kane mused as he checked the calculations he had scribbled on a small map. The fold-out map looked tired and worn, and so did Kane. He also looked irritated as hell.

Kane was a tall man in his early thirties, well-built with broad shoulders and long, rangy limbs. His dark hair brushed at his collar, tousled atop his head as the wind caught it, and the dark trace of a beard was beginning to show on his square jaw. There was a thin line by Kane's left eye where something had cut him recently, and he brushed at it in annoyance as the breeze played against it.

"So what do you suggest we do?" asked the woman to Kane's side. "Run away like scared little girls?" In her mid-twenties, the woman had an olive complexion, with long dark hair that trailed halfway down her back, and a wicked glint in her chocolate-brown eyes. Rosalia had been Kane's almost-permanent companion over the past few weeks since an altercation up in the Bitterroot Mountains of Montana.

The final member of the group—an imposing man with dark skin, short hair and the grizzled look of a fighter—chuckled at that, turning to the woman. "If you really believe that then you don't know Kane so well, Rosie," Grant said, his voice a deep basso rumble. "Me, either," he added after a moment. "We never ran away from anything."

Grant had been Kane's combat partner for longer than either of them cared to admit. A little older than Kane, Grant still deferred to his colleague in moments like this, trusting the other's uncanny instincts to keep them safe. He brought his hand up, brushing it against the drooping gunslinger's mustache that he wore over his top lip, feeling the dark growth of stubble that was forming all around it.

Brushing her hair from her face as the wind caught it, Rosalia shot Grant a contemptuous look. "From what I've seen so far, all you Magistrates are the same. Big men when you're safe in your villes with your special armor on and backup just a street away, but you run like schoolgirls when you're faced with anything you didn't plan for."

The three of them were hunkered down at the edge of a ridge overlooking a ramshackle settlement constructed of wood and sun-dried clay bricks, with several struggling fields as its surround. Made up of two dozen buildings, the little run-down town was locked in the gully between two towering cliff faces, their sandy orange sides bright in the midmorning sun. A thin ribbon of river wended its way through the center of the town like a main street, and people could be seen moving along its edges.

The trio on the cliff top wore shadow suits weaved from a high-tech armorlike material that could deflect blunt trauma and act as a self-contained environment, keeping its wearer hot or cool depending on the needs of their surrounds. Over the shadow suits, the three of them were dressed in indistinct clothing that showed the wear from long days on the road. Kane wore a beaten leather jacket in a tan color turned dark with sweat and dirt, Grant a long black duster with a bullet-blunting Kevlar weave in its thread, and Rosalia was wearing a beaten-up denim jacket with loose threads dangling from its cuffs and collar and a light summer skirt that swished just above her shapely ankles, which in turn were encased in black leather boots.

Kane checked the map again, running his hands across the creases to brush away the dusty sand that had blown across it. "Damn ville wasn't on the map. Must have sprung up in the last eighteen months. But our next closest parallax point is fifty miles eastward," he explained. "We're looking at a heck of a trek, and we'd have to find a way across the Rio Grande."

"The big villes have been vomiting out people for a while now, forcing little shitholes like this to crop up all over," Rosalia told them both, pushing her dark hair out of her face as the wind snatched at it. "You Magistrate men seldom notice what's going on in front of your eyes," she added contemptuously.

Kane shot her a look before turning back to watch the people moving around in the ravine below them. Twenty-four buildings meant maybe seventy people in total, he guessed, could be more as a refugee settlement, but it seemed as if it had taken a while growing up. The structures certainly looked sturdy, perhaps it had been here for years—who could say?

Grant turned his eyes from the settlement below to Kane. "Let's keep our heads down and act friendly to the locals," he rumbled, pointing to the little town between the cliffs.

With that, the imposing ex-Mag pushed himself up, snagging the cloth knapsack sitting behind him in the dirt and hooking it over one of his massive shoulders before leading the way down the steep path that led to the gully. The others followed a moment later, but Rosalia stopped at the top of the path for a moment, peering behind her.

"Come on, stupid," she huffed, irritation in her voice.

From close by, a dog came tromping out from behind a crop of drooping bushes, their leaves wizened from lack of water. The carcass of a cony lay behind the bushes, and the dog had been sniffing at it, wondering if it could still be eaten. The dog was a mongrel with mottled fur and a long snout, and Rosalia suspected that it had more than a hint of coyote in it. Most remarkably, it had the palest eyes that she had ever seen, their irises a creamy washed-out white like mozzarella cheese. She had "owned" the dog for seven months, finding the creature wandering alone out in the Californian desert. In all of that time, the woman had never given the animal a permanent name, hoping to avoid any attachment.

"Stupid mutt," Rosalia cursed as the dog trotted along at her heels down the dust path. "Always thinking about your stomach."

A dozen paces ahead, Grant was talking with Kane, polychrome sunglasses protecting their eyes as they walked into the sun, keeping their voices low.

"You look worried, old friend," Grant observed as Kane fiddled with the Sin Eater pistol he habitually wore at his wrist.

Once the official side arm of the Magistrate Division, the Sin Eater was an automatic handblaster that folded in on itself to be stored in a bulky holster strapped just above the user's wrist. Even at full extension, this remarkable pistol was less than fourteen inches in length, and it fired 9 mm rounds. The holsters reacted to a specific tensing of the wrist tendons, powering the pistol automatically into the gunman's hand. The trigger had no guard; it had never been foreseen that any kind of safety features for the weapon would ever be required. Thus, if the user's index finger was crooked at the time it reached his hand, the pistol would begin firing automatically. The absolute nature of this means of potential execution was a throwback to the high regard with which Magistrates were viewed in the villes—their judgment could never be wrong. Though no longer a Magistrate himself, Kane had retained his weapon from his days as one in Cobaltville, and he felt most comfortable with the weapon in hand.

Grant, too, had one of the remarkable blasters hidden beneath the sleeve of his Kevlar duster, though he carried other weapons, as well, secreted in the lining of the long coat. Primary among these, Grant carried his favored Copperhead close-assault subgun, tucked just out of sight.

Kane shrugged at Grant's observation as the pair shuffled sideways along a narrow section of the steep pathway. "I just don't like entering new places these days," he said. "Seems things are getting more and more hostile."

Then, as Kane spoke, his booted heel slid on a loose

stone and he began to slip toward the edge of the path. "Whoa!"

Grant instantly reached out, grabbing his friend in a firm grip just above his left wrist. "No need to expect trouble," Grant said as he pulled Kane back onto the path. "And I've always got your back if things do turn nasty."

"Humph," Kane grumbled. "We used to say the same thing to Baptiste—and look how that worked out."

"We'll find her, Kane," Grant assured his partner. "If she's out there, we'll find her."

Kane nodded. "Damn straight we will."

Until recently Brigid Baptiste had been the third member of their field team, accompanying Kane and Grant on numerous adventures across the globe and beyond. Baptiste was a gifted archivist with remarkable talents. However, in a recent attack on the Cerberus redoubt—the headquarters from which Kane and his companions had operated—Baptiste had gone MIA. Despite their best efforts, her current whereabouts remained unknown.

The gradient of the path eased for the last thirty yards, and Kane had returned his Sin Eater to its hiding place beneath the right sleeve of his jacket by the time the trio reached its foot. They walked three abreast, with the dog skulking at Rosalia's side as they made their way along the last part of the dusty roadway that led into the hamlet itself.

A single thoroughfare dominated the village, running parallel to the thin river. People dressed in light clothes were walking along that main street, a few youngsters paddling at the stream's edge. A bearded man in simple clothes was leading a mule down the street, its back laden with two great baskets full of the leaves of some edible root crop or other. It seemed normal enough.

As they neared the closest of the buildings, the companions could hear the tink-tink-tink of a blacksmith at work. Kane turned and saw an open-fronted shed beside the single-story house. Inside a man worked at shaping a horseshoe that glowed white-hot at the end of his tongs. The man peered up from his work as the companions passed, eyes narrowing as he watched the strangers entering the village.

"By my reckoning," Kane told his companions, keeping his voice low, "our parallax point should be in the northwest corner of this place." He pointed. "Over by that storage silo, maybe?"

Parallax points were a crucial part of a system of instantaneous travel that was employed by the Cerberus rebels. The process itself involved a quantum inducer called an interphaser, which could fold space upon itself, granting its user immediate teleportation to another location, either on Earth or beyond. Though portable, the interphaser units could only be engaged in set locations. The units tapped into an ancient web of powerful, naturally occurring lines of energy stretching right across the globe, much like the ley lines of old. On Thunder Isle the Cerberus crew had discovered the Parallax Points program, which encoded all the vortex points. The interphaser relied on this program, and new vortex points were fed into the interphaser's targeting computer.

Frequently the specific sites of interphase induction had become sacred in the eyes of primitive man. However, over time many of these parallax points had become forgotten or buried beneath the rise and fall of civilizations. As such, they often turned up in the most unlikely of locations.

The Cerberus organization had several of the portable interphase units. When they had evacuated their redoubt headquarters, Kane's team had taken one of the units for ease of transport while they went undercover. Right now, Grant carried the foot-high unit in its protective case inside the rucksack on his back.

Rosalia's dog whined plaintively as the companions continued to stride along the dusty street. It was a simple path marked out on the ground by the basic virtue of repeated usage. A woman in her thirties sat in a weather-beaten rocking chair outside the front door to one of the tumbledown shacks, her fingers moving deftly as she knitted a pair of baby booties. Grant acknowledged her with a dip of his head, touching his fingers to his brow for just a second.

"Things don't feel right here, you guys," Rosalia said, her voice a whisper.

Kane looked over to her and a lopsided smile touched at his lips. "Weren't you the one who was complaining about we ex-Magistrates skulking around like frightened schoolgirls?"

In response, Rosalia showed him her teeth in a sarcastic imitation of a grin. "Just an observation, Magistrate Man," she said, subtly stretching her arms out as if to yawn. "Don't jump at shadows on my account." As she did so, she shifted two hidden knives that were located beneath her sleeves.

With the open stream running to the right of them, Kane continued on, making his way toward the crop silo he had pointed out a few moments before. "Keep the interphaser to hand," he instructed Grant out of the corner of his mouth. "I want to be on our way as soon as."

They were heading for a meeting high on the Californian coast. A coded message had been piped through to Kane a few hours before from their old Cerberus leader, Lakesh, providing them with coordinates of a meeting point where he hoped to set up a temporary base.

As the three of them rounded the corner of the silo and a simple lean-to building that stood at its side, Kane spotted a small chunk in the sandy dirt at the external edge of the silo itself. It looked like an ancient mile marker, a little hunk of rounded stone sticking up about eighteen inches from the soil. The marker sat in the lee of the lean-to, obscured by the shadow that the tall silo cast.

"Five'll get you ten that that's our parallax point," Kane stated, indicating the marker stone half-buried in the ground.

As Kane spoke, a figure appeared from the far side of the silo fifteen feet away, striding into view before halting, his eyes locked on Kane and his teammates. The man was tall and wore a rough-hewn robe made of a dirty brown material that covered him from neck down to his ankles like a cassock. The robe featured a voluminous hood that the man had pulled up over his head, hiding his features in shadow so that only his eyes glinted in the fierce morning sunlight. His right fist was held loosely clenched at his side, and Kane could tell immediately that the hooded stranger was clutching something within that balled fist. The man's fustian robe featured a red badge pinned to the left breast, and the insignia flashed as it caught the sun's rays.

"Can I help you gentlemen?" the robed figure asked, challenge in his tone.

"We're just passing through, friend," Kane stated, feeling a disquieting roiling in his stomach.

Beneath the hood, the man closed his eyes for a moment, reaching out with uncanny senses. Kane and his companions watched as the strange figure shook his head infinitesimally as if confused by what he could feel. "Cannot…" the man muttered before opening his eyes once more. "This is a sanctified town, sirs," the man said in an authoritative tone. "Are you faithful?"

Kane stared at the robed man in disbelief. "I…I…" How could he possibly answer that question?

"I suspected as much," the robed man stated, his tone rising in fury. "Mr. Kane, is it not?"

Kane became aware that figures were massing behind him. Where moments before they had seemed to be wary of the strangers but simply going about their workaday lives, now the townsfolk appeared to be closing in, subtly blocking the street and hemming the Cerberus teammates in at the alleyway between the silo and the one-story lean-to beside it.

Kane took a steadying breath. "You seem to know me, but I don't think I caught your name," he told the robed figure at the farther end of the silo.

The hooded man nodded once in acknowledgment. "I am stone," he stated.

Kane had heard the phrase before. It was something of a battle chant for an expanding class of warriors who fought in the name of a sinister being called Ullikummis. In speaking the phrase, the hooded figure had not merely confirmed his allegiance, but he had also entered a meditative state whereby his physical attributes would change.

Kane's eyes darted to the subtle movement as the man unclenched his right fist and a simple cord of leather with a cuplike design at the farthest extension of its loop sagged from his hand.

"And you are an enemy of stone," the hooded figure said. Even as he spoke, the leather cup whirled around the man's arm as he launched a cluster of lethal projectiles at Kane and his teammates.

Chapter 2

"Get down!" Kane shouted as he dived out of the path of the hurtling missiles.

A handful of sharpened pebbles had been flung from the simple slingshot that the robed man had hidden in his fist, and the rocks picked up speed as they whipped through the fifteen-foot distance separating the man and Kane's team. The stones cut through the air and, by the time they reached the space where Kane had been standing, the half dozen pebbles had taken on a lethal velocity similar to bullets fired from a gun. The projectiles had been aimed at Kane's face, but by then Kane had dropped out of their path, his left palm slapping against the dirt even as he called his Sin Eater pistol to his right hand with a practiced flinch of his wrist tendons.

To either side of the dark-haired ex-Mag, Grant and Rosalia also flung themselves out of the path of those vicious rocks, and Grant snarled as one of them clipped against the swishing tail of his Kevlar-lined duster as it leaped high in the air.

Across from Grant, Rosalia kicked out as she ran at the high, curving wall of the silo. Suddenly she was running up the side of the silo, her skirt tearing as she kicked out again and flipped herself high into the air, over the path of the hurtling stones and onto the low roof of the lean-to beside it, her back to the man in the robes.

She landed with catlike grace, looking out at the gathering crowd on the main street, two short blades appearing in her hands from their hiding places in the ragged sleeves of her denim jacket.

As Rosalia landed, Kane's index finger tightened on the Sin Eater and a stream of 9 mm bullets cut through the air toward their mysterious attacker. The red badge at the robed man's breast caught the light once more as the bullets streamed toward him. Kane realized what the badge meant: it was a symbol of authority, a mockery of the Magistrate badge that he and Grant had worn when they were in service.

Kane was moving for cover as he unleashed that flurry of bullets, but he watched as the robed man held up his free hand. The bullets struck against the man's outstretched arm but incredibly—impossibly—the man let out no sound of pain; he just stood there, jaw set as four bullets cut through the hemp sleeve of his robe and rattled against his flesh. His other arm arced behind him and he launched a second salvo of stones from his slingshot as Kane's admirable figure disappeared behind the wall of the lean-to.

Kane looked down for a moment as he almost tripped over something. Rosalia's mongrel was there, lips peeled back in a fearsome snarl as it looked at the approaching crowd of townsfolk. A bearded man wielding a claw hammer was leading the charge at the strangers, drawing the hammer back in a vicious arc. The dog jumped then, jaw snagging around the man's arm and pulling him to the ground in a cloud of disturbed earth.

Grant meanwhile had spun to his right, slapping his back against the curved wall of the silo as the bullet-like stones cut toward his companions. They had met these hooded figures before, and Grant knew that they could be tenacious opponents. They'd need something with a little more stopping power than the Sin Eater, and Grant had just the thing. While stones clashed against the clay wall of the silo and the sound of Kane's bullets cut through the air, Grant had reached into his long coat and pulled loose the Copperhead assault subgun from its hiding place strapped to the lining of the coat. The barrel of the subgun was almost two feet long. The grip and trigger of the gun were placed in front of the breech in the bullpup design, allowing the gun to be used single-handed. An optical, image-intensified scope coupled with a laser autotargeter were mounted on top of the frame. The Copperhead possessed a 700-round-per-minute rate of fire and was equipped with an extended magazine holding thirty-five 4.85 mm steel-jacketed rounds. Besides the Sin Eater, the Copperhead was Grant's favored field weapon, thanks to ease of use and the sheer level of destruction it could create in short measure.

Gun in hand, Grant dodged from cover and unleashed a firestorm of shots at the robed figure at the far end of the alley between the buildings. The hooded figure staggered for a moment under that vicious assault, before finally toppling backward into the silo wall. Grant depressed the trigger again, unleashing a second burst of fire as the robed figure began to pull himself up off the ground.

"Stay the hell down," Grant said as the Copperhead drilled another burst of lead into the robed assailant.

Just a few feet away, Kane was moving among the mob beside the lean-to when Rosalia's voice rang out.

"Kane, watch your six!"

Kane dodged and turned even as something whizzed through the air toward his head. The object glowed white and orange as it cut the air, missing Kane's head by the narrowest of margins. Heart thudding against his rib cage, Kane glanced behind him where the projectile clanged against the wall of the lean-to—it was a horse-shoe, red-hot and launched with a flick of the black-smith's tongs. The burning-hot horseshoe left a smoking indentation in the wooden wall even as it tumbled to the ground.

Overhead, Rosalia leaped from the roof of the lean-to like some graceful bird of prey, knives slashing the air as she dived at the blacksmith. With a vicious sweep of a blade, Rosalia cut through the man's throat in an explosion of blood as she barreled into him. The blacksmith let out a howl of pain as he toppled backward under the weight of the hurtling woman, but his scream was cut short as the knife sliced through his vocal cords.

Then the blacksmith slammed against the hard-packed soil of the roadway and Rosalia used her momentum to leap away, bringing her knives up to face their next challenger. Her mongrel hound was already at her side, letting out a savage bark as the townsfolk crowded around them. The townspeople had armed themselves with makeshift weapons, sticks and loose bricks, here a large ax made for chopping logs.

Rosalia smiled. "Come on, then," she goaded, "let's see what you're made of."

The man with the hammer brushed himself down as he regained his footing, snarling back at the dog that had felled him. Then he was rushing at Rosalia, brandishing the long-handled hammer like a club as he swung it at her head. Her dark eyes fixed on the hammer's arc, Rosalia ducked, allowing the metal head to whisk through the air just inches above her head. Then her left arm snapped up, forearm meeting forearm and using the hammer wielder's own momentum to knock him away. The bearded man staggered a little in place, surprised that this slender girl had struck him with such precision. As he did so, Rosalia spun on the spot, bringing her left leg up and around, delivering a beautifully executed roundhouse kick that ended when her foot connected with the man's face. The bearded hammer man was flipped over by the force of Rosalia's brutal blow, but she was already leaping away to face the next crowd member who dared attack the Cerberus companions. Rosalia's confrontation with the hammer wielder had lasted all of three seconds, start to finish.

As Rosalia leaped, Kane rolled forward, Sin Eater raised as he assessed the threat level that the crowd posed. There were perhaps sixteen people here, with more rushing to join them from the buildings all around. These people were in the eerie grip of the false religion, the promised utopia that Ullikummis had drummed into his loyal subjects. It was as if they were brainwashed.

A broad-shouldered man came at Kane from his left, swinging a two-by-four plank from some nearby construction project. Though renowned for his combat sense, Kane almost didn't see the man approach, ducking only at the very last second as his attacker lunged at him with the length of wood. The board hurtled overhead as Kane snapped off a quick burst from his blaster, sweeping his attacker's legs out from under him. The man cried out in agony as he crashed into the soil, a bullet shattering his right kneecap. These outlanders were innocents mixed up in a sinister cult created by a being far more powerful than themselves, and Kane would rather not kill them if he didn't have to.

Then Kane was standing, the black muzzle of the Sin Eater stretched out in front of him like a warning. "I'm asking all of you to back off," he commanded, "so no one else gets hurt."

"Enemy of stone," one of the crowd facing Kane cried in reply. "Enemy Kane!"

That was the second time in less than three minutes that a stranger had called him by name, Kane realized. Whatever was going on with these cultists, they seemed to recognize him.

"When the hell did I become public enemy number one?" Kane muttered under his breath as the foremost members of the crowd rushed at him, their mismatched weapons raised. With a sigh of resignation, Kane began selecting targets and squeezing the trigger of the Sin Eater. Four perfectly placed rounds blew out the knee-caps of the nearest of the approaching crowd before they swarmed on Kane.

To THE SIDE of the silo, Grant was having his own problems. He hurried along the alleyway between buildings toward the stone marker half buried in the dust. Two feet away, the hooded figure who had attacked them was lying on his back, limbs flailing like a bug where Grant's shots had taken him down once more. Yet already the man seemed to be recovering. These cultists—"firewalkers" was one term that had been popularized among the Cerberus personnel—could miraculously change the density of their flesh in some way that Grant and his teammates had yet to fully comprehend. The trick required fierce concentration, and all of these fire-walkers had to keep their minds still to reach the condition of stonelike flesh. One way to stop them retaining such a degree of meditation had been to use concentrated sound, which irritated the firewalkers so that they could not achieve proper concentration.

Grant shrugged out of his rucksack as he knelt by the stone block poking up out of the ground. Swiftly he undid the straps on the cloth backpack and reached inside, pulling out a metal pyramidal device of roughly one foot in height, its protective cloth sleeve dropping free and wrapping over itself as the wind dragged it a few feet across the ground. Grant ignored it, his attention fixed on the chrome pyramid itself. The metal was scuffed and marred from where it had been hurriedly stored, and Grant brushed dirt from its surface as he flipped down a control panel close to the base of the interphaser unit. Grant watched as the tiny display came to life, a series of lights flickering on in quick succession.

Suddenly, Grant saw movement from the corner of his eye and turned his head in time to see the robed man leap off the ground and spiral toward him like some vicious ballerino. Leaving the interphaser in place by the stone marker, Grant rolled aside, and the robed man's kicking feet slapped against the ground where Grant's hand had been just a second before.

From his crouched position on the ground, Grant swung the Copperhead up one-handed, the bullpup design ideal for such a move. But even as he depressed the trigger, his robed assailant shoved the muzzle aside with a violent flick of his wrist. Grant's shots went wild, slamming against the grain silo and drilling through the brickwork with powdery little orange bursts of dried clay.

Then the robed man's fist struck Grant across the jaw with the force of a thrown brick, and the huge ex-Magistrate blinked back hot tears as his vision blurred. Blindly, Grant lashed out with his left palm, slapping the robed figure away with a mighty sweep of his limb. Grant felt more than saw the figure fall from him, heard as he struck against something hard with the sound of breaking wood.

Wiping a hand across his eyes, Grant pushed himself to his feet, bringing the Copperhead to bear once more as he searched for his target. Before Grant could react, the robed figure came leaping out of the shadows of the lean-to, barreling into the ex-Mag like a cannonball. The pair of combatants crashed back to the ground once more, and Grant's breath was driven out of him in a loud gasp. To the side of his head, Grant saw the flickering lights of the interphaser as it tried to lock on to the parallax point. Come on, good buddy, he thought, let's make us a door out of here, already.

Then the robed figure's hands clamped around Grant's throat, exerting tremendous pressure as he attempted to snap the ex-Mag's neck.

KANE FOUND HIMSELF struggling under the pressure of the mob, a heavy man clinging to his back and weighing him down. It reminded him of the worst moments of the obligatory Pit patrol, back in his days as a Cobaltville Magistrate. Each time he shoved one person aside, another rushed to take his place, kicking and clawing at him—ineffective against his shadow suit but still enough to wear him down so he couldn't get back to the interphaser. With one determined shove, Kane wrenched the man from his back, tossing him over one shoulder in an urgent flexing of muscles. The heavyset man rolled away across the ground, tumbling over and over until he splashed into the shallow stream.

Before Kane could extricate himself from the angry mob, he felt someone clutch at his Sin Eater, a pair of hands yanking at his right arm. He pulled his hand free, then swung the blaster around to shoot his attacker. Kane's finger depressed the guardless trigger, but he whipped the pistol aside with just a fraction of an inch to spare. His attacker—attackers, in fact—were two children, a blond-haired boy and his sister, the elder of them perhaps eight years old.

Kane's bullets went wide, blasting harmlessly into the sky as he cursed under his breath. Bad enough that the adults had become indoctrinated into this cult of stone worship, but Kane wouldn't forgive himself if he went and shot an indoctrinated child.

With the echo of his wasted shots still fresh in his ears, Kane crashed forward as someone tackled him from behind, sacking him like a quarterback. Again Kane hadn't noticed the attacker coming at him from his left; he had somehow been blindsided. Kane flailed for several steps before slamming into the ground with bone-shaking force. And suddenly he was breathing nothing but water, the clear stream washing into his mouth and nose. Kane choked as someone slammed him with a savage punch to the back of his head.

Just a few steps away, Rosalia spun on her heel as a young woman came at her, slashing something at her face. It was the same woman whom Grant had noticed on their walk through the village, thirty-something years old with a weather tan to her features. Rosalia dipped out of reach as the woman slashed at her, recognizing the nine-inch knitting needles in the woman's hands.

Off to Rosalia's left side, a man was rushing at her with a cosh in his hand, raising it overhead to bring down on her head. There was a blur of motion, and something leaped at the man. When Rosalia looked again she saw her faithful dog had clamped its jaws around the man's arm, wrenching him around and around as it snarled angrily.

Rosalia ducked again as the woman with the knitting needles whipped one of them at her face. Then Rosalia's left leg stretched out and whipped back in a blur, catching the other woman's ankle and tripping her off balance. The woman cried out as she slammed against the ground, but Rosalia was already moving, turning back toward the alleyway beside the silo.

"Come on, you slow poke," she snapped at her dog as she rushed toward where Grant had set up the interphaser. *"¡Vamanos!"*

As she ran down the alleyway with her scruffy-looking dog at her heels, Rosalia saw Grant struggling beneath the pressure that the robed figure was exerting on his throat. Grant was urgently raising the Copperhead, but he was unable to bring it around enough.

In a blur of movement Rosalia brought the fingers

of her left hand up to her lips and blew, unleashing a piercing whistle that caused her dog to whine even as she drew her right arm behind her in a graceful arc.

The robed figure turned at the noise, and Rosalia saw his lips were pulled back in an animal snarl. The knife shot from Rosalia's right hand like a dart, cutting through the air and embedding itself beneath the robed figure's hood. The robed man cried out in a splutter of pain, falling away from Grant as he reached for the thing embedded in his face.

As his assailant's hood fell back, Grant saw that Rosalia's knife had pierced his left eyeball, burying its point there to an inch or more of its shining length. "Nice aim," Grant acknowledged as he rolled out from under the hooded man.

"There's always a chink in an opponent's armor," Rosalia said, "if you know where to look."

Kane had done something similar to this before, using the piercing noise of a warning alarm to break the concentration of these so-called firewalkers. For a moment, the sound had caused the faux-Magistrate to lose his stonelike powers.

The hooded figure was screaming in agony now, his meditative calm already a distant memory. Grant knew that if these firewalkers lost their concentration, even for just a second, they became vulnerable. With a wrench of his mighty arm muscles, Grant hefted the robed figure aside, plucking him from the ground like a toddler before whirling him around and finally slamming him into the solid wall of the silo before letting go. The figure sagged down the wall, head swaying in semiconsciousness. Grant glanced at the figure for a moment, confirming the thing he already knew: the man had a tiny ridge in the center of his forehead, a puckering of the skin where many religions believed the third eye was located. Beneath that ridge, the ex-Mag knew, lurked a stone, subtly altering the man's thoughts and granting him his superhuman powers.

"Where's Kane?" Grant snapped, his eyes scanning the crowd massing at the end of the alleyway. Two sturdy young men rushed down the alley, farming tools raised in their hands like clubs.

"You concentrate on getting our gateway open," Rosalia instructed, dropping low and felling both of the young farmers with a leg sweep. "We'll get him."

With that, Rosalia pointed toward the gap between the buildings, and her mongrel hound scampered ahead to where she indicated. "Get Kane," she told the dog. "Go find him, boy." The dog yipped excitedly as it rushed back down the alley.

Though it seemed to spend most of its time in a dreamworld, the dog was able to follow commands without any encouragement. Rosalia suspected that the dog had previously been owned by a now dead dirt farmer out in the Mojave Desert, but beyond that she knew little about it.

As the dog wended through the legs of another of the farmers, Rosalia's second knife blade glinted and she leaped from the alley with all the fury of a wildcat.

KANE KICKED and struggled as his own opponent shoved his face down into the silt at the bottom of the shallow stream. Though the water barely came over the back of his head, Kane was reminded of that adage that a man could drown in an inch of water—curse it all, if it wasn't just the kind of random fact that Brigid Baptiste would have spouted by way of reassurance as Kane struggled for his very life. His eyes were wide open and he saw the big bloated bubbles pass by his face as another blurt of breath was forced from his aching lungs. He renewed his struggles, trying desperately to flip his attacker from him as the man held his head under the water with a viselike grip.

As Kane struggled, the Sin Eater in his right hand kicked as a random shot blasted from the barrel. Through wide eyes, Kane watched as the bullet cut through the water beneath the surface of the little stream, burying itself in the far bank with a puff of silty debris. I need air, dammit, and I need it now.

Then the weight on Kane's back became heavier for a moment, and rather than freeing himself he was forced farther into the water, his chin scratching against the tiny flecks of stone at the bottom of the stream.

But almost as soon as it started, it was over, the weight disappearing as the man above him was wrenched aside. Kane pushed himself up, taking an urgent breath as he broke the surface. An instant later something came splashing into the water beside him, and Kane saw a dull-faced man rolling over in the silt, red trails of blood immediately clouding the water around his throat.

Kane turned and was shocked to find himself face-to-face with Rosalia's mongrel dog. The mutt had blood on its teeth as it pulled its lips back in a wolfish snarl.

"Good boy," Kane reassured the dog, realizing it had been his savior.

Water streamed down the ex-Magistrate's face and he brushed his hair back in irritation. His face felt cold from his brief dip in the water, the bone chilled at his left cheek, and he winced as the sensation bit against his eyetooth.

Behind the hound, more of the villagers were waiting, warily watching as Kane pulled himself out of the crystal-clear water of the stream that ran through their ramshackle hamlet, their eyes fixed on him, pure hatred burning in their glare. These people had been converted, a whole community pledging allegiance to Ullikummis, even the children. Some had marks on their wrists where the obedience stones had been inserted beneath their flesh, forcing them to submit to the faux god's will, but not all of them. Perhaps—Kane realized with indignation—some had chosen this religion.

Kane's eyes darted across the crowd as, from somewhere among them, spoken words drifted to his ears. "I am stone," a woman said.

"I am stone." This time it was a man's voice.

Then an elderly man stepped forward, shuffling his feet like a clockwork thing. "I am stone," he said proudly, his watery blue eyes meeting with Kane's in grim determination.

Then Kane was running at the crowd, the dog issuing a low growl from deep in its throat as it rushed ahead of him on its four shaggy legs.

Kane shunted the old man aside, ducked a driving fist from a younger-looking man, before kicking his leg out and knocking that man in the gut with such force that he doubled over and rolled to the ground in pain.

Concentrating on the battle, Kane was only peripherally aware of what Rosalia's dog was doing. The mongrel moved with such speed that, for a few moments, that ragged-looking mutt seemed more like something ethereal, a ghost-thing not fully of this world. The dog leaped at the massing crowd, batting people to the ground with its weight. It barked once, and for just a second it seemed that the hound expanded, became somehow more in front of the startled eyes of the crowd, like a swelling cloud of steam.

KNEELING AT THE EDGE of the silo, Grant played his fingers across the control console of the interphaser, inputting the coordinates that Lakesh had forwarded. A few paces away, Rosalia drove the sharp point of her stiletto blade into the gut of another would-be attacker, snarling as the blade pierced his clothes and flesh. At least this one had not assumed the properties of stone. That seemed to be a quality reserved only for the hooded figures that she had met over the past two months.

"Come on, Grant," Rosalia urged, flipping the bloody farmer's body to the ground. "Hurry it up."

"It'll be ready in a moment," Grant said without looking up. "Just finding a suitable destination…"

"Screw that." Rosalia glared at Grant. "Just get us out of here already."

Grant's thumb brushed the final key in the sequence he had been programming into the unit, and the interphaser seemed to move without truly moving, as if in the grip of an earth tremor. "Gateway's opening now," Grant said calmly, a grin appearing beneath the drooping crescent of his gunslinger's mustache.

Beside Grant, the pyramid shape of the interphaser

remained static yet the world seemed to swirl around it as a lotus blossom of inky rainbow light surged forth, twin cones of color bursting from above and below. Lightning played without those impossible cones of light like witch fire, tendrils sparking like clawing fingers reaching out from the mists.

At the entryway of the alley beside the silo, Rosalia put her finger and thumb to her lips and let out another piercing whistle. Her dog cocked its head at the call, and the ghostly apparition that it seemed to have become evaporated as if it had never been, and it was just a scruffy-looking mongrel once more. Perhaps that strange ghostlike form had never really existed at all; perhaps it had just been a trick of the light.

"Come on, Magistrate Man," Rosalia hollered, "our ride's here."

Kane's fist snapped out as he punched another of the villagers on the jaw. The woman's head snapped back with an audible crack as something broke in her neck. Then he was leaping up into the air, booted feet kicking out to connect with the chest of a man wielding a pitchfork. The man toppled back into the dirt, and finally Kane could see a clear path to where Rosalia, her dog and Grant were waiting. Behind the beautiful Mexican woman, Kane saw that familiar blossom of colors as the interphaser carved a door in the quantum ether, opening an impossible corridor through space.

Kane's empty left hand lashed out, slapping into the head of another grizzled local and casting the man aside in a tumble of flailing limbs. Then Kane was clear, ducking beneath a swinging length of hose pipe as he made for the alleyway.

Up ahead, Rosalia walked gradually backward, making her way to where Grant was waiting by the functioning interphaser.

"Damn unfriendly locals," she said with irritation.

Grant shook his head. "Whole bunch of them are *stoned*," he told her. "This Ullikummis thing is way, way out of control."

"You two always attract this much trouble?" Rosalia asked as a breathless Kane appeared at the end of the alleyway, blasting shots from his Sin Eater behind him to force the angry locals to retain their distance.

"Kane has a knack for it," Grant admitted, with a hint of reluctance in his tone. "Still, it does kinda look like we've been promoted to the New World Order's most wanted list."

"Let's move," Kane said breathlessly as he hurried down the short length of alleyway toward the burgeoning lotus blossom of light. A moment later he had leaped into the upward-facing cone of light, with Grant, Rosalia and Rosalia's dog stepping to follow him.

An instant later the twin cones of light collapsed and the triangular interphaser unit disappeared along with Kane and his companions. The angry locals were left scratching their heads as they found themselves alone in the alleyway, finding no trace of the targets of their hostility other than the fallen forms of the hooded figure and three farmhands. It was as if Kane's team had never existed.

Chapter 3

Snakefishville smelled of flowers. Their heady, luscious scents swirled through the air like urgent whispers in a hospital ward.

"Name and purpose of visit?" the Magistrate on the south gate asked, sounding bored. He wore a hooded robe of coarse material with a simple belt around his waist from which a small bag hung, bulging but no larger than a man's fist. A small red-shield insignia, the familiar symbol of Magistrate office, shone at his left breast as it reflected the morning sunlight.

A petite woman stood in front of him, head down in supplication. She had white hair and a chalk-white face, and she wore a loose summer dress whose hem shimmered just above her bone-pale ankles. "Mitra," the chalk-white woman said, "here to give thanks to our lord and master, as is his holy right." Her name was not Mitra, and while she planned to visit the newly built cathedral in the center of the ville, she had no intention of giving thanks, holy right or not.

The Magistrate nodded, barely glancing at the woman who had called herself Mitra. He gave a brief, formal smile as he ushered her through the wide gate and into the vast compound that made up the walled ville. The south gate was wide enough to accommodate three or four of the Magistrates' tanklike Sandcat vehicles driving side by side, a huge opening in the high-walled city of the ville. The white-skinned woman was just the latest of a whole crowd of refugees who had been made to wait at the gate while the Mags processed them. She'd waited two full hours in the warming June sun, beads of sweat forming at the back of her neck where her pixie-short hair brushed at its nape, but curiously she had not seen a single person rejected from entering the ville.

Within, garlands of flowers had been strung across the high walls and on the facades of the towering buildings that lined the ville's central thoroughfare, their pink-and-white petals fluttering in the warm summer breeze. The woman who had given her name as Mitra peered at them as she strode through the main gates and entered the busy street, letting the bustling crowd flow around her as she admired the pleasant juxtaposition of the natural and the artificial. Behind her, the two Magistrates continued their work at the surveillance booth by the gate, wearing fustian robes over the black armor of their office, smiling as they welcomed newcomers to the ville on this day of worship. Buzzing honeybees flitted from flower to flower along the decorative garlands, delving lustily at their sweet contents before moving on in their restless dance through the warm air. There were other people on the street, dressed in light summer clothes, hurrying to and fro just like the bees, their clothing bright and clean in the midmorning sunlight.

The white-faced woman stood still for a moment, feeling out of place as she watched the people hurrying by all around her, each with a purpose, a destination. Her name was Domi and she didn't belong here.

The last time Domi had been in Snakefishville—the last time it had been called Snakefishville—it had all been very different. As one of nine magnificent walled cities dotted across North America, Snakefishville had lost its ruler when the hybrid barons had evolved into the Annunaki Roverlords two years ago. Baron Snakefish himself had transformed into cruel Lord Utu. Without the baron's influence, the ville had fallen into confusion and, most recently, it had been all but destroyed by a subterrene, an underground engineering device that replicated the effects of an earthquake and sent the towers of Snakefish crashing down into a crater. When Domi had last visited here four months ago, what little remained of the ville itself looked like something from a nightmare. All that had remained of its once-majestic buildings were a few rotten struts clawing the skies at awful angles, and the wrecked streets were filled with the decaying bodies of the dead.

Yet now, just a few months on, the ville was miraculously reinvigorated. And not just reinvigorated, Domi reminded herself—renamed. Like all things Annunaki, Snakefishville had been reborn, this time as Luilekkerville where freedom was everything and its citizenry considered themselves carefree.

Domi didn't like it. When things changed rapidly like this it was seldom for the better, she knew. The guards on the gate were all too friendly, far too welcoming for Magistrates, and Domi could tell with a glance that neither was combat-ready.

Luilekkerville's buildings were universally lower than those of Snakefishville, and the towering Administrative Monolith that had dominated the center had been replaced by a two-story cathedral. But the cathedral's tower strove higher, reaching up over the new-built city, a circular stained-glass window dominating its front like some all-seeing eye, its panes made up of reds and oranges and purples, just like the old disk on the Administrative Monoliths.

Different but the same, then, still following the old street map that had been created during the Program of Unification, the same regimented plan on which each of the nine villes had been based. A child of the Outlands, Domi had never felt comfortable caged inside the high walls of the villes. They did something to people, she felt sure, muddled their senses and made them susceptible and docile—gave them "tanglebrain," as she called it. Recently, her friends in Cerberus had begun to suspect that there was more to the ville blueprints than met the eye, that the symmetrical design of the cities—with their towering structures that peaked at the center—created some kind of sigil, a magical symbol that could genuinely affect a person's thinking. Cerberus archivist Brigid Baptiste had told Domi that such symbols were commonplace back before the nukecaust, that an ancient political organization called the Nazi Party had used one as a rallying point to recruit their members, a symbol called the swastika.

Domi shivered for a moment despite the warmth of the sun, recalling that excited look in Brigid's eye as she explained this over dinner back in the Cerberus redoubt. Domi had been sitting at the edge of the cafeteria table, while Kane, Grant and Lakesh had all been discussing the implications of what Brigid's discovery might mean in the seats beside her. Domi missed Brigid; she had been her friend, and Domi found friends hard to come by. But Brigid had disappeared during a raid on the Cerberus redoubt, and now she was numbered among the missing while the mountain headquarters itself had been abandoned until it could be rebuilt and made secure.

Domi peered around, watching the smiling faces of the passersby as they made their way to their destinations. Everyone was dressed in light clothes, simple but elegant, the women in long skirts or summer dresses, the men in loose cotton shirts and slacks and shorts. Many of the men wore flowers in their shirt pockets, and some of the younger women had flowers in their hair, here and there in a complete ring like a fairy's crown.

As the crowd flowed all around her like the current of a stream, Domi halted, closing her eyes and taking in the sweet scents of the flowers. Flowers decorated so much of the ville: flowering creepers wound up the ornate streetlights that lined the main street; flowers peeked from their perches in the hanging baskets that decorated the lights; flowers grew from pots lining the center of the road.

Domi relied upon her other senses as much as her eyes, and she allowed her mind to go blank in that moment, letting her impressions take over. Domi was a unique figure among the hurrying populace of Lu-ilekkerville. Her skin and hair were the chalk-white of an albino, the hair trimmed short in a pixie-ish cut that highlighted the sharp planes of her cheekbones. She was a petite woman, barely five feet in height with bird-thin arms and legs. The floaty sundress she wore was colored burnt umber, sleeveless with its hem brushing the tops of her white ankles above bare feet, the small swell of her breasts pushing at its simple bodice. A matching ribbon of material had been wound around Domi's left wrist, its lengths dangling down as she swung her arms. Although small, Domi was wiry, her body muscular beneath the unrestrictive flow of the material. She had secreted her favored weapon beneath the masking lines of the dress, a hunting knife in a sheath just above her left ankle. The blade was well hidden from a casual search, but she had been surprised that the Magistrates hadn't even frisked her. With hindsight she wondered if she might have sneaked a blaster in Luilekkerville, too, but that had seemed too much risk for what should be a simple surveillance mission. She was out in the field alone here, and the last thing she wanted to do was to attract any extra attention that her ghoulish appearance didn't already demand.

Domi breathed deeply for a moment, scenting the air and listening to the contented buzzing of insects amid the fluttering petals. The whole settlement had been rebuilt, constructed from the ashes of Snakefishville at a furious rate. Even now, behind the buzz of the honeybees and the chattering of conversation, Domi could hear hammering and sawing as construction workers continued to build the towering edifices that would dominate the skyline of Luilekkerville out here close to the Pacific coastline.

With its fresh air and happy population, the change in the ville seemed almost a bewitchment.

As Domi stood there, one of the passersby stopped in front of her. When Domi lifted her eyelids, two scarlet orbs reappeared like glistening rubies in her elfin face as she turned her attention to the stranger. The stranger was a beautiful woman of indeterminate middle years, a golden tan to her skin and smile lines around her eyes with a long lustrous mane of blond framing her pretty face. A small wicker basket depended from its hard straps under the woman's right arm, its open bowl filled with freshly picked flowers. Domi watched in surprise as the woman reached into the basket and handed her a flower, its trimmed stem just an inch or so in length.

"For you," the woman said, smiling brightly as she offered Domi the flower.

Domi reached out and plucked the flower from the woman's hands, nodding in gratitude. "Thank you," she said, surprise clear in her tone.

"Our love is solid as rock," the woman recited with a warm smile before stepping past Domi and moving on down the street.

It was not often that a stranger approached Domi in such joyous circumstances. She had grown up a wild child of the Outlands and she was used to being singled out as a freak thanks to the albinism that distinguished her from the people around her. As Domi watched, the blonde woman continued along the street, handing out more flowers to the people crowding there, offering her chanted words before moving on to the next.

Domi peered at the flower, sniffing at its rich scent for a moment as she twisted its stem around and around between her fingers, making it spin. There was something going on here, just beneath the surface—an all-pervading attitude that seemed to have affected the populace of the born-again ville. The nine villes had always acted as a sort of safe haven, a shelter from the ravages that man had brought upon himself with the advent of the nukecaust and the Deathlands era that followed. They had grown up as a part of the Program of Unification, and had brought a much-needed regimentation to the lives of their residents. In total, forty-five thousand people had been spread equally across nine walled cities, and they had lived a harmonious existence. Yet the happiness on show here, the undercurrent of joy, was something Domi had never seen before. It was a happiness that transcended logic, a primitive happiness at simply being alive. It was sinister somehow, as if a mass brainwashing had taken place.

Domi stepped out of the way as three gallivanting children came hurrying past, laughing as they threw a weighted cloth bag back and forth among themselves. The oldest of them was perhaps nine years old, and she wore a daisy chain in her flowing black hair, in unconscious imitation of many of the adults who wandered along the street.

Domi watched as the children hurried on, wrapped up in their game of mutie-in-the-middle. Then she turned her attention back to the other people on the street, looking for patterns of behavior. The vast majority seemed to be heading in the direction of the center of town, and Domi scanned the broad street ahead until her eyes met with the cathedral that towered above everything. Its red window seemed to glow like the evening sun, a single bloodshot eye observing the populace of the ville. Even as she watched, Domi became aware of the tolling as a bell was struck, and then it came again after a few seconds' pause, and again.

As the bell tolled, the citizenry of Luilekkerville

seemed to turn as one, making their way more determinedly down the street toward the looming cathedral in the town center. Casting the flower aside in a waste receptacle at the side of the road, Domi joined the crowd, keeping her head down in that most simplistic of disguises—hiding in plain sight—as she made her way toward the cathedral.

Up close, the cathedral looked rough, its walls hewn from hard rock of a miserable brown-gray mix. Shingles covered its facade in a swirling pattern, as if washed up by crashing waves on a beach. The basso bell continued tolling from within, its single note calling the locals to worship, and Domi walked with them, furtively looking around. The locals seemed happy enough, laughing and jolly as they continued their friendly conversations. There were adults and children, old folks who needed sticks to help them walk just shuffling to the open doors of the cathedral that waited in the center of the ville. Some of the children ran or skipped along, and several of the adults skipped, too, one young couple laughing as they skipped hand in hand through the wide archway into the structure of the building. Other than the central tower, the cathedral was just two stories high, and the archway dominated its frontage, almost two stories at its apex and wide enough to drive a Sandcat assault vehicle through without touching the sides. There were no doors, Domi noted—the doorway remained open day and night, allowing free passage for those seeking entry. Perhaps that was a throwback to the days when this settlement had been Snakefishville, as the Program of Unification allowed for no locks on doors, no privacy for the individual, for privacy showed a lack of trust in one's fellow man and lack of trust had been the overriding rationale of the Deathlands, that terrible time that had preceded this.

With one last glance behind her, Domi padded beneath the towering archway and into the body of the cathedral itself, the distinct aroma of flowers coming to her nostrils even as she stepped beneath the arch. It was darker inside, away from the morning sun, and it took a few seconds for Domi's eyes to adjust, a blur of green sparking momentarily in front of her retinas. The sunlight drew a deliberate pattern inside the church itself, the archway of the open door cast in an elongated line across the floor, stretching two-thirds of the length of the main aisle leading to an altar that Domi estimated had been placed close to the center of the building. Some trick of the light turned that bright pattern into the roughly hewn form of a man, and Domi checked behind her once more to confirm that the arch was still an arch; it was. She realized there must be subtleties to the carved structure to generate this illusion, the towering stone man was drawn by the brightness of the sun across the floor like some giant carrying the worshippers on his broad back. She knew what it was, of course—it represented Ullikummis.

Domi made her way into the main chapel, its walls stretching two stories up to the high rafters of the building, creating a generous feeling of space. As outside, the interior walls were carved of rough rock, and they had an unfinished feel to them, their surfaces pitted and mottled like sand. The floor was flat like slate, and Domi winced as her bare feet padded from the warmth of the sun through the arch to the icy coolness where the floor had remained in shadow all morning. She peered down, seeing patterns painted on the floor, dappled in whisker-thin lines of red as if veins or arteries.

The sound of the clanging bell was loud within the cathedral, its droning note echoing from the hard surfaces of the walls and floor. Behind the altar, Domi saw a towering structure made of glass, hexagonal with a diameter of twelve feet or so, stretching up into the highest reaches of this tower that dominated Luilekkerville's skyline. The glass tower looked like something medical and it contained the chiming bell, its heavy cone swaying back and forth like a lily in the wind, its petals just beginning to open for the spring. High up in the bell tower, the single circle of stained glass glowed a fearsome red where the sun struck it, turning the sides of hexagonal glass red where the panes met, like lines of blood dripping down from the heavens—the blood of the gods.

The wide aisle stretched up toward the central altar, abutted by two broad columns of chairs, simple things carved of wood. The people of Luilekkerville were filing into these, the chairs filling up like a theatrical audience. As they sat, Domi saw other aisles leading up to the altar from all sides, ten spokes converging on it with lines of chairs dividing them, each one containing the same sunlit illusion of the fallen man-god for the communion to walk upon. She estimated that the cathedral could seat eight hundred or more at any one time, and it seemed to be almost full even now. Domi slowed for a moment, eyes roving over the crowd, halting here and there as she spotted that familiar shade of vibrant red hair she was hoping for. A woman sat just a few rows away, her back to Domi, a cascade of red-gold curls tumbling freely down her back. Domi watched for a moment as the woman sat there, then saw her turn to talk to a child tugging at her arm, revealing the hard planes of her face more clearly to Domi. For a moment Domi's breath caught—but no, it wasn't who she had hoped, not Brigid Baptiste, just a stranger with hair the color of the setting sun.

Her long skirt brushing at her ankles, Domi took an aisle seat two-thirds from the back. She pulled her legs in to allow others to shuffle past, take the empty seats in the row—she was an interloper here and she wanted to keep a clear path for herself to the exit. Instinctively, Domi's hand reached forward, brushing at her skirt for just a moment, feeling the blade sheathed just above her left ankle.

Domi sat and watched, listening to the loud chimes of the single bell as it swung to and fro. High in the rafters, Domi saw more garlands of flowers had been stretched, lining the walls and twirling like creeping vines down the rough stone pillars that held the structure up. It was strangely simple, beautiful in a naive way. It reminded her of some of the more simplistic outlander rituals she had witnessed.

The cathedral was abuzz with voices, no one person's standing out but all of them together generating a low blanket of muffled words that seem to fill the theater with a sense of camaraderie, of joy. It was a celebration, an expression of the love of life by the living. Domi sat dour-faced, letting the noise wash over her.

A couple of rows ahead of Domi, a fresh-faced couple laughed, their hands intertwining as they gazed into one another's eyes. The lad was perhaps nineteen or twenty, a thin blond beard barely tracing over his chin, while his girl looked a little younger, a circlet of flowers weaved in her lustrous black hair, shining pips of metal hanging from her earlobes. Their faces came close, noses brushing for a moment, and they laughed once more before kissing. Domi looked away, only to spy more couples— young and old—in similar joyful states.

At the meeting point of the aisles, just in front of the glass tube that held the swinging bell, a figure in a hooded robe strode to the altar area, rising up a small flight of steps to stand before the congregation. His hood was up over his features, his robe a creamy white with red braiding like lines of trickling blood.

In silence, the hooded figure on the podium held up his right hand, spreading the fingers like rays from a stylized sun, and the bell ringer stopped pulling the bell rope, ceasing its chiming with a final tuneless clang. For a moment the hall was still, the congregation falling silent in anticipation. Domi waited, wondering what would happen next. Nervously, she glanced over her shoulder, confirming that the arched doorway was still open, that she could escape if she needed to.

The cathedral remained silent for almost a minute, the robed figure at the altar standing there with his hand still held high, the red-filtered sunlight playing through his outstretched fingers. The congregation began shuffling just a little, a few of the children becoming restless as they waited for what was to come next. Domi watched, eyes narrowed as she traced the red lines that played across the hooded figure's cassock like bloody veins.

Finally the robed figure spoke, his voice loud in the echoing chamber of the cathedral. "Friends," he began, bringing both hands up to his head and pushing back the white hood of his robe. Beneath, he was middle-aged, a square face, clean-shaven with the hint of a tan on his balding pate, a ruddy redness to his cheeks. "Utopia is here, opening before you like a flower in the springtime, paradise on Earth."

Domi turned her head a moment, saw the beatific smiling faces of the crowd to either side of her. The members of this congregation were pleased; they felt safe with these words.

"And what has brought about this utopia?" the man in the white robes asked rhetorically. "Not a baron, that's for sure. We need no barons here, now that we have god. But what is god? you may ask."

The priest left the question hanging in the air for a few seconds, and Domi heard the mumblings of several people around her as they whispered the familiar answer, speaking it quietly to themselves.

"God is love," the white-robed priest announced, spinning around at the altar and sweeping his arms through the air to encompass every person in the vast audience. "This is god, this thing you feel here, among your fellow men and women."

"And children!" a voice shouted from over to Domi's right, and several of the audience members laughed with embarrassment. It was a child's voice, a little girl, excited and restless at the communion.

"Indeed." The priest smiled. "Children, too. We mustn't forget them." He turned, waving to the part of the audience where the girl's voice had emanated from before turning back to address everyone. "I don't think she's going to let me forget them anytime soon," he said with the faux secrecy of a true showman.

Some of the audience laughed at this, several applauding just for a moment.

Up on the podium, the white-robed figure was turning once again, raising his arms to indicate the rough-hewn walls of the cathedral. "God promised to bring heaven to Earth, and so he has. You are safe, well fed, you are loved. He demands nothing in return, your strength is his strength.

"Our love is rock, and a rock never breaks."

Domi felt her breath catch in her throat. The rock god was the thing that had almost destroyed Cerberus, had killed her teammates and left Brigid Baptiste among the missing, possibly dead. His name was Ullikummis and his influence now stretched to whole villes, reshaping them to worship him. And such was his power, Domi realized, that now his people need not even speak his name. He was rock, and rock was love. Domi felt the cobra-creeping fear in her belly as she looked once more at the joyful faces of the congregation all around her. Ullikummis was in their hearts now, his bloody form of salvation sweeping them up like the tide.

For just a moment a breeze blew in from the open door behind Domi, and it seemed Arctic-cold despite the warmth of the June morning. Domi sank into her seat, listening to more of the preachings of this priest of the New Order.

Chapter 4

There came a warm sensation in Kane's eye and his vision blurred for a scant second. When it cleared, a monstrous child-thing was standing in front of him, his lizard-slit eyes staring into his own. Kane recoiled and tried to pull himself away, but the thing with lizard eyes continued to stare, holding his gaze.

Kane studied him.

His flesh was dark and calloused, hardened like something hewn from stone. He stood as if uncomfortable, limbs held awkwardly, the shoulders hunched as though his back was in pain. He wasn't standing in front of him, Kane realized with a start—he was standing in a tall square frame of glass, a mirror. The mirror was set into a wall carved of stone, the glass turning dark and smoky at its edges, a decorative affectation to the design. The wall itself was of a bright stone the color of sand, and a crimson band had been painted through it like the bloody slash of a knife. The wall radiated heat as fierce sunlight played across its surface. They were indoors, but it was still bright, with square, open windows lining the wall opposite the mirror.

Where am I? Kane wondered.

The statuelike figure in the mirror smiled, a frightful rending of the rock that clad his face, his primitive features turning him into something even more hideous.

It took a moment for Kane to recognize it, or at least he thought that he did. Though a child, the creature was tall—towering even—yet he still carried himself with the awkwardness of a child getting used to the changing shapes of his forming body. The tall child turned from the mirror, trudging down a flight of steps and into the darkness. It was cooler here, as they went underground, away from the sun. Kane seemed to be seeing all of this, yet he was traveling with the monstrous child, as if he was a part of him, as if the thing in the mirror *was* him. It was like a dream, a vivid story that Kane was being swept up by.

The child walked and Kane remained with him, feeling the weight of his stone cladding, the hideous aches that fought for attention in his muscles. He felt stretched, pulled almost to breaking point, his muscles screaming as if shot through with influenza.

His feet—which is to say, the child's feet—clomped heavily on the brick floor, stone on stone as he descended the steps. Strange noises flittered to his ears from the foot of the stairs, and Kane marveled as they entered a vast laboratory set in the windowless room there. Clay containers hissed and burbled, naked flames playing on their bottoms and sides. The flames were mostly blue or orange, but Kane noticed that two of them were a fearsome green and a disarming lilac, neither color natural. A plain wooden bench waited in the center of the room, a high side table next to it like a bedside cabinet. A network of glass tubes ran along one wall, multicolored liquids turning to gas or being refined into solid lumps of crystal at various apertures along its glistening, sleek lines. A figure stood there amid the bubbling tubes, his back to the child, his green scaled flesh the color of jade. Kane looked at the figure with fascination—it was an Annunaki, the enemies of mankind. Kane tried to leap, to attack this hated enemy, but he was unable to move, still watching events as though watching a stage play.

Without warning, the scaled figure turned and Kane saw a strange apparatus masked the top half of his lizardlike face. The apparatus was made of circles of glass, lenses on metal arms that could be brought in front of his eyes to magnify his vision, one in front of another. The lens arrangement stood out almost six inches from the Annunaki creature's face, and some of the metal arms remained in the upright position, the lenses not in use by its wearer. Behind the magnifying lenses, the creature's eyes were as green as his skin with twin vertical slits down their centers in the bottomless black of the grave. The monster admired the stone child who was Kane for a moment, gazing up and down as though admiring his handiwork.

"You're looking tall," the creature with the magnifying lenses stated. Kane got the indefinable impression that this Annunaki saw him not as a living creature but as simply a slab of meat on which to experiment, a chef meeting a farm animal.

After a brief exchange, the child lay on the wooden bench, a slab of meat on the butcher's block, and Kane seemed to be lying there with him, two as one. Then the Annunaki with the strange eyewear checked at some solution that was bubbling close to Kane's ears, and he heard the hiss of steam as some superheated liquid expanded and tried to escape its container.

"Calm yourself, child," the jade-scaled Annunaki instructed, his tone soothing. "I can hear your breathing from all the way over here."

"I'm sorry, Lord Ningishzidda," the child said, bringing his breathing down to a more normal level.

Kane waited, helpless as if strapped to the bench where the child remained free. Then the Annunaki, the one that the child had called Lord Ningishzidda, strode over to the bench, wielding a syringe tipped with a vicious-looking needle. Within the syringe, an orange concoction bubbled and steamed like lava, a trail of hot mist whispering at its edges.

"You must keep your eyes open, mighty prince," Lord Ningishzidda explained. "There is no other way."

Then the green-scaled Annunaki came at Kane with the syringe, watching with sick delight as he drove its needle deep into Kane's left eye. It felt like liquid fire being pumped into his eye, burning all sense and reason away. Kane cried out, loosing a scream that seemed to echo beyond the walls of the underground chamber itself, shattering them as he watched. Colors swirled there for a moment.

Around him, the multicolored lotus blossom of the interphaser was fading, lightning strikes firing across its depths like electricity-firing neurons.

Shunted two hundred miles through quantum space by the interphaser, the three companions emerged on a tranquil, grassy plain beneath a cloudless azure sky. Kane staggered forward, clutching a hand to his face where his left eye continued to burn. The eye was watering and he could feel warm tears burning at the dam of his tear duct, swelling as they clamored to burst free.

He rubbed at his eye with the ball of his hand, wiping at the tears as he stumbled blindly forward, two steps, three, before tumbling to the ground, the bright green grass rushing up to meet him with its fresh-cut smell so strong that Kane could taste it.

"You okay, man?" Grant's voice came as if from far away. Beneath that sound, threatening to obscure it, a dog barked repeatedly—Rosalia's mutt, excited at the instantaneous transition through space-time. And beneath that, distant like a shushing hush in a library, the waves of the sea crashed against some nearby shore.

"Kane?" Grant asked again, reaching for his partner where he lay facedown on the grass.

Kane rolled over at his partner's gentle shove, and Grant saw the tears streaming down his cheeks. "You okay, buddy?" Grant asked.

Kane's eyes flickered and he nodded, his head feeling suddenly sore as he moved it. "Jump dream," he explained.

The human body had not been designed for the instantaneous transportation of the teleport, and one side effect was the so-called jump dream that threatened a user's sanity. Mostly associated with the mat trans, a man-made teleportation system that the Cerberus team had employed on numerous occasions, jump dreams were accompanied by nausea and a sense of disturbed reality. However, the interphaser units had rarely generated such jump dreams, and Grant was surprised to hear his friend refer to such a thing after so long.

"You need some time?" he asked, concerned.

Kane brushed at his face, swiping at the tears. "I'll be fine," he said. "Let's keep moving." His face looked red and his left eyelid was puffy, the eye itself blood-shot. "I'll be fine," he repeated as Grant looked at him.

Turning then, Kane led the way up a subtle incline that led to a one-story building set amid the quiet grounds. His companions followed, Rosalia's dog scurrying ahead excitedly to scope out this new place. Off to their left was a simple wooden fence, a long strip of two horizontal boards attached to wide-spaced posts like a farmyard gate. Behind the fence, a sheer drop fell away, ending in the pebble-dappled shore of a tiny beach.

"Looks like a nice spot," Rosalia observed as she peered over the cliff side. "Quiet."

"Work on your tan later," Kane growled as he marched onward. "We have us a meeting to attend."

He was angry, he knew—not with Rosalia but with himself. Whatever that vision had been, that "jump dream," as he had called it, it had left some mark inside him, an indelible burning behind his eye. He blinked, forcing back the salty tears that welled there once again at the memory.

IT WAS A FEW MINUTES after dawn in Tibet and the watery yellow-white orb of the sun was just starting to nudge itself over the towering mountains that dominated the landscape. The woman with the fire-red hair pulled her cloak around her as she ascended the rise that led to the cave opening, striding the final few miles of the snow-dusted mountain path, her horse abandoned with exhaustion. It was cold out here in this mountainous range where Tibet bordered China, bitingly so. In fact it was cold enough to freeze the flesh of the woman's steed almost three hours before. She hadn't cared—the armorlike properties of her shadow suit kept her warm, regulating her body temperature beneath the scarred black leather of the supple armor she wore like a second skin. The cloak that she wore was made of animal fur, a dead thing cinched around her throat, encasing her with its ghosts. Hung inside the cloak, a bag slapped against her hip, a large leather satchel containing something heavy. It had been better when the satchel had been contained in her horse's saddlebag where it couldn't irritate her, but it mattered little.

The wind blew around the woman as she clambered along the rough path, her booted heels breaking the night frost that covered it before sinking into the layer of snow that dwelled beneath like a bloated egg white. Her name was Brigid Haight and she had made this approach before, several years ago when she had been a member of the Cerberus team. That had been before Ullikummis had remade her, showing her the true path and filling her head with a secret knowledge that had always seemed just out of reach before.

Back then she had been known as Brigid Baptiste, an archivist from Cobaltville who had formed one-third of the seemingly inseparable trinity that lay at the heart of Cerberus. Where Kane had brought his integrity and Grant his strength, Brigid had brought knowledge. Blessed with an eidetic memory, Brigid had the ability to recall information to the smallest detail with photographic accuracy. She had traveled the globe under the aegis of Cerberus, expanding her experiences and her knowledge and challenging her archivist's mind with the most complex of conundrums. Alongside Kane and Grant, Brigid Baptiste had learned of the secret history of the Earth, uncovered a conspiracy that stretched back millennia and placed the star-born Annunaki at the top of the evolutionary tree. In those days Brigid had thought that humankind should rebel against this notion, that Cerberus was engaged in a noble fight to turn these alien usurpers away and free humanity from the shackles of their subjugation. She had been naive.

Ullikummis had changed all that, his words bending her prodigious mind, letting it achieve its full potential for the first time. Now she stood reborn, and had chosen the new name of Haight. The role of the Annunaki was deeper than she had ever suspected, their tentacles reaching out beyond this simple plane of existence. The things she had seen as Brigid Baptiste had been nothing more than performances on a stage, but Brigid had been too ignorant to think to look past the curtain, beguiled to think that the play was real without ever considering the activity backstage that created the illusion in front of her eyes. Ullikummis had changed that.

Brigid Haight took a deep breath of the icy air as if challenging it to harm her, to make itself felt. Ignorantly, the air remained cold, caring nothing for the affairs of man or Annunaki.

She had come here before in search of a mythical city called Agartha. Buddhist and Taoist legends had spoken of this city, a secret enclave beneath a mountain range on the China-Tibet border from which strange gray people emerged to influence human affairs. In actuality, the city had once housed a race of aliens called the First Folk, among whom a long-lived creature called Balam had been witness to many of the most pivotal points of human history. Balam had befriended the Cerberus team, welcoming them into his underground city that stood all but deserted hundreds of years on from the days when those initial legends had first sprung up. Balam remained in the city even now, living there with his foster daughter, the hybrid spawn known as Little Quav.

It was Little Quav that brought Brigid to Agartha on this occasion under the instructions of her master, the fallen god Ullikummis. The half-human girl child was actually an Annunaki in chrysalis state. The members of the Annunaki royal family had been reborn in hybrid form on Earth, their tweaked DNA hiding their true nature until a catalyst download was applied by their mother ship, *Tiamat.* The two-and-a-half-year-old child known as Little Quav housed inside her the genetic sequence of the goddess Ninlil, child bride of Enlil and mother to Ullikummis. When the Annunaki, those terrible children of the serpent, had re-emerged on planet Earth, Lord Enlil, the most fearsome of their number, had sought out Little Quav to complete their ghastly pantheon. The Cerberus warriors had protected the child until an agreement could be reached that placed her in the custody of Balam until such time as she came of age. It had been a tentative solution at best, and Balam had been forced to return to hiding with the child so that she would come under no further scrutiny. Ullikummis was determined to bring his mother back to his side in his war against his father—the full nature of his scheme, however, remained unknown. While Ullikummis could not enter the secret city of Agartha without alerting the child's watchdog, Balam's longtime ally Brigid should be able to without raising any undue curiosity.

For a moment Brigid stopped, searching the shadow-painted mountains as they towered above her. There was an access point near here, she recalled, a physical entryway that led into the ground itself. Her emerald eyes narrowed as she peered into the darkness, scouring the base of the mountains until she found the place she sought. It was lodged within her eidetic memory, the location still vibrant despite the rudimentary change in the mountains' snowy covering.

There was something else in her memory, too, appearing for just a fraction of a second as she delved for the hidden location in her mind's eye—a series of golden circles disappearing into the blue, regular highlights of red and green dotted all around the pattern like a Julia set.

Then, her red-gold hair billowing around her like a lion's mane, Brigid made her way to a familiar indentation in the snow-covered foothills, her emerald eyes seeking the opening that was hidden in the shade. Her boots slipped for a moment on the shifting snow, and then Brigid had located the path, clambering down to a clump of rocks that waited like sentries, timeless and eternal.

A few months ago the Ontic Library had gifted Brigid knowledge she had never accessed before, and it had opened her mind to new pathways into Agartha, places that had been hidden before. Standing at the hard rock wall, Brigid twisted her leather-sheathed body, and somehow an opening appeared in the wall where there had been none just a moment before. It was not a mechanical thing, nor a supernatural one; it was simply a way of looking for things that Ullikummis had taught her, a way to comprehend the world as the Annunaki did, no longer constrained by just three dimensions.

Brigid stepped into the open mouth of the cave, and found herself in a tunnel, barely five feet in width with a low ceiling, its black basalt walls faintly lit by a ghostly blue luminescence. There was the distinct metronome sound of dripping as snowmelt plip-plopped down into a puddle that pooled along the floor of the tunnel. The puddle itself was so cool that, in turn, the water would freeze again, creating a glistening silvery sheen on its surface like some slug's midnight trail.

Brigid moved down into the tunnel, descending as it clawed a pathway beneath the surface of the Earth. As she went farther, the rough-walled tunnel opened up and the ceiling became higher overhead, the blue luminescence becoming fainter through its distance from her. Brigid closed her eyes, recalling the map of the area in her prodigious mind's eye. As she did so, she thought she heard something—a voice—and she stilled her thoughts, filtering through the noises around her, the dripping echoes, until she could be sure. It was a child's voice, joyful, laughing, awake with the crack of dawn and hungry to live and to play and to experience.

Brigid opened her eyes and moved on down the incline, making her way toward the far exit of the tunnel. After a while, the tunnel widened even more, and then instead of a tunnel it was a chamber in its own right, a vast room whose shape was like a funnel with the narrow tunnel as its spout. High above, stalactites reached down from the ceiling like grasping talons, many of them wider than a man's body. The child's laughter was louder now, like a musical instrument being playfully plucked and strum.

It took almost four minutes to stride across the vast cavern before Brigid reached a staircase hewn directly into the rock. The staircase was narrow and without sides, and went down another fifteen feet into a far larger cavern. More of that ghostly blue luminescence spilled from the high, arched roof, tiled here in square light panels like a child's jigsaw of the sky, with some pieces still waiting to be placed. Beneath, a grand settlement stretched off through the enormous cavern, its squat, windowless buildings carved of the same black basalt as the cavern itself, radiating like the spokes of a wheel from a central tower—yet again, the towering-center-and-lower-surrounds pattern that had repeated itself throughout history. The outskirts of the settlement sloped gently upward to meet with the stone stairwell that Brigid was descending.

The city was eerily quiet, not a single sign of movement across its vast entirety. Then, as Brigid reached the bottom of the staircase, a small figure came charging through the street in front of her, appearing from behind one of the black stone buildings, her short legs pumping as she hurried to greet the stranger. The girl was human in appearance and not yet three years old, wearing an indigo-colored one-piece suit and carrying a rag doll with red hair and a dress that matched the child's clothing exactly. The girl had snow-blond hair hanging loosely to past her shoulders, and her large blue eyes were wide with excitement. Behind the little girl, another figure strode at a more languid pace, shorter than a man with grayish-pink skin and a bulbous, hairless head. Two huge, upslanting eyes dominated his scrunched-up face, black watery pools like the bottom of two wells lost in shadow. Beneath these, twin nares lay flat where a man's nose would protrude, and a small slit of mouth held the faintest expression of pleasure, the corners turned up infinitesimally.

"Briggly," the little girl said, laughing as she ran up to the woman in the black leather armor.

Brigid knelt on the floor, stretching her arms wide to clasp the girl and pull her toward her.

"Welcome, Brigid Baptiste," the gray-skinned creature acknowledged from behind the little girl.

It was all so easy.

Chapter 5

"Just when you think it's done it starts again," Grant growled as he took a seat in Shizuka's winter retreat. He was a large man, so large in fact that he made the seat he sat in look comical, like something out of a cartoon. Dressed in a skintight shadow suit, Grant was a well-built man with broad shoulders and skin like polished ebony. He still wore his long duster over the shadow suit, black Kevlar that looked like leather, and his dark eyes betrayed his exhaustion. His jaw was dark with the start of a beard beneath the drooping lines of his mustache, his hair close-cropped to his skull. "Damn snake-faces keep popping up every time we try to move."

Shizuka looked at him, gracing him with the slightest of smiles as the other people in the room made themselves comfortable. They had had all of two minutes to get reacquainted once Grant and his team had arrived via the quantum window opened by the interphaser, and the hulking ex-Mag made little secret of his irritation. There were seven other people in the room besides Grant and Shizuka, including four guards standing equidistant from each other in the corners of the large reception room.

Located on a remote part of the coast overlooking the Pacific Ocean, the building was of classic Japanese design, reaching two stories aboveground with a pleasing curve to the roof like a folded ribbon. A simple wooden balcony surrounded the winter retreat, and several more guards from Shizuka's loyal Tigers of Heaven patrolled along the balcony, keeping watch for any approach.

"Tiger Isle has had a few castaways turn up on her shores over the past three weeks," Shizuka explained, referring to the Pacific island home of her Tigers of Heaven. "Missionaries, they initially claimed to be lost, the victims of shipwrecks and the like. We offered them hospitality, but each one eventually revealed himself to harbor a hidden agenda to convert my people."

Shizuka was a beautiful woman, petite of frame—seemingly more so when sitting in front of Grant across the low table that rested in the precise center of the room. Dressed in a simple silk kimono, its wide sleeves swinging several inches below her wrists as she gestured, Shizuka had flawless golden skin accented with peach and milk. She had full-petaled lips beneath a stub nose and her dark eyes showed the delicate almond lilt of her Asian ancestry. Despite her small stature, Shizuka was a fearsome warrior, a full-blooded samurai who ruled her people with firmness tempered with mercy. She was also Grant's lover.

"One of these missionaries tried to push a stone into the face of my majordomo," she continued in her trilling, singsong voice. "It was most strange."

"They worship a rock creature," Kane stated by way of explanation, his voice betraying his irritation. "Big fucker name of Ullikummis, yet another member of the endless Annunaki royal family."

Shizuka nodded once in acknowledgment. Like

Grant, Kane wore a shadow suit, which he had chosen to augment with a battered old leather jacket of a worn brown color, its slick surface scuffed and bearing a patch across one elbow. The jacket was still dusted with the soil of the little village between the cliffs where he and his companions had been ambushed by the worshippers of Ullikummis. He also wore his favored black boots—also scuffed—one of the last survivors of his Magistrate days, and dark pants held up by a belt with a large buckle of dull, gunmetal finish.

Kane stood by one of the windows, his broad shoulders leaning back against the frame, his legs crossed at the ankles. Over six feet tall, Kane looked imposing when he stood to his full height, his steel-gray eyes boring into you like a laser beam beneath his dark brows. With his long and rangy arms and legs, there was something of the wolf to Kane's physical appearance. There was something of the wolf in his nature, too, both a natural pack leader and a loner as the need arose.

Kane had been Grant's brother-in-arms for more years than either cared to admit. Shizuka had known Kane for as long as she had known Grant, and the two ex-Mags had often seemed inseparable. Kane looked tired now, dark lines around his eyes, his poise just a little flatter than Shizuka had ever noticed before. Several days of stubble darkened Kane's jaw, a hint of ginger beginning to make itself known at the edges of his lips. Kane had left his hair to grow out since the last time she'd seen him, and it brushed against his collar with an untidy kink, as if he had not had the chance to comb it before arriving for this meeting.

The other man in the room spoke up then from his

position in a soft seat at the end of the table. "Ullikummis has been something of a thorn in our side over the past few months," Lakesh said. His refined voice had a pleasant, almost musical quality. Lakesh was the founder of the Cerberus organization. Mohandas Lakesh Singh was a master cyberneticist and physicist born in the distant twentieth century. A combination of cryogenics and surgery had kept him alive well into his third century, yet he sat with them now as a man who appeared to be no more than perhaps fifty-five years of age. His dusky skin looked flawless, and his blue eyes shone with vitality. His sleek black hair was slicked down to his scalp over a high forehead, betraying just a little white at the temples and over the ears.

Until very recently, Lakesh had been suffering from a degenerative time-bomb that had been hidden in his DNA by Enlil, the Annunaki overlord. However, less than two weeks ago a chance encounter with a Quad V hybrid mutant called Priscilla had reversed the genetic curse in the elderly scientist's system, retarding the aging process and granting Lakesh yet another lease on life. That encounter had brought Lakesh's physiology back to that of a man of roughly fifty-five years of age, and he felt nothing less than reinvigorated at the hands of such a miracle. Dressed in casual clothes, Lakesh had arrived separately from the other three visitors, making his way to this hidden rendezvous under his own steam and appearing about an hour prior to his colleagues. He sat with a large travel bag at his feet, in which he had stored a powerful laptop computer among other items.

"The exiled son of Enlil," Lakesh elaborated, referring to the loathsome Annunaki overlord who had proved to be Cerberus's fiercest and most long-lived opponent, "Ullikummis returned to Earth in a meteor shower almost four months ago. As with all Annunaki, Ullikummis is indoctrinated to believe that he is a god here on Earth, and he began recruiting followers almost immediately. His methods of recruitment have been nothing less than brutal. The stone you refer to was most likely an obedience stone—a semisentient piece of Ullikummis's own body that burrows under a host's skin and is able to dull the thoughts of the host, as well as grant them incredible physical properties such as the rigidity of stone itself."

Rosalia, the remaining member of the group, spoke up. Like Kane and Grant, Rosalia's trim, long-limbed body was sheathed in a shadow suit, which clung enticingly to her curves like body paint. She had shucked off the torn skirt and jacket that she had arrived in, better showing the way the material hugged her trim body and firm muscles. A mercenary by trade, Rosalia had found herself siding with the Cerberus rebels after Ullikummis's troops had infiltrated the Cerberus redoubt. She crouched on the wooden boards of the floor, stroking the neck of her faithful dog to calm it after the journey through the quantum gateway.

"Some of the stones have different properties," Rosalia explained in her husky voice, the trace of her Mexican accent showing in the way she stretched her words. "The real nasty ones, they turn people into firewalkers, able to resist pain and even deflect bullets from their skin. I've seen them do it. Those people, they're bad news—they're where the whole thing starts up. You get one of those in your house, and he'll recruit or kill anyone he can get his hands on."

Shizuka listened as the beautiful Mexican woman continued. She had not met Rosalia before, had been surprised when Grant and Kane had arrived without their usual traveling companion, the red-haired Brigid Baptiste. For now, the samurai warrior woman would hold her tongue, but she wondered how much this dark-haired woman could be trusted—her body language gave so little away.

"But there are other stones, too," Rosalia continued. "Lesser ones that just shit with your mind. Well," she said, laughing, "they all do that, especially if you're dumb enough to let them. But they have other properties, too. Some of them function like hidden keys beneath the skin."

"Sort of like an infrared remote," Grant elaborated in his deep rumbling voice.

"Exactly," Rosalia agreed before turning her attention back to the dog at her feet.

Kane picked up the story then, unable to mask the anger in his voice. "A bunch of these stone lovers attacked Cerberus," he explained. "They had help from inside—some of our own people had been turned."

Shizuka gasped. "It hardly bears thinking about."

"Well, we have to think about it," Kane said. "We had to evacuate the redoubt, get the hell away from there before Ullikummis came back to wipe us out entirely. He's already figured we're a threat. When he took over the redoubt he thought he had us contained. Bad mistake."

Shizuka looked from Kane to Grant, seeing the weariness in her familiar friends' bearing, the changes they seemed to have gone through in the past few weeks since she had last seen them. While Kane was prone to a little bravado at times, his statement that this was a "bad mistake" seemed somehow more a hopeful revision of the situation than a reflection of the truth. Shizuka dismissed her suspicions for now, allowing them to fade into the background. "And what has happened to the rest of the Cerberus personnel?" she asked, looking from Kane to Grant to Lakesh.

"The team is currently in a number of locations," Lakesh explained, "keeping on the move as much as possible. An associate of ours has been immeasurably helpful in hiding our teammates while we took stock of our changed circumstances."

The associate to whom Lakesh referred was an independent trader called Ohio Blue, who worked out of the Louisiana/Tennessee border area. Ohio Blue's network of mercenaries, thieves and ne'er-do-wells numbered in the dozens, with numerous other allies hidden among the gray markets that operated outside of the old villes. Blue had agreed to hide the Cerberus team in scattered locations for a fee, and while that fee was high it was notable that Cerberus—or Kane, at least—trusted her. As Kane had put it when they had settled on this course of action, "I trust these bottom feeders about as far as I can throw them, but Ohio's pretty light so I figure I can throw her further than most." With no better options presenting themselves, Lakesh had taken that as a recommendation.

"But, of course," Lakesh continued after a moment's

consideration, "you already received my message or we would not be here, Shizuka."

Shizuka nodded once. "The Tigers of Heaven own many properties across the globe," she said. "This winter hideaway here on the Californian coast has been held by my family for over three hundred years."

Lakesh smiled, choosing to say nothing. To him, three hundred years was his lifetime plus some small bills in change.

"The winter palace suffered extensive damage during the nukecaust and the horrors that followed, but craftsmen have worked laboriously to remake it just as it was," Shizuka continued. "From your message, I understood that you had need of somewhere hidden away from prying eyes. Will this suit your purposes?" she asked Lakesh, gesturing around the room with a graceful sweep of her hand.

Lakesh looked around, a broad smile forming on his face. "It seems ideal," he said, patting his hand on the large travel bag he had brought with him, "and a very generous offer. It is my hope that we can set up a semipermanent base of operations here where we might regather the Cerberus group and from which we can aggressively pursue Ullikummis and the other Annunaki."

"You believe there are others still out there?" Shizuka asked.

Lakesh nodded.

"Those snake-faces don't die easy," Grant reminded his lover.

"I thought they had all expired in the explosion of *Tiamat*," Shizuka said, referring to the Annunaki's mother starship that had begun a self-destruct sequence while she was aboard about a year ago.

"We've bumped into Lilitu again recently," Grant said, "and we had a run-in with Marduk last year over in Greece."

"By establishing a definite headquarters," Lakesh proposed, "we can tap the satellite feeds and begin monitoring for trouble once again. Our final encounter with Ullikummis showed us one thing—we had, all of us, become lax."

From his position by the window, Kane nodded wearily, rubbing a hand over his face. "The world got a whole lot nastier while we were taking a vacation," he said. "Ain't going to happen twice."

WHILE SHIZUKA WENT through the plans with Lakesh, Kane's field team took the lull in activity to get cleaned up. It seemed they had been going nonstop for longer than any of them cared to remember, and for Kane and Grant that period of activity stretched back to the meeting with Lilitu that Grant had alluded to.

Still rubbing at his face, Kane made his way to one of the winter retreat's bathrooms, locking the door behind him. Alone, he removed his jacket and stripped off the top portion of the shadow suit, leaving his chest bare. His chest was scarred and marked, and the shadow suit itself had tears in its weave where it had suffered some savage trauma. He still half felt as if he was trapped in a prison cell, as he had been just a few weeks ago when Rosalia had shown him a way to break free. His muscles ached, not from overuse so much as from the almost constant tension he felt.

He looked at himself in the mirror, taking in the untidy visage he presented these days. He had been a Magistrate—and a damn good one at that—in the barony of Cobaltville. A peace-keeping and law-enforcement force, the Magistrates were instilled with the discipline of soldiers, and took pride in their abilities and their appearance. Seeing himself looking so unkempt, his hair uncombed and the dark stubble that was already closer to a beard than he'd like, made Kane feel a sense of shame.

Below the mirror there was a basin shaped like a deep lotus blossom, its petals reaching up to contain the water from the faucet. Kane reached for the faucet, fitting the stopper and filling the basin with cool water, watching himself in the mirror as the basin filled. Then he reached for the faucet, turning it until the flow of water stopped.

Eyes on the mirror, Kane splashed water on his face, feeling its coolness waking his pores like the first shock of winter. He stood there for a while, splashing water over his face and feeling it enliven his tired skin. There was something there, in his eye. He couldn't see it, but he could feel it there, like a deadweight tucked behind the socket.

Kane leaned forward, bringing his hand up to his face and pulling down the flesh beneath his left eye, gazing at himself until he blinked. There was nothing there. Just tiredness. Tiredness weighing him down.

ROSALIA WAS SHOWN to a guest room by one of the Tigers of Heaven, a narrow-shouldered man defined by his erect poise and the *katana* blade sheathed at his hip.

After pulling back the paper door, he bowed curtly to the woman and left her, assuring he would provide anything she required—she need only ask.

Rosalia pulled the door closed and made her way to the bed, sitting on its side before lying back to gaze at the ceiling. Her dog sniffed at the door and the creamy white walls of the room, licking at the paper sheets that made up the sides of the room.

"Stupid mutt," Rosalia muttered, shaking her head in irritation. The dog had become her familiar companion in recent months, yet she had little time for the beast, whose purpose and reasoning seemed at best contrary and at worst nonsensical.

She lay on the bed and pushed back the left sleeve of her shadow suit, searching for the little scarlike ridge that was all but hidden on her skin. Rosalia ran her finger along the inside of her wrist until she felt it, the little bump that indicated the presence of her obedience stone. It was an infiltrator in her body, a souvenir from the brutal attempt to indoctrinate her into the cult of Ullikummis.

The stone had remarkable properties that made Rosalia retain it, including acting as a key for specific doors relating to the Ullikummis faction, and hiding her presence from other indoctrinated worshippers of the stone god. However, the thing worked like a parasite, fueled by her own body, drawing blood to keep itself alive. Unchecked, it would spread tendrils within her body, take control of her mind and make her see the world in a different manner, and so she had to keep a steady watch on it.

As her dog settled itself on the floor, turning around

three times before finally lying in a spot close to the door, Rosalia reached for her jacket and pulled out a portable sewing kit, its fabric case no longer than her ring finger. She unfolded the casing, pulling out one of the long sewing needles that resided within. Then, taking a deep breath to steady her nerves, the beautiful dark-haired Latino plunged the tip of the needle into her wrist and began to work it in a tiny circle, probing for the vampiric stone that had buried itself in the flesh that ran alongside her ulna bone.

ALONE FOR THE FIRST time in more than a week, Grant left Lakesh to sort out the details while he made use of the bath that rested in an en suite arrangement off the master bedroom he would share with Shizuka. The bath was a vast circular bowl, finished in white and set at the same level as the floor, a mixer faucet at its edge. He filled it with steaming water, stripped and dipped beneath its surface, letting its warm embrace soothe his aching muscles. His body was immensely powerful, all muscle with not an ounce of fat, a few old scars puckering his mahogany flesh. This wasn't just the first time he had been alone in more than a week; it felt like the first time he had been off his feet in all that time. His knees had cracked as he sank into the bath, and he was all too aware of the kink in his back muscles.

"I'm getting too old for all this running around," Grant grumbled to the empty room, sinking back into the bathwater. He was only a few years older than Kane and had always been stronger than him, but there were occasions when he envied Kane's speed and enthusiasm just a little. Lately, however, Kane's enthusiasm seemed to be waning; the man was clearly grieving for their missing companion, Brigid Baptiste.

Grant lay in the bath, the water still running from the faucet, allowing his thoughts to drift along with the eddies of the water, until the door slid back on its runners and Shizuka came to join him on whispering feet.

Grant peered over his shoulder, watching Shizuka shuffle into the room on her wooden sandals until she stood in front of him. She bowed once in acknowledgment, her face emotionless.

"You need me out there?" Grant asked. "I kind of lost track of time. How long have I been here?"

"No," Shizuka assured him. "Lakesh and I have agreed upon the essential workability of the project now, and Lakesh is putting together his plans so that he can call upon and gather your people."

"Oh," Grant said. Being on the run with Kane and Rosalia, it had become easy to forget that they were part of a larger organization. He had grown accustomed, however briefly, to calling the shots without worrying about the rest of the team. His thoughts brightened as he admired Shizuka properly for the first time since they had arrived at her winter vacation palace. "Still as beautiful as ever," Grant observed, "only more so than I ever can actually remember."

Shizuka smiled timidly, her silky black hair falling over her face for a moment as she leaned forward. Then she ran one of her delicate hands through the bathwater, letting it play through her widespread fingers. "It's getting cold," she said.

"It's been a while since I got to do this," Grant said. "Hot or cold doesn't come into it awful much."

Making her way around the edge of the sunken bath, Shizuka adjusted the mixer faucet, turning its trickle back into a gush until it ran steaming hot, replenishing Grant's bath with warmth. She was closer to his head now, in line with his chest, and she peered openly at his face for a half minute.

"Something on your mind?" Grant asked finally.

Shizuka stroked her hand across her own chin, holding his gaze. "You look different," she said, meaning his beard.

"It's a new world out there," Grant told her, "more dangerous than it's ever been before. Ullikummis and his followers have got a mad-on for Cerberus—me and Kane especially. Not had much time to stay neat and tidy, but I figure it doesn't hurt to change my appearance a little, just to keep them on their toes so they don't know quite who they're looking for."

Shizuka reached forward and, very gently, ran her fingertips through the hair of Grant's scalp. The sensation made his head tingle, and he felt suddenly relaxed, as if he could fall asleep at any moment. "I like the beard," Shizuka told him with simplicity.

Grant closed his eyes, languishing in the warmer water that was topping up the bath. "It's good of you to do this for us," he said. "For Cerberus, I mean. It could bring down a shedload of problems on your house, you know."

"I know," Shizuka whispered, her voice close to his ear.

Grant sighed, the images of the past few weeks playing across his closed eyelids. "We didn't see it coming," was all he said, deep resignation in his voice.

Then Grant felt a movement beside him, and when he opened his eyes Shizuka was right next to him, stripped naked and dipping herself into the wide pool of the bath beside him. He smiled, pulling his arm around her and leaning in to kiss her gently on her rose-petal lips. They kissed for a while, with increasing urgency as they rediscovered one another in the flowing waters of the bath. When they were done, Shizuka pulled away, resting her hands on Grant's broad chest.

"Grant?" Shizuka asked. "You said that you and Kane were wanted by this Ullikummis thing and his followers. But what about Brigid? Kane never travels without her, and you rarely travel without him. Is she in hiding? Have things become so bad that the three of you have had to split up so as not to be recognized?"

Grant shook his head, and suddenly it seemed as though all the life had left him. "Brigid's missing," he said. "She disappeared during the assault on Cerberus. We haven't seen her since. We tried tracking her by the transponder implant," he explained, referring to the subcutaneous transponder that had been injected beneath Brigid's skin. It should have been instantly traceable via the Cerberus mainframe anywhere on Earth. "It seemed to have been switched off or blocked somehow. Lakesh has people working on it."

"If the transponder is no longer broadcasting," Shizuka said, "could that mean that Brigid is…?" She stopped, either unable or unwilling to state her fear aloud.

"No," Grant said, shaking his head wearily. "Kane thinks he'd know somehow if Brigid was dead. Says their *anam-chara* link would warn him."

The nature of the *anam-chara* had never been fully explained, but in essence it meant that Kane and Brigid were soul friends, mystically bonded throughout eternity, ever vigilant for the other's well-being. Some assumed it meant they were destined to be lovers, too, though Kane and Brigid had discouraged such speculation, preferring to keep their own counsel on the matter.

Below the surface of the water, Shizuka's hand reached across until she found Grant's, her fingers entwining in his as she looked in his eyes. "And what do you think, Grant? Could Brigid still be alive?"

"I think the snake-faces have come back from the dead enough times that we shouldn't write anything off just yet," Grant replied, "and we'll know when we know."

Shizuka leaned into Grant's body and he pulled her closer, letting go her hand and wrapping his mighty arms around her as the faucet splashed hot water into the tub. "Who is the other one you brought with you?" she asked, gazing up at the ceiling as she leaned back into Grant's arms. "I do not recall seeing her in my visits to Cerberus."

"Rosalia?" Grant asked. "She's a... Kane found her. She's a substitute."

"Can she be trusted?"

"Ask Kane," Grant replied. "He vouched for her."

Turning her head, Shizuka peered over her shoulder, up into Grant's eyes. "Do *you* trust her?"

"The first time we met she tried to kill me," Grant said with a tight smile. "The second time she was part of the group that locked me in a cell and tried to starve me to death. We might have some unresolved issues."

"But...?" Shizuka prompted, knowing Grant still had something on his mind.

"But Kane's vouched for her," Grant finished, "and I'd trust him with my life—and yours—a dozen times over."

Shizuka stretched as she lay in Grant's arms, kissing him urgently on the mouth once more, and together they drew closer, making up just a little for the time they had been apart.

Chapter 6

The sermon in Luilekkerville cathedral lasted a little under an hour. To Domi, who was naturally restless, it seemed a little like eternity. She neither wanted to be here, nor did she feel comfortable snooping on this performance while she was still worrying about Lakesh's health. She had been with Lakesh when he had been granted a physical reprieve by the Quad V hybrid out in the Las Vegas territory, and she was having trouble shaking her natural concern for the man. They had been lovers for several years now, and her feelings ran deeply for the aging physicist.

Shortly after the Quad V incident, Lakesh had received the response he had been waiting for from Shizuka—confirmation that she could provide a suitable hiding place for Cerberus. At the same time, intriguing reports were coming through to the Cerberus network that Snakefishville had been somehow reborn. With the Cerberus team split across the country, it had been most efficacious for Domi to leave Lakesh's side to check out Snakefishville.

The sermon itself had been surprisingly personal given the size of the minister's audience. Minister Morrow had described himself as a high priest in the glorious New Order. He had spoken on things like love and consideration for one's fellow man, and the way he

had described Ullikummis made the monstrous alien
sound like an angel fallen from heaven. Having been
on the receiving end of Ullikummis's fury, Domi found
this benevolent characterization both fascinating and
disturbing.

However, the vast majority of the sermon had been
about love, about the nature of their unconditional love,
and great emphasis was placed on how the new love was
a love built on rock, sturdy, unbreakable. The congregation cheered and applauded at times, chanting of their
love—and Domi felt she must join in, too, for the sake
of appearance, but she could see the sinister undertones.
Ullikummis was a creature of rock, and his will could
change the nature of stones, moving them and shaping them to form mighty structures. He had used this
power to reshape the Cerberus redoubt into the prison
structure known Life Camp Zero, almost destroying the
Cerberus organization in the process. Ullikummis used
stones in other ways, too, such as the obedience stones
that budded on his body and sapped an individual's will.
Even as Domi thought of this, her hand moved to the
brightly colored ribbon of material that she had wound
around her left wrist. The material masked a length of
almost four inches of her wrist, beneath which was a
puckered scar where she had once had one of the stones
implanted. Domi had used her own nails to pluck the
stone from her body before it could take hold, gouging
out a chunk of her own flesh and leaving a bloody trail
across her arm.

Minister Morrow had encouraged questions, and he
had answered each of them patiently, never once show-

ing irritation, even when two children had asked the exact same question just moments apart.

"Remember that love comes from without," Morrow had concluded. "Broadcast love from your soul, like a radio broadcast, and it will be felt by all around you. Love is the future, and our love is a rock." And then he asked all members of the congregation to reach out and express their love to the person beside them.

There was a low buzz as people said kind words to their neighbors all around the vast hall, and Domi watched as some of the people in front of her embraced or kissed one another on the cheeks. Then, to Domi's surprise, the woman sitting to her right leaned over and hugged her, pulling her close like a mother with a baby. The woman was in her fifties, streaks of gray in her once-dark hair. "Our love is strong," the woman whispered, her lips brushing at Domi's bone-white hair as she spoke. Domi nodded, feeling a little overcome with emotion. With her strange appearance and outlander nature, she had never experienced anything like this, strangers opening their hearts to others so freely.

With that, Morrow had bowed his head and led the congregation in quiet prayer before urging everyone to think on the lessons they had learned today as they began filing from the building.

While the sermon had disturbed Domi on one level, knowing as she did the horror that Ullikummis had brought with his arrival on Earth, it seemed curiously benign. She reflected on this as she rose from her seat to exit the cathedral with the people around her. There were people of all sorts here, and while it was a reasonable assumption that the majority were survivors from

Snakefishville, where they had likely lost everything, it was notable how friendly everyone was. There was no sign of the rigid, almost oppressive class structure that had dominated the old ville. Where once those on Alpha Level had looked down upon the people on Cappa and the filthy slums of the Tartarus Pits at the base of the ville, now it seemed everyone was equal. Truly, they had embraced Minister Morrow's message of love; it dominated not just the congregation but the way the whole of Luilekkerville presented itself.

And more than that, Domi realized, she was being welcomed not as an outsider but as a new friend. Of course she had received several strange looks from people at the cathedral, especially from a few children who had sat close to her; with her chalk-white skin and ruby-red eyes that was inevitable. Yet the old concepts of muties and outlanders seemed far from people's minds here; it was as if they were ready to embrace all people to create their new society, their promised utopia. Domi had spent her life as an outcast, so to suddenly find complete strangers embracing her was something of a shock.

Domi made her way toward the exit of the cathedral that dominated the skyline of Luilekkerville.

"Minister Morrow is a wonder," Domi heard one of the people behind her exclaim.

Other voices cheered their agreement, and there was a friendly buzz in the air.

Domi kept her head down, striding determinedly beneath the open arch and out of the towering building of worship, but then someone stood in front of her, blocking her path. Domi looked up and saw a man standing there, mid-twenties with an untrimmed beard on his chin. The man stretched his arms wide, effectively blocking the wide exit from the cathedral. Domi tensed. If she tried to run, she would call attention to herself and potentially the whole of this brain-addled congregation might turn on her, all eight hundred of them, realizing they had a spy in their midst.

Then the man blocking the entrance smiled, his arms still stretched wide in front of him. "Love is our god," he exclaimed, taking a step toward Domi. His arms reached around her, pulled her close in a friendly embrace. "Spread the message of love, sister," he said. "Spread love across the land."

Automatically, Domi flinched, feeling constrained within the man's broad-shouldered grasp. She had been a sex slave for a while in the lowest slums of Cobaltville, and she still felt a certain sense of disgust at being touched by strangers, despite her seemingly casual attitude toward most things physical.

"Spread love," Domi muttered, feeling self-conscious as the man at the entrance hugged her.

Then he let go, and Domi thanked him and moved toward the exit. Behind her, the man was hugging another stranger from the crowd, an elderly man who needed a walking cane to shuffle along. "Bring love to the world, my brother," the man said.

Outside, the sun was just beginning its languid afternoon descent toward the horizon. It was hot—June hot—and she was glad of the thinness of the material of her dress, the way the skirt swished over her legs to fan her. She would prefer to be in her usual clothes in this heat, of course—for Domi, shorts and a vest top was constraining enough. She began to sweat immediately, a little trace of water glistening across her shoulders and bare back.

Behind her, set near the apex of the towering cathedral structure, the circle of red glowed brighter, the high sun making it sparkle like some scarlet lighthouse, a vast homing beacon for stragglers. When the sun was at its zenith in the sky, the twinkling window could be seen for miles around, its red eye visible as many as twenty miles away on a clear day.

Domi peered behind her for a moment, examining that red eye in the sky, her pace slowing just a little. The red of blood, of life, shining across the surrounds, burning like a sun over the infant city of Luilekkerville.

Outside the church, people were gathering, talking about the sermon, about this new utopia, this Heaven on Earth that they were now a part of. Domi could well believe it, as there was a sense of freedom and cooperation in this ville that she had never known before, not in all her years in the Outlands and in Snakefishville. But Domi suspected that the promised perfection would come at a price—the people of Luilekkerville may not realize it, but Ullikummis was a force of evil, another of the snake-faced Annunaki who had manipulated and subjugated humankind for time immemorial, and whose only care was for himself. While these fools in the villes may believe they had found utopia, Domi felt sure it had to be a part of something else.

As the albino girl took a stride away from the cathedral entrance, someone called to her. "Hey, miss? With the white hair…miss?" It was a man's voice and it had an authoritative tone like a Magistrate's.

Domi tensed. Had her ruse finally been discovered, that she was a spy in the house of Ullikummis?

She turned, offering a fixed smile as she answered. "Help you?" Domi said. The sentence was clipped, abbreviated in the manner of the wild people of the Outlands, an unconscious habit of Domi's during times of stress.

The man was tall and broad of shoulder, in his midthirties with a tanned face. He looked like a farmer or fisherman, some kind of outdoors type anyway. "We're going to have a late lunch out on the plains," the man said. As he spoke his blond-haired wife turned from the cathedral entrance where she had been talking, with two children under five hurrying behind her skirts. "I noticed you were alone, and wondered if you would perhaps care to join us, break bread together."

"In the name of love," the man's wife added in a soft voice, wrapping her arm in his.

Domi looked over the couple for an instant, her eerie red eyes scanning them for tricks. They seemed genuine enough, so much so that Domi actually felt just a little bit touched by their offer. A new philosophy really had taken hold among these people, a new sense of liberty and of consideration for their fellow man. "I…er…I can't," she stuttered. "I have to be… I have a place I have to go to. My father will worry if I'm late and he cannot cook for himself with the sickness."

It was a simplistic excuse, but one with all the evasion and vagary of familiarity: a young woman rushing home to care for a sick relative, a story heard a dozen times every single week.

The albino woman slinked off, continuing along the

main thoroughfare as the man and his wife wished her well, wished her love. Domi made her way past a construction site where people cheerily worked on skeletal scaffolds, the men bare-chested and shining with sweat as they hammered at the newly made walls.

Before long, Domi was walking toward the East Gate. Domi thought back, recalling the rigid old layout of the villes. This area would have been a residential block in the old structure of Snakefish, one of the vast enclaves that sprawled out from the Administrative Monolith as though bowing in subservience to that colossal structure. The new buildings were the same but different, still bowing before the mightiest of their number in the center, only now that tower was the cathedral with its cyclopean red eye.

Domi moved on, feeling the breeze play across her neck where sweat glistened, marveling at how the rebuilding was different, yet just the same as it had always been. Brigid's theory came back to mind for just a moment, the idea that the villes were constructed in a way that locked the minds of the citizens into a certain pattern of thinking, a mandala writ large across the landscape.

As at the South Gate, where Domi had entered the ville, a Magistrate in a fustian robe stood at the gates, his arms folded across his chest, the hood of the robe pulled up so as to mask his features in its shadow. He wore a simple belt around his waist, just a length of rope knotted in the center. A bag hung from the rope belt, made of leather and just a little bigger than Domi's fist. Inside, she knew, the bag would contain a clutch of stones, their edges sharpened, flecks of Ullikummis, either a part of his body or something he had produced with his uncanny mastery of stone. The rocks were ammunition. The man would also have a simple slingshot hidden in one of the pockets of the robe, a strangely primitive weapon yet devastatingly effective when combined with the stones. Domi had been on the receiving end of those slingshots less than a month before, when Cerberus had fallen. The Magistrate was one of the warrior class that Ullikummis had trained, and his hood likely hid the bulge on his forehead where an obedience stone was buried.

The robed man was speaking to two people as they exited the ville. It was the young couple from the cathedral that Domi had noticed earlier, the girl with the crown of flowers in her hair. Their hands were intertwined and the dark-haired girl leaned against the lad, her crown of daisies coming up to the point of his chin, brushing at the whiskers of his thin blond beard. The girl wore a dress of purest white cotton, its hem swishing just above her knees, sandals on her feet. The lad was wearing a loose cotton shirt, breeches and a tie-dyed cape that fell to the base of his spine. The man at the gate nodded the couple through.

"Love be with you," the pretty young lady said as they passed.

"And with you," the hooded figure replied.

Domi followed the young couple, and as she got closer, the robed man turned and she saw something glinting on his left breast. Her eyes snapped to it, recognizing the design immediately—a red shield, the symbol of office of the Magistrate. With the collapse of the baronies, the Magistrates had struggled to keep order, and their authority had dwindled over the two years that followed. Now, Domi realized, the old symbols were reappearing, reborn under the yoke of Ullikummis. The symbols had power, and Ullikummis was turning their familiarity to his advantage, branding his new model army as Magistrates for the world he was building. Everything old was new again.

Domi nodded as she caught the Mag's eye, inclining her head as she made her way to the gate that he guarded. The gate was open, and the Mag watched sullen-faced as she exited the ville.

In the old days the villes had kept all gates closed and guarded, vast towers watching for the approach of strangers to the villes, preparing for any hint of attack, any threat of disruption to their citizenry's ordered lives. Now, Luilekkerville left its gates open, welcoming all comers to the burgeoning society they were creating, so long as they were here to worship this cult of Ullikummis, to confirm their love of love. It seemed like a natural progression, in some ways, for the Program of Unification had specified the need for openness, that no citizen may lock his or her door for they should never have anything to hide. Here, in the infant Luilekkerville, the concept had been taken to its logical conclusion, the gates left open for any who agreed to embrace the future.

But there was more to it than that, Domi intuited as she made her way out onto the dirt road beyond the gates. It wasn't simply about letting people in, hooking them into this new religion the way an angler hooks a fish—the open gates allowed people to leave and so let the message be spread across the Outlands beyond.

Up ahead, Domi saw the young lovers making their way along the dirt path that led from the gates. Their laughter carried as they walked, linked hands swinging back and forth. Domi slowed her pace, not wanting to catch up with them or anyone else using the roadway on this hot afternoon.

Domi trudged along the path toward the trees in the far distance. Other people were approaching the towering ville via the roadway, called by the insidious siren song of that red, unblinking eye atop the cathedral. Domi had approached from the south but had chosen to leave via a different gate, a natural way of covering her tracks just a little to make her movements in and out of Luilekkerville that little bit more difficult to trace. When she was sure that the Magistrate at the gate wasn't watching her, she stepped off the pathway and made her way up toward the line of trees lining the ridge beside the newly rebuilt ville. She had left her interphaser unit there after journeying here, with its remarkable capacity for instantaneous travel for a human subject.

Domi checked around her, preternaturally aware of her surroundings. Up ahead, the young couple had halted, the young man leaning down to kiss the girl at his side. Then, as Domi watched, he bent down until his torso was almost horizontal, parallel with the ground, his short cape falling to the side. Laughing, the girl with the long dark hair clambered onto the lad's back, hitching her legs up so that he could hold her around the knees. The young man straightened then and he began to run up toward the trees, his girl laughing hysterically as he gave her a piggyback. They seemed happy, and not just that, Domi realized—they seemed free.

Domi put the couple to the back of her mind, making her own way up toward the dark clump of trees that waited patiently in the middle distance. Among the smaller deciduous trees, a crop of towering redwoods stretched into the air, their colossal trunks as wide as whole buildings. Between them, much lower to the ground, poplars and beech trees populated the soil, so much shorter than the redwoods that they seemed almost like toys. As she stalked through the grass and up into the tree line, Domi saw churned earth hither and yon, signs of the damage that the subterrene had wrought just a few months before. An underground boring machine, the subterrene had created a crack in the earth that had plunged Snakefishville into a crater. But its effects had stretched out farther than the fallen ville itself, disrupting portions of the ground for miles around. Even now, the immediate area was still prone to cave-ins.

As she walked, Domi engaged her Commtact, a radio communications device hidden beneath her skin along the line of her mastoid bone. The subdermal device was a top-of-the-line communication unit, the designs for which had been discovered among the artifacts in Redoubt Yankee several years before. Commtacts featured sensor circuitry incorporating an analog-to-digital voice encoder that was subcutaneously embedded in a subject's mastoid bone. Once the pintels made contact, transmissions were picked up by the wearer's auditory canals, and dermal sensors transmitted the electronic signals directly through the skull casing, vibrating the ear canal. In theory, even a user who was completely deaf would still be able to hear normally, in a fashion, courtesy of the Commtact device. Like most of the members of the Cerberus field teams, Domi had had the Commtact surgically embedded beneath her skin as standard, a relatively minor operation that allowed her to keep in real-time contact with her companions and home base in any given situation.

With the Cerberus personnel now scattered across the continent and beyond, the hidden communication devices had become more crucial than ever, but the decision had been made early on to use them sparingly. Lakesh had tasked his right-hand man, computer expert Donald Bry, to create a scrambler for the devices, disguising Cerberus's radio communications with a randomizer. With the group now wanted by Ullikummis and his expanding New World Order, it had seemed prudent that the Cerberus personnel do their utmost to keep their communications untraceable.

"Hello, Cerberus," Domi said, her voice barely above a whisper. The Commtact would pick up and boost any spoken word, thus limiting the necessity to speak loudly when engaging the device.

For a moment there was silence from the hidden Commtact, and Domi struggled over a churned-up ridge of dirt before wending between the trees beyond. A wide crack ran across the soil here, opening two or three feet wide in places.

Then a familiar voice spoke to Domi, seemingly from just beside her ear as the Commtact relayed the signal. It was Lakesh. "Hello, dearest," he said, genuine concern clear by his tone. "How are things going out there in Snakefishville?"

"Kind of weird, but everything went okay," Domi told him, speaking softly as she made her way through the filtered lines of sunlight cast amid a dense copse of deciduous trees. "Just leaving the site now and on my way to pick up the interphaser. By my chron, I'll be ready to phase back in about six minutes. Can you remind me of the coordinates?"

Lakesh related the coordinates of Shizuka's winter retreat, roughly ninety miles north of Domi's current location, reminding her of the code for the local parallax point that her interphaser would need to target.

Committing the coordinates to memory, Domi crossed the broken ground and made her way into the forest to the place where she had left her interphaser and its carrying case, well hidden from view.

THE SUN WAS HIGH in the sky, casting abbreviated shadows like freak-show people on the ground as Kane made his way out of the winter lodge guarded by Shizuka's Tigers of Heaven. The lodge sat in its own grounds, overlooking the angry Pacific at a sheer cliff face, where the waves crashed against it with the relentlessness of a hornet trapped behind a windowpane.

Kane pushed open a side door and stepped out onto a low wooden veranda that ran all the way around the building. The building itself was mock-Japanese in style, imitating the vast manses from the seventeenth century, with a harmony of sloping roofs that looked like upended books left open at their center pages. An elaborate balcony penned in the veranda, its carved woodwork like filigree lace, a red-painted circular banister across its top. Kane looked at the barrier for just a moment before placing a firm hand on its banister and launching himself over it in a swinging movement of fluid muscles. He landed in the garden below, his booted feet crunching against the shinglelike gravel that formed the path.

Kane peered down a moment, saw that one foot had crushed a tiny, mosslike fern, its pale green leaves arranged in pairs that seemed to stand in opposition to one another. When Kane sniffed at the air he could detect just the faintest scent of mint, and he removed his foot from the plant with a muttered and self-conscious apology.

Above him, several members of the samurai-like Tigers of Heaven stood guard, patrolling the balcony in slow sweeps. There would be more in the vast grounds, Kane knew. It didn't matter—he just needed a little time to himself, where no one would bother him.

The winter lodge was set in its own grounds, and a delicate herb garden had been tended at the rear of the lodge itself. Kane stalked through the garden with the prowess of a jungle cat, glancing briefly back at the lodge to assure himself that no one was following.

Finding a small wooden bench tucked behind the masking fronds of a fern, Kane took a seat, staring off into the middle distance as he gathered his thoughts.

Something strange had happened as he waited for Grant to engage the interphaser back in the hostile village. And it wasn't the first time, either. Something had been bothering him for a week or so now, his muscles tensing up when he had least expected. He was becoming aware of a dull ache in his face, too, across the left side, not a pain so much as a lack of sensation. That jump dream hadn't helped, that vivid tale of burning inside his eye.

Kane narrowed his eyes, watching the way the sunlight played in and out of the shadows cast by the swaying fronds. His right eye adjusted to the bright green effect of dazzling sunlight as it smashed against the rods and cones that painted imagery for the brain. But his left eye seemed duller, as if watching the same scene through a haze, a subtle clouding of the lens.

The burning after the jump dream had been like an allergic reaction, as if something had become caught beneath his eyelid and made it swell, clouding his vision with a web of mucus. Heat and mucus, man's defense mechanism against infiltration.

Kane opened his eyes wide once more and the mist abated, returning to the very edges of his vision, hiding in the corners of his left eye.

Just a few weeks ago he could have asked Reba DeFore, the Cerberus physician, to check over his eyes, identify and treat whatever infection he had picked up. Now, with the Cerberus redoubt abandoned and their forces in disarray, such resources were no longer within easy reach.

"Damn," Kane muttered, shaking his head in irritation.

It had all become so very complicated.

DOMI HAD WISELY hidden the interphaser a long way from the road, further assuring it would be safe from casual discovery. With her heightened senses, she would have little trouble locating where it sat in its protective carry case again among the dense forest of towering redwoods and poplars. But as she clambered over a fallen tree, Domi spotted movement up ahead. Instinctively, the

albino warrior adopted a crouch, reaching her hand to
the hidden blade sheathed at her ankle, her nose twitching with alertness. The hilt of the blade appeared in her
hand as she warily peered all around her, flashing as a
stray beam of sunlight glinted from its edge. It was a
combat knife with a wickedly serrated nine-inch blade,
and it was the only memento that Domi had kept from
her time as a sex slave in the Tartarus Pits of Cobaltville.

For a moment the forest was eerily still, just the
shushing sound of the wind as it caressed the leaves in
the trees. Domi waited, her ruby-red eyes flitting back
and forth, searching for signs of movement she felt sure
were there. She heard traipsing footsteps off to her left,
crunching against the covering of decaying leaves.

Then suddenly, a noise from close by echoed to
Domi's ears. It was laughter, high-pitched—a girl's
giggle. Domi inclined her head toward the sound,
searching for its source amid the dense cover of the
forest. After a second Domi spotted a flash of white material between the tree trunks, a woman's dress. Domi
moved silently, taking just a single step in a crouch so as
to get a clearer view, peeking over the gigantic, lopped-
off limb of one of the redwoods where it lay in the dry
brown leaves that covered the ground like skin. The tree
limb was colossal, larger across than a grown man's
torso. Domi peered over it, watching that flash of white
amid the greens and browns of the forest. It was the girl
with the black hair, clapping at her boyfriend's back as
he gave her a piggyback through the undergrowth. She
laughed gleefully, and her head bobbed back and forth
as she clung to her boyfriend's back. Then the daisy
crown fluttered free, tumbling past her shoulders and

dropping to the ground even as the pretty girl reached for it.

The lad was laughing now, too, almost losing his footing as he spun around and around, whirling until he finally slumped over with dizziness. When he did so, the black-haired girl fell with him, giggling again as she rolled on the soft leaf cover that carpeted the ground, her joyful giggling echoing through the forest like a bird's cry.

But wait. There was another sound, too, Domi realized, and it really was a bird's cry—harsher than the girl's laughter, with an angry, discordant edge. Even as Domi's eyes searched for its source, a large shadow dropped out of the upper limbs of the trees and swooped down at the young couple.

The diving bird cawed once as it plummeted at the couple on the ground beneath it. Its movements were so swift that Domi could just barely get a sense of its enormous size, and she estimated that the wingspan was eight feet or more. Then the grotesque bird's vicious claws snagged at the girl's bright dress, tearing it and pulling her up into the air, even as she began to cry out.

"No." Domi pounced forward and charged toward the couple.

Chapter 7

Domi sprang forward with the fluidity of a jungle cat, leaping over the fallen limb of the redwood that lay in front of her and sprinting for the gap in the forest where the young couple had stopped. Domi could see the bird more clearly now, and though the surrounding redwoods gave a false impression of the creature's size, she still viewed it with trepidation. Its wingspan was over eight feet from tip to tip, the wings swooping back like vast sails. The wings were covered in a russet down that looked leathery—more like a bat's wings than the feathered limbs of a normal bird. Its clawed talons had grabbed hold of the teenage girl, one of them hooked around her arm while the other jabbed into her torso, spilling blood as it pierced the flesh. Each of those clawed feet was as large as the girl's head, the vicious-looking toes striped in red and black.

The pretty girl cried out, struggling as the bird pulled her up, mighty wings flapping as it sought to pluck her from the ground. Next to the girl in the white dress, the bearded young man was waving his arms back and forth, trying to shoo the monstrous bird away. It ignored him.

The bird cawed once again, an angry screech in the enclosed covering of the forest, its vast mouth opening wide to unleash that discordant shriek as it pulled the girl off the leaf-covered ground. Its beak looked like a pair of twinned scythes, their great hooked lines over a foot in length, snapping together with a mighty savagery that chilled the bone. Above that vicious implement, two beady eyes the color of midnight glared straight ahead, no emotion in their soulless depths.

Domi leaped as the bird took off, kicking her bare feet against the hard-packed ground and launching herself up into the air. Domi twisted in the air, and her body slammed against the flailing form of the girl, knocking her from the monstrous creature's grip. The girl swung for a moment, her dress still hooked on one of the bird's wickedly sharp talons as it ascended with mighty beats of its huge wings. With a slash of her knife, Domi cut the material of the girl's dress where it was caught, and—twelve feet above the ground—the two of them plummeted earthward. Domi and the girl caromed toward the ground in a tangle as the bird cawed in irritation, taking flight as it was relieved of its burden.

The girl cried out as she crashed against the ground. Her dress was covered in blood, its white turning red as she bled from the wounds she had suffered with the talon attack. Domi rolled away as she landed, coming up in a crouch, the knife poised in her hand.

"What th—?" the lad asked.

Domi didn't bother to look at him. "Get back, find cover," she ordered. Her eyes were fixed on the high branches of the trees, watching as the red-black bird became lost in the shadows there.

Then Domi spotted movement above as the bird adjusted its flight path and began to swoop down at the people below once more. Only this time it was accompanied by seven more of the gigantic creatures, each of them unleashing an unearthly cry as they lunged for the trio on the ground.

IT WAS LATE afternoon when Rosalia finally pushed herself up from the bed. After working at the stone that lurked beneath the skin of her wrist, she had sewn up the rip in her skirt, pleating it subtly to disguise where it had torn before lying back on the bed, enjoying the quiet. But her dog was becoming restless stuck indoors, and it whimpered as it lay by the door, watching her with its eerily pale eyes until she finally relented.

Reaching for her jacket, she made her way out into the corridor, the dog trotting along at her heels. She shot it a look as she shrugged her arms into the worn sleeves of the denim jacket, the dark material of her skirt swishing against her ankles. "Always after something, aren't you?"

A guard stood rigidly at one end of the corridor, his leather armor polished and his sword held in its ornate hilt at his waist, eyes locked straight ahead as the beautiful woman and her dog marched past. Woman and hound made their way through the lodge, Rosalia's natural sense of direction bringing her to the main room, which in turn led to a set of French doors that opened into the gardens surrounding the construction. Lakesh had set up a small notebook-type computer at a desk by the wall, and he was tapping at the keys furiously as Rosalia strode past, a portable Commtact hooked over his ear. The computer was a rather dated DDC model, with scrapes and wear showing across its casing, but its memory had been augmented with a card insert, granting the user a phenomenally powerful network in the deceptively small unit. Lakesh glanced up for a moment, offering a few polite words of acknowledgment before returning to his furious work at the computer terminal. He was resetting the Cerberus uplinks that controlled the surveillance satellites they relied upon, running a subroutine so that their access point could not be traced. Rosalia left him to it, observing the lines of code running across the flip-up screen in a single glance.

At the far end of the room, ornately beaded twin French doors had been propped open, allowing for a pleasant breeze to run through the room. Rosalia's dog peered up at her hopefully with those strangely expressive eyes and she nodded, following as the mongrel ran through the doors and out into the warmth of the garden air beyond.

The lodge was set in its own grounds that covered more than two acres in total. A line of trees at their edges provided additional privacy from prying eyes on the side away from the cliff. Several more of Shizuka's guards, the Tigers of Heaven, patrolled the area, marching in long circuits through the main gardens and its surrounds.

The lodge itself was set on raised wooden housings, lifting it a couple of feet above the ground with a wood balcony running its full perimeter. An abbreviated flight of five simple wooden steps led down into a small garden that smelled of herbs and was enclosed by low walls. Beyond the low walls stretched a vast expanse of land dominated by carefully trimmed grass and pruned trees. The dog leaped down the wooden steps and rushed to sniff at the plants and low trees there, so eager it couldn't seem to stop moving to the next thing. Rosalia followed, moving with a little more dignity as she made her own way down the stairs. She spied the figure sitting alone in the garden area immediately, despite the masking effect of the shrubbery. It was Kane, sitting on a two-seater wooden bench, gazing down at his feet in contemplation.

A stone path wound languidly around the garden area leading to a simple water feature by one of the walls, a bubbling stone in a waterfall arrangement that stood three feet high. Rosalia's dog scampered up to this, lapping at the clear water that drizzled into the pool at its base for a few moments. Then, its thirst quenched, it ran on, leaping through the neat rows of herbs until it was at the nearest of the low walls, peering out into the open area beyond.

As Rosalia approached, the dog barked once, looking up at his mistress for confirmation. She swept her arm out, pointing vaguely past the low wall to the area beyond, and the dog yipped before hurrying off to explore. Rosalia left the dog to it, instead making her own way toward where Kane sat.

Kane looked up as Rosalia's shadow crossed over him. "Penny for your thoughts, Magistrate Man?" she prompted.

"Don't waste your money," Kane dismissed, his steel-gray eyes meeting with hers for just a moment.

He hadn't shaved yet, she saw, instead sporting a rugged stubble across his jaw, with his dark hair still in disarray.

"You look like shit, you know?" Rosalia told him, edging toward the bench.

Kane nodded with little enthusiasm. "Thanks."

Then Rosalia sat on the cozy little bench with Kane, the seat so tight that her hip brushed against his. "What's bothering you, Kane?"

"Just thinking about stuff," he told her after a moment's consideration. "Cerberus and everything that happened there."

Rosalia snapped her fingers in front of Kane's face, just an inch from his nose. "Hey, you're free of all that," she said. "We got out, didn't we?"

"Yeah." Kane nodded heavily once more. "But where's Baptiste?"

Rosalia began to reply, "Maybe she didn't..."

But Kane stopped her with a ferocious look, the fury clear in his narrowed eyes.

Rosalia held his gaze, taking a slow breath before she spoke, her voice soft. "She might not be alive, Kane," she said gently. "It's a possibility and one that you should accept. I've had friends die on me before now..."

"Not Baptiste," Kane interrupted.

"It's been a month," Rosalia pointed out reasonably.

"She's alive," Kane assured the woman, speaking with conviction. "I'd feel it if she wasn't."

"Is that what you really think," Rosalia asked, "or just what you hope?"

Kane opened his mouth to speak, but stopped himself. Closing his mouth, the ex-Magistrate gazed out over the gardens for a long time, watching the bubbling stone waterfall as clear water trickled over its sides, filling a small, dark pool at its base. "You were a part of it, Rosie," Kane said. "You saw what they were doing in that Life Camp we were held in. Surely you must know what happened to her, where they took her, why she wasn't…"

With a gentle firmness, Rosalia placed her hand on Kane's leg, the dark pools of her brown eyes fixed on his. "You've asked before and I don't, Kane," she said. "I'd tell you if I did."

The ex-Mag stared at her, waiting for her to flinch, to show some sign that she might be lying. But she didn't. Ultimately, Kane nodded in resignation, accepting the sad reality that Rosalia was trying to tell him. "If she's alive, we'll find her," was all he said, and Rosalia smiled sympathetically.

"Of course," she said quietly.

In losing Brigid Baptiste, Kane had lost his *anamchara,* or soul friend. The nature of their link was something Rosalia didn't truly understand, but she recognized Kane's loneliness and his need for reassurance. Rosalia reached up, stroking a hand along the rough stubble that dotted the man's jaw as he looked away from her.

"You're becoming less like a Magistrate every day," she told him.

"And you sound less and less like a mercenary," he replied, giving her a lopsided grin.

Rosalia smiled mischievously as she looked up from under, into Kane's eyes. "You can be so naive, Magistrate Man," she said, her words barely a whisper. "But it's sweet," she added before he could reply, and she leaned forward and kissed him on the cheek, her tongue brushing along the line of his jaw for a long, lingering touch.

Rosalia gazed out over the tranquil gardens, her rich

chocolate eyes narrowing as she searched for her dog. As she did so, Kane looked at the woman beside him as if for the first time. Lithe of limb with dark eyes full of promise, Rosalia was certainly an intriguing companion for any man to find himself with. For a moment Kane found his eyes drawn down her body, admiring the way the shadow suit painted itself over her curves like a second skin.

INSIDE HIS CHAMBERS in the lodge, Grant sat very still as Shizuka brought a razor blade toward his scalp. He had already shaved away his stubble, trimming it into a goatee-style beard that surrounded his lips like dark strokes from an artist's brush. It had become a very hostile world out there and the encounter at the valley-based settlement only served to remind Grant of just how dangerous it really was. It seemed that the whole world had been turned against him and his colleagues in the Cerberus organization, and he and Kane were now wanted men. A deliberate change in appearance seemed like a smart move under those circumstances.

"Stay still, Grant," Shizuka advised him gently, running the safety razor over his soapy scalp. She had kneaded soap into his hair, bringing it up to a frothy lather before taking the safety razor from his meager possessions and flipping off its plastic catch.

"You sure you know what you're doing?" Grant asked as he sat in a seat in front of the bathroom sink.

"My ancestors have been masters of the blade for over a thousand years," Shizuka reminded him. "I think I can handle it."

"Yeah," Grant said thoughtfully. "But did these ancestors of yours perform any decapitations? Didn't you once tell me your great-granddaddy was the shogun's executioner?"

"Just pillow talk, my love," Shizuka said sweetly, dismissing his frivolous questions. "Now keep still." Then she was running the razor through his hair.

Grant felt her run the razor over his head, shaving away his hair and leaving a hairless streak across his scalp. He smiled at the sensation for just a moment, the feeling of intimacy as Shizuka fussed over his appearance.

Pulling the blade away, Shizuka let out a little laugh, a gentle trilling in the quiet intimacy of the warm room.

"What are you doing up there?" Grant asked, his voice edged with a note of suspicion.

Shizuka reached at Grant from behind, her fingers playing across Grant's lips for a moment, hushing him. "Making it harder for them to find you," she whispered, and Grant felt the razor play over his scalp once more, a lock of black hair tumbling to the floor.

Grant closed his eyes, letting his beautiful samurai companion perform her barber work.

EIGHT OF THE hulking birds swooped down toward where Domi stood by the lad and his wounded girlfriend, wings tucked behind their bodies as they rocketed toward the ground. Domi stilled her thoughts, focusing on those swiftly moving creatures as they blurred in front of her ruby eyes. Her head darted left and right, searching for the nearest tree trunk. Then, as the first of the birds snatched at the ground, Domi began running, weaving out of range even as the bird cried out in irritation.

"Come on, birdie," Domi muttered. "Come to mama."

As the sounds of that discordant caw filled her ears, Domi ran for a nearby beech tree, her chalk-white feet slapping at the earth, arms pumping as she hurried forward. Behind the albino warrior, the flustered bird was lifting its head, bringing its body upward to swoop up and away from the ground where it had tried to attack her, its plumage brushing less than two feet above the ground itself. Domi's left foot slammed against the sturdy tree trunk and she seemed to continue to run, using her momentum to sprint a half dozen steps up the side of the tree before flipping out and backward, arms outstretched as she sailed through the air. Clutched in her pale hand, Domi's combat blade flashed for a heartbeat as sunlight licked across its shiny surface.

Then Domi was rolling in midair and she landed astride the lead bird as its powerful wings cut at the air. With the sudden increase in weight, the bird swayed erratically for two beats of its enormous wings before righting itself. At the same time, Domi found herself falling backward, and her right hand slapped down toward the bird's back, driving her nine-inch blade between the elephantine bones of the bird's spine. They were ten feet above the ground and Domi's legs swung left and right as the knife drove through the bird's flesh, struggling to find purchase. Domi felt the blade judder as it ripped over one of the massive vertebrae, then another and a third before finally lodging firmly in the ghastly creature's back.

Seven more of the grotesque monsters were zooming

toward the ground, screeching angrily as their companion was attacked. They weren't used to prey that fought back, and they sure weren't happy about it.

The russet bird let out an angry caw, struggling to stay in flight as Domi's blade cut into it. With her free hand, Domi snagged a handful of the monstrous avian's leathery tail feathers as the creature spiraled between tree trunks. Domi looked up just in time, some sixth sense warning her, as the disoriented bird went hurtling toward the wide podium of a redwood's trunk.

Domi leaped, pulling her knife free in a rupture of spilled blood as the bird slammed headfirst into the tree trunk. Then the albino warrior herself was hurtling through the air, body twisting as she reached for a jutting branch of the redwood. She snagged it with one hand, flipped over it to quell her momentum before bringing herself up and around so that she crouched on the mighty bow of the towering tree.

"Domi to Cerberus," Domi said out loud, engaging the Commtact unit buried behind her jaw. "Situation is urgent. Please respond."

As she spoke, Domi was scanning the leafy cover around her, watching as the other birds swooped around in dazzling formation. Twelve feet below her, the young man pulled his bloodied girlfriend close to a tree as the birds rushed at the ground one after the other, unleashing angry cries as they grasped for but missed the young couple.

Then Domi dropped from her branch, falling feetfirst toward the next bird as it swooped up toward her, its reddish-brown wings cutting the air in majestic arcs.

"Hello, Domi." Lakesh's voice came over the Commtact. "What seems to be the trouble?"

Domi landed with a grunt on the neck of the swooping bird, driving the sharp point of her knife into the creature's left eyeball. The creature shrieked—though whether in surprise or pain, Domi couldn't be certain—and tried to shake her from where she clung to the downy feathers around its neck. Domi's left hand bunched tighter in the feathers there, securing her grip as she twisted the knife that had been rammed into the creature's coal-black eye.

"I've run into some local trouble," Domi explained breathlessly over the Commtact as she worked the knife. "Weird stuff—monstrous birds attacking in flocks. I'm going to need backup or a cleanup crew."

"Am homing in on your transponder now, dearest one," Lakesh replied over the Commtact link.

As Lakesh spoke, Domi let go of the bird's neck and yanked her knife free. The bird cawed with frustration, wings flapping as it took itself upward, the glossy remains of its eye smeared across its face and beak, loosened feathers fluttering from its neck. Domi dropped from the creature's back and fell through the air away from the ascending bird. Its vision impaired, the giant bird crashed into the branches of the nearest tree, scattering the leaves there, its wings tangling in the larger limbs as it struggled to get free with a frightful shriek.

Domi fell eight feet as the next bird swooped into view. And then her hand snapped out, grabbing a tree limb and using it to flip herself around.

Lakesh's precise voice came over the Commtact again as Domi shifted her balance on the thick branch of the redwood. "Would you please elaborate on the nature of these birds you've found?" he instructed, ever polite.

Her body twisting around the tree limb, Domi lashed out with both feet, kicking the next bird in the face even as its beak widened and it let loose a piercing cry. The knock pushed the bird off course, and it went careening off into another tree letting out a desperate "urk" as its neck snapped.

Domi was swinging around a second time, as the bird crashed into the tree trunk, bringing her legs around and around as the next bird swept up toward her from the ground. "There are a whole flock of the things," Domi related as she gathered momentum. "They look like birds of prey, heavy bastards and almost as big as a man."

Down on the ground below, the young lad toppled to the soil as another of the fiendish birds snagged his face with its sharp talons. Blood sprayed the air as he fell, spitting a loose tooth from his mouth.

High above, Domi's legs snagged around the neck of the next bird as it passed, and she twisted them together in a scissor movement. There was a sickening crack and the bird's neck broke, though it felt as if she had been trying to break a log in two. The creature's wings flapped once more and it went rolling away, losing all sense of direction. Legs still wrapped around the flying creature's wide neck, Domi was forced to let go of the branch before her body was ripped in two.

Hanging upside down, Domi released her leg grip on the monstrous bird as it hurtled upward through the canopy of branches. In an instant, the albino girl was dropping earthward from over twenty feet in the air.

"Their wingspan is maybe eight or nine feet across," Domi explained over the Commtact as she fell, turning the knife in her hand until it pointed ahead like the bowsprit of a sailing vessel.

Ahead of Domi—which is to say down closer to the ground—another of the giant birds was flapping its wings as it came around toward her, crying out as it spotted this tender morsel of white meat. The falling Domi struck it with the force of a jackhammer, her right arm delving into its open mouth as it clamped to snap its beak shut around her. A line of blood formed around Domi's trapped hand immediately where the beast's beak pierced her flesh. Domi's other hand came up, pushing the scythelike beak aside as she worked the knife inside the monster's mouth even as it flapped its powerful wings to gain altitude. The keen edge of the blade tore through the ligaments at the side of avian's mouth, tearing a hole there in the space of two seconds. The beast cried out as blood pumped from the wound that had suddenly appeared at side of its mouth, and it brought its talons up, clawing the air as it grabbed for the pale and twitching form of Domi.

Her hand still trapped in the creature's vicious-looking maw, Domi swung her legs away as those razor-sharp talons grasped for her. One claw nipped at the floating hem of the summery dress, ripping a three-inch line in the light material as Domi twisted herself clear.

Then the creature cried out again and Domi's hand came free. Suddenly she was dropping once again, batting at the leaves and twigs as she fell through the cover of the trees.

How high up am I? she wondered with sudden realization. Even as that thought struck her, so did something else—but this was something far less ephemeral; it was the thick limb of a redwood and it struck Domi with the force of a hammer blow to her head as she continued to drop.

Chapter 8

Lakesh spoke as his fingers played across the keys of his portable DDC computer. "Domi? Domi, please respond."

He didn't stop working at the keyboard as he listened for Domi's response, bringing up a detailed stream of data plucked from her transponder. The transponder display showed that Domi's heart was still beating, her brain-wave activity still peaking and troughing as it should. Yet no response came from their linked Commtacts.

"Domi?" Lakesh tried again, his voice rising a little with anxiety. Lakesh was naturally a calm man, but any risk to Domi cut him deeply. She had put his life before her own on more than one occasion, and even after their recent altercation with the Quad V hybrid, she still acted as a watchdog when she was around him, protective and loyal to a fault. Losing contact with her while they were so far apart was barely endurable.

"Come on, dearest," Lakesh whispered. "Please respond."

Still nothing. Lakesh checked the connections on the Commtact headset he wore while his typing fingers brought up a diagnostic of the Commtact communication network. To his dismay, everything was normal.

Lakesh was not a man to overreact, and he knew that

he was leading with his heart when it came to Domi's well-being, yet he suspected that she was in real trouble out there on the outskirts of Snakefishville. Setting the computer to alert him if Domi's Commtact should respond, Lakesh lifted himself out of the chair—a joy to do so with such ease after his recent health problems— and hurried to gather his companions. Used to giving orders, Lakesh turned to the samurai-styled guard who waited by the door and told him to fetch Grant and Shizuka. The guard genuflected an acknowledgment, then slid open the nearest door and disappeared into the winter lodge to call his mistress. At the same time, Lakesh made his way to the French doors that led into the garden, the ones he had seen Rosalia go through just fifteen minutes earlier.

A light breeze was blowing in the garden around the lodge as Lakesh made his way past the carefully trimmed bushes and herbs, searching the area. He spied Rosalia's dog first, bounding across the grassy plain beyond the low-walled garden, and he raised his voice, calling for Rosalia.

The dark-haired woman materialized at Lakesh's side a moment later, appearing with such silence that Lakesh almost jumped in surprise. "You called?"

Lakesh nodded. "We have an emergency on our hands. I wonder if—"

At that moment Kane joined them, appearing from behind Rosalia, running a smoothing hand over the black T-shirt he wore.

"Aha," Lakesh finished. "That's answered that question."

Lakesh looked at the ex-Magistrate, and Kane recognized the grim look to the set of the older man's jaw. "What's going on?" Kane asked.

"I believe that Domi is in trouble, my friend," Lakesh explained as he hurried Kane back to the building. Rosalia followed them both, calling to her dog in an irritated hiss as if the beast was embarrassing her at a fine restaurant.

Less than a minute later the three of them had gathered in the main room of the lodge along with Grant and Shizuka.

Shizuka had dressed in combat wear, supple leather armor that had been molded to fit her petite form, curving softly over the breasts and tucking in neatly at the waist. The brown leather covered her torso and flared in a short skirt over her hips, leaving her arms and legs free to move with ease. Like the others, she had opted to wear a shadow suit beneath this, its thin black weave protecting her limbs. She also wore an ornate scabbard attached to her belt, gold filigree running along its three-foot length. The scabbard held a samurai sword called a *katana,* its blade razor-sharp.

Grant looked different now, too. His mustache had been trimmed to form a goatee-style beard that surrounded his mouth and his head had been shaved bald, the dome shining like polished mahogany in the sunshine that filtered in through the windows of the room. Kane acknowledged the change in his partner's appearance with a querulous tilt of his head.

"New disguise for the new world," Grant explained as he took a position close to Lakesh.

The long-lived cyberneticist had brought his laptop computer over and was tapping out a sequence on its flat keyboard. "I was speaking with Domi not five minutes ago," Lakesh explained as the Cerberus team settled around him. "She had been investigating the state of play at Snakefishville."

"Isn't that nothing more than a burned-out shell now?" Kane asked.

"It appears not," Lakesh said, "but that is not the reason for this gathering. Domi was making her way to the parallax point via which she planned to join us here on the Pacific coast when she stumbled upon what she described as a flock of monstrous birds. From what she told me over the Commtact, these creatures are almost as big as a man and they appeared to have turned on Domi. Her communication link to me halted abruptly at—" Lakesh checked the computer display "—15.03, prior to which she sounded as if she was in considerable distress. I would ask you, as my friends and as Domi's, to investigate this matter immediately while I try to raise Domi again over the Commtact."

The room was silent for a breath as Kane and the others considered Lakesh's words. Then there was a flurry of movement as everyone began to get ready for departure while Grant made his way across the room to grab their interphase unit.

As he picked up his Sin Eater and holster, Kane looked over Lakesh's shoulder, peering at the display map that showed the location of Domi's transponder. "How close is she to the parallax point?" the ex-Mag asked.

Lakesh tapped a key and an overlay map appeared on-screen, showing the nearby parallax points as flashing red beacons. "We're talking yards rather than miles.

She would be no more than two minutes' walk, by my reckoning," he explained frantically.

Kane put a reassuring hand on Lakesh's shoulder. "Easy, old man," he said, "we'll be there before you know it. It's probably nothing, just a glitch on the comm."

"I think I should…" Lakesh began but Kane stopped him with a look.

"If you're going to say 'come with you' then you can forget it," the ex-Mag said grimly. "Let us do the dirty work while you man Cerberus Mark II here, okay?"

Reluctantly, Lakesh nodded, turning his attention back to the Commtact as he tried to raise Domi.

Shizuka spoke up then, her voice tranquil in the rustling urgency of the room as the others prepared themselves. "Domi's my friend," she explained. "I'd like to join you."

Kane shook his head. "You're needed here, Shizuka," he explained. "Lakesh has to concentrate on the new setup, and he may need you and the Tigers of Heaven if he runs into trouble."

Reluctantly, the petite samurai woman took a single bow. "Your words are wise, Kane."

From close beside the still-open French doors, Rosalia's dog barked joyfully. Rosalia leaned down, scratching the mutt behind its flea-bitten ears.

Busy strapping on the wrist holster that contained his Sin Eater pistol, Kane looked up at the woman and her dog. "What's got into him?" he asked.

Rosalia's eyes shone as she looked at the thing hanging from Shizuka's belt. "Still be handy having a sword with us," she suggested.

Shizuka smiled at the woman's words. "You are trained in the use of the *katana?*" she asked, surprised.

"A little." Rosalia shrugged noncommittally.

Shizuka issued a brief order to one of her guards. With a bow of his head, the man immediately unbuckled the sword he wore at his belt and laid it flat across his palms, presenting sword and sheath to Rosalia.

Rosalia bowed her head graciously before accepting the sheathed blade. As the others readied themselves, Rosalia drew the blade and tested its weight. The *katana* sword was the traditional weapon of the samurai, twenty-five inches of tempered steel honed to a razor sharpness. The blade was solid but felt light and perfectly balanced, making it easy to wield. Rosalia weaved it through the air for a few seconds, getting a feel for its weight before she resheathed it and strapped the sheath to her waist, leaving the sword's hilt at an angle low to her hip like an old-style gunslinger. The hilt itself was decorated with an intricate gold pattern between strips of wound red leather, creating a striped pattern of crimson-and-gold like a hornet's abdomen.

At his computer terminal, Lakesh was speaking into the Commtact, once again hoping to elicit a response from Domi. Embedded beneath her skin, the Commtact did not need sound to activate, Lakesh knew, which meant that Domi should be able to subvocalize her response if she was in a position where silence was paramount. Lakesh waited an anxious few moments, yet still there was no reply.

His face set grimly, Kane led the way to the open doors with Grant and Rosalia following just a few paces behind him, the woman's straggly-looking hound trotting along at her feet, tail wagging and its engorged tongue hanging out of its mouth with excitement. All three were armed now, their workaday clothes augmented with the armored weave of the shadow suits once more, and Grant had shirked back into his protective Kevlar duster. As they passed Lakesh, the elderly cyberneticist informed them of the coordinates of the parallax point that was closest to Domi's current location.

"Keep in touch," Kane said. "We'll be the ones on the ground, but you're our eyes and ears once we get there."

Lakesh nodded as CAT Alpha left the winter lodge and made their way out through the garden at a fast trot. It had taken upward of a dozen personnel at any one time to man the Cerberus control room and keep the field teams safe. Now, in reduced circumstances, he was expected to monitor all the feeds from a single laptop, advising his team and protecting them from harm. That was a tall order in itself, but to make matters worse, the life of his lover was at stake. Lakesh bit at his lip with nervous anxiety as he brought up the map and satellite feed of the Snakefishville area and its immediate surrounds.

DOMI HAD FELT the bird's claw strike her head as she plummeted between the thick leaves of the redwoods, poplars and beeches. Something had snagged her, plucking her from the air even as she hurtled toward the ground. It had all been over in the space of a second, perhaps not even that long, and she had blacked out before she had even been able to order her thoughts. Now, the albino girl woke dazedly, feeling something jabbing into her side. She was lying on a rough surface, the sound of the wind in the trees all around her.

She moved, slowly at first, her muscles tender. Beneath her body it felt as if she was lying on a bed of thorns, sharp protrusions jabbing into her soft flesh. She opened her eyes, and was reassured to find that the sun still lit the sky. It was darker here, the thick cover of the leaves forcing the sun's rays to cut like the strike of a flashing sword wherever it discovered a gap.

How long have I been out of it? Domi asked herself.

The ground beneath her had sharp edges and she stared at it for a moment, trying to make sense of what it was she saw. It looked like a bed of branches, plaited one against another to form a vast bowl with high sides. The torso of a gutted wolf lay by the rounded stick wall, teeth bared, dried blood on its fur.

Domi heard something moving behind her and she whipped around to face it, reaching for her knife where it should rest in the leather sheath at her ankle. The knife was gone, dropped at some point after she had blacked out.

A clutch of eggs waited behind her, three in all, blue-shelled and each one a little larger than her torso. One of the eggs was wobbling, and Domi perceived the crack that was widening on its surface. She was in a nest, the nest of one of those gigantic birds she had struggled with in the forest.

"Domi? Dearest, are you there?" Lakesh's voice came from the internal mechanism of her Commtact, sounding loud as it reverberated through her reeling head.

"Moment," Domi replied, her voice low. A child of

the Outlands, Domi had slipped into the abbreviated patois of the true outlanders.

Lakesh expressed his relief over the Commtact, and instructed her that Kane's team was coming to join her shortly. As she listened, Domi made her way stealthily to one of the bowl-like sides of the ten-foot-wide nest, glancing overhead to see if any of the colossal birds was approaching. A moment later she was pulling herself up the side of the nest and peering over it.

The nest sat in the fork of two branches of one of the giant redwoods, presumably better to hold its weight. The branches stretched off left and right, each one as thick as the widest part of Domi's torso.

"I'm inside a bird's nest," Domi explained when Lakesh had finished filling her in. "Big as a room."

Her movements punctuated by the sound of Lakesh's astonished gasp, Domi climbed over the edge of the nest until she was crouched on the ridgelike branches that formed its side. Two of the mighty birds were spiraling a little way below her, fighting over some bloody hunk of meat while several more feasted on the gore-drenched remains of their brethren—the ones Domi had caused to crash into the trees.

IN THE TRANQUIL GARDENS surrounding Shizuka's winter retreat, twin cones of light suddenly blossomed as if from nowhere as Grant, Kane, Rosalia and her dog waited. Lakesh glanced up for a moment from his position in the back room of the building, watching through the glass of the French doors as the interphaser opened a window through quantum space and sent his three teammates on their way.

The cones of light spread wider in front of his eyes, one expanding up into the air while the other seemed— counterintuitively—to expand into the very ground itself. The light was multicolored, as if cast through a prism, and witch fire played deep within its eerie, oily wash.

As suddenly as it started, the light abated, closing in on itself until nothing remained, not even the three people and the dog who had stood there moments before.

"Good luck, my friends," Lakesh muttered, "and Godspeed."

DOMI DUCKED BACK as one of the flying birds pulled suddenly away from the other with an angry squawk, yanking the bloody morsel away with a splatter of blood and flesh. Then the huge bird lunged upward with a majestic sweep of its vast wings, cawing as it did so. The bird held something beneath its belly, clutched in its claws.

Domi crouched inside the nest, pushing her back to the side and wishing she hadn't lost her combat blade. To her right, the bird's flapping wings became louder as it cut through the air back to its nest. In a moment, its dark shadow obscured the sun, wings flapping like mighty sails as it brought itself in for a landing.

Lakesh's voice came over the Commtact in that moment, an oasis of calm amid this world turned upside down. "Kane's team have just opened the gateway now," he said. "Is there any message you want me to pass on?"

Domi watched as the bloody torso of a human being dropped into the nest from the claws of the huge bird, rolling beside the dead wolf. Both legs were missing as was one of the arms, but Domi recognized it, even with the white material of the gossamer dress turned red with spilled blood. It was the pretty teenage girl who had been prancing in the woods when the birds had appeared. She stared at Domi with lifeless eyes, a bloody streak obscuring one half of her face.

"Tell Kane to be quick," Domi whispered as the girl's body rolled against her feet. "Tell him it's urgent."

THE JOURNEY was instantaneous. A moment before, the three of them had been standing in the cliff-side gardens of Shizuka's lodge. Now, just a single heartbeat later, they stood in a wooded area that overlooked the vast settlement of Luilekkerville, its towering structures jutting into the clear blue sky like shoots from a nascent plant. And as for the space in between—it was a nonspace, an impression, a blur, like stepping through an emotion.

The transition was smooth enough, but as the Cerberus team emerged from twin cones of inky light with arcing thunder in their fractal depths, Kane unleashed a terrible cry of agony before slumping to the ground, his hands to his face. It was so sudden, so quick, that it took Grant and Rosalia a few seconds to react, momentarily disoriented as they were from the journey through the quantum ether. Beside her, Rosalia's dog let out a yelp and hurried across to Kane's side, sniffing at him as he rolled on the leafy ground. Kane was breathing hard through his clenched teeth, rolling this way and that like a man on fire trying to put out the flames.

The swirling light of the interphaser was still churning behind him as Grant hurried over to his partner with Rosalia just a step away. Rosalia reached down for the dog, pulling it away from Kane by the scruff of its neck. "Come here, animal," she cursed, "give him space."

"Kane? What is it?" Grant demanded. Automatically, Grant's Sin Eater blaster had shot into the palm of his hand from its hiding place in his sleeve, and he was scouring the area with narrowed eyes.

Kane remained doubled over on the bare soil, his body shaking and his hands clutched to his face as he rolled back and forth on his back like a stranded turtle. Had he been shot?

Grant could not detect any immediate threat. Warily he lowered his pistol, keeping it in a ready position. Close by, Rosalia was already checking the area, sprinting around the immediate circle of trees to ensure no one was in hiding, the dog at her side.

"Kane?" Grant urged, the rising concern clear in his voice.

Still lying atop the mulch of the leaves and soil in the clearing amid the woods, Kane turned his head to face his partner. For a moment he held his hands in front of him still, and Grant could see thick beads of sweat washing down his forehead with the force of a cloudburst. Then Kane tentatively pulled his hands away, and Grant saw his face properly for the first time. The right side of Kane's face seemed normal enough, tousled hair behind the ear and the dark trace of stubble lining his square jaw, his blue-gray eye peering out from beneath his dark brow. But the left side seemed locked, immobile, just the occasional spasm like a man in the midst of some terrible stroke. And there, just above Kane's cheek, his left eye had turned darker, a gray the color of rain-slick slate.

"I can't see," Kane said with a trembling voice. "I'm blind."

Chapter 9

The island sat low to the horizon, like the husk of a long-dead insect dried in the unforgiving sun. The boat seemed small by comparison as it rode the rolling waves of the Atlantic, two miles out from the eastern seaboard of the territory that had once been known as the United States of America. Once, the towering statue of a woman had stood in this bay, torch thrust aloft, promising liberty for all who visited these shores. Her torch and her city were long since departed, reduced to rubble two hundred years before when the nuclear hostilities between East and West had come to a head in a single orgy of radioactive fire.

The boat continued past the jutting struts of the old bay and out into the ocean. The boat was a forty-foot fishing scow that had been converted into a ferry barely a month before, its owner turning his life over to the glory of the New Order and his master, Ullikummis. The boat bobbed up and down over the blue-green waves, continuing away from the shore on its slow journey to the island of Bensalem.

The passengers numbered almost sixty in total, crammed on the deck like an old-fashioned game of sardines, leaving barely any space for the fisherman himself to guide his vessel to its strange destination.

Three months ago, the island had not existed. Back

then, the ocean had stretched away from the shore in a seemingly endless line, swaying back and forth as the currents altered, rising and falling with the movements of the moon. Then Ullikummis had come, a mighty god from the stars, and he had reached out, speaking to the rocks that lay beneath the ocean in some archaic language only he seemed to know. Ullikummis had abilities far beyond those of mortal man, and if one needed proof that here stood a god, then this act was it. He had generated a psionic bond with the rocks beneath the ocean, calling them, teasing them, encouraging them to rush to the surface and do his bidding. The rocks had loosened themselves from the ocean bed and spun through the waters of the ocean, spinning over and over as they hurried to obey this clarion call. First one pebble, then two, then four until a veritable swarm of rocks had rocketed up from the ocean depths to surface in the baking rays of the sun. Under Ullikummis's instruction, the rocks had massed, forming this strut of land where there had been no land before, the new island of Bensalem.

Almost two miles across, the island seemed like a fort, struck out in the ocean as if to defend the land behind it. The people on the boat had been jubilant as they boarded, but now they fell silent, watching as that monstrous island hove into view. Its stone walls were sheer, harsh lines jutting up from the water on all sides, high cliffs looming above the boat as if in judgment of its human cargo. The rock was mottled, browns and grays and chalk-white, like some huge calico cat reclining in the sea. The boat came closer, making its way through a channel that ran through a section of the stone island like a vein. Bathed in shadow, the channel was dark and it took a moment for the fisherman's eyes to adjust to the sudden gloom. The fisherman had been down this channel several times, ferrying passengers to and fro in the name of his master. Down below, he knew there were juts of rock, poised like teeth beneath the surface, just waiting to rip through the hull of an unwary boatman's vessel. Thus, he navigated the channel slowly, feeling as much as seeing the perils that lay beneath. His name was Alfredo and he had once believed in a different god.

Like his brothers and sisters, Alfredo had fallen into step with his mother's religion, kneeling before the painting of the pale-faced woman with the headscarf and saying his prayers each night, thanking her for the bounty he had received. He had made a living as a fisherman, enough to feed his family and still have something to sell to the passing outlanders who often went on to sell it to the gated communities of the villes. Then, six weeks ago, Alfredo's wife had been approached by a wandering nomad. The man had been dressed in rags and looked half-starved, but he had a steely determination to his gaze. A kindhearted woman, Alfredo's wife had invited the man to join her and her family over a meal, and Alfredo had welcomed him, too. Despite his ragged appearance, the man had spoken long and eloquently about the world that was coming, of the fall of the baronies and the manner in which that had opened a gateway to utopia, to heaven on Earth. The man's words had been encouraging and he had spoken then of the lord of this forthcoming utopia, a mighty god called Ullikummis. Alfredo had listened to the man's words as his wife sang their firstborn child to sleep in his cot. The future had sounded wonderful, a place carved out of love where the world they came from seemed so full of hatred.

"All it takes is belief," the bearded stranger had explained, reaching into his coat pocket.

Alfredo had watched with intrigue as the man produced two tiny flecks of stone from his pocket, each of them no bigger than his thumbnail. The man had smiled, a line of yellowing teeth amid the whiskers of his beard. "Take one," the stranger had said. "Take one and you can begin your journey into a new world."

Tentatively, dark sweat patches still lining his work shirt, Alfredo had reached for one of the stones like a child stroking a dog for the first time. In front of him, the ragged-looking stranger had nodded once in singular encouragement. "The future awaits," he had said.

As Alfredo's fingers brushed the surface of the tiny stone he felt a jolt, like electricity running through him, playing over the hairs that lined his fingers between the knuckles. His wife had come back then, smiling benignly as she poked her head around the living-room door and asked if either man would like coffee or tea.

"Why don't you come join us, 'Nita?" the old hobo had said, and he had the understated forcefulness of a man who ruled the roost rather than came here as a visitor.

Juanita had come in meekly, taking a seat opposite her husband, her lustrous hair tied back in a bun.

Beside her, Alfredo's eyes widened as the stone began boring into his skin, biting through the flesh of his palm as it sought a place to lodge itself. For a moment Alfredo felt fear run through him, and his lips moved, mouthing the word "stop," but no sound came out. Then the stone was inside him, clawing at his flesh and at his thoughts, bringing a newfound calmness where for so long he had felt anxiety. Alfredo closed his eyes, leaning back in his chair as the wave of euphoria had taken him. Entheogen, the god within.

Devoted to the Virgin, the fisherman's wife had been more reluctant to imbibe the stone and feel the power of Ullikummis blossom inside her. Converted, Alfredo had held her down while the hobo made an incision with his knife along her left wrist and forced the stone inside her, tamping it down as the swelling blood tried to push it away. Juanita had screamed for a moment, waking the baby as the obedience stone took effect. Then it was over, and Alfredo and Juanita had been converted, the old religion forgotten. The baby needed no stone, the hobo had explained. He would learn from his parents, learn to serve Ullikummis and help build the new utopia.

Now Alfredo ran a ferry service to Bensalem, the self-made island where god had constructed his home.

The cramped fishing scow sailed on through the choppy waters between the towering cliffs, occasional stripes of sunlight catching the water, plucking at the spume on the waves. The boat wended slowly down the channel, following its tight curves as the fisherman guided his way to the island's single dock. They turned a sharp corner where the boat listed, threatening to overturn for a long five seconds before finally righting itself at the gentle guidance of its captain. Then a rocky cove appeared up ahead, the shore coming out of the water

at a ramped incline, its beach covered with thick shards
of rock the gray color of ash.

There, standing at the edge of the beach stood Ullikummis, his bare flesh the same color as the ashy rock.
He presented an uncanny figure, more like a crude
statue than a living being. Eight feet tall and magnif-
icently proportioned, two magmalike eyes glowed in
deep pits within the craggy rock mask that made up
his face. The face itself was rudimentary, more like the
weather erosion of a rock than something intentionally
carved. An angry slash of mouth sat low to the face,
and that same magma glow emanated from it as from
those terrible eyes. Beneath that, the thing's body was
a ragged conglomeration of battered rocks, brutally
smashed together as if in anger. Twin arrays of vicious-
looking stalagmites reached up from the god's shoulders like the horns of a stag. Ullikummis's crude body
seemed longer than it should, with tree-trunk-like legs
ending in flared stumps, giving the impression that this
impressive figure had no feet to speak of. The rippling
edge of the ocean lapped against those massive legs,
washing the rock darker where it left its fleeting signa-
ture.

Aboard the boat, the already silent passengers seemed
to hold their breath in unison as they spied their god
standing in front of them, awaiting their arrival. Turning the scow's wheel, Alfredo smiled; he had made this
journey with other parties and the reaction was always
the same—breathless anticipation and reverence.

The great god Ullikummis nodded once as the boat
pulled up to the shore, the boat's movement churning
the waves so that they tumbled over his legs before

scurrying fearfully back down the beach to the ocean's embrace. The stone giant's eyes glowed brightly as he scanned the people aboard the fishing vessel. They seemed strong, healthy. Perhaps half of them would live this time.

THE GIRL known as Little Quav clung tightly to Brigid as the red-haired woman wrapped her in her arms.

Behind the girl, Balam came pacing in his ungainly manner, his short legs hurrying to power his long torso toward their visitor. Completely hairless, his bulbous head tapered to a pointed chin, his low features leaving a vast expanse of gray cranium tinted with a faint blush of pink. The last of the Archons, Balam was the product of a pact between the Annunaki and the Tuatha de Danaan. For a moment, the strangely proportioned humanoid stared at Brigid, his dark eyes like limpid pools beneath the glistening blue luminescence that served as a faux sky for the underground city of Agartha. He seemed to be analyzing her, as if already he suspected something had changed inside this woman whose face he knew so well.

"Hello, Balam," Brigid said, nodding her head gently as she hugged Little Quav for a moment longer.

Balam ducked his own head in reply, its great bulbous shape moving as if too heavy for his thin neck to support. "Brigid," he repeated in a voice that sounded as if he was in pain, a scratchy hoarseness mixed with a cat's meow.

Brigid fixed her eyes on Balam's, watching the curious creature even as he studied her. He was a telepath, she knew, and he might even now be probing the edges of her prodigious mind. She tempered her thoughts, her muscles tightening as she held everything inside. Balam was the little girl's foster parent; she had been entrusted into his care over two years ago shortly after her birth, ostensibly to protect her from the threat posed by her destiny as one of the Annunaki pantheon.

Balam's fingers flexed for a moment, six long spidery digits on each hand like the branches of some nightmare tree, and then a beatific smile appeared on his lips. The smile, like Balam's mouth, was small and seemed almost lost amid his bulging, gray-pink head.

As Balam smiled, the little girl let go of Brigid and hurried back to her foster father, singing to herself as she ran on her short little legs. "Briggly's here, Uncle Bal-bal," the girl announced, her voice playful like notes from a piccolo.

Balam nodded once more as he took the girl's outstretched hand. "You look healthy," Balam stated by way of greeting. "Come." Then he turned and began to lead the way into the deserted city of Agartha, Little Quav trotting along at his ankles, still clutching his hand and holding her rag doll in the other.

After a moment Brigid followed, the heels of her boots clacking against the hard rock floor as her long-legged strides ate up the distance between the buildings. Agartha was built to a wheel design, the tallest structure in its center. Again, however, this city was built to that immortal Annunaki plan.

Brigid watched as Balam of the First Folk made his way through the empty streets of dust, his long indigo robe brushing below his knees as he led the way to his stone dwelling. Beside him, the girl seemed human at first glance, but Brigid now saw her for what she truly was. She had never seen this before, never comprehended the Annunaki the way they should be comprehended. They were multidimensional beings, their existence emanating further than the lines that human physics could draw. Where Quav had once looked normal to her old eyes, to the eyes of Brigid Baptiste, now she seemed to glow, her echo stretching out across the infinite. Ullikummis had shown her this, had taught her to see things in the Annunaki way, expanding her mind and making her realize for the first time how misguided her war had been against them back when she had been a part of the Cerberus team. Now Brigid saw the truth of the Annunaki world, and in much the same way that she had detected the door that had seemed to not really be there, the one that had allowed her access to this underground lair, so, too, did this secret vision open up gateways for her to pursue.

The Annunaki had ruled the Earth over millennia ago, where they had been treated as gods by the primitive humans who populated the planet. When finally they had left Earth's shores, their essences had been stored in a mighty organic system, access to which came via the mother ship, *Tiamat*. Reentering the solar system after millennia away, *Tiamat* had issued a download command that reignited the Annunaki personalities where they had been hidden within the shells known as the barons. These barons had been hybrid creatures, possessing both human and alien DNA in a delicate mixture that made them both intellectually superior and physically more fragile than the average human. But these hybrids served only as staging posts, body templates for the magnificent final forms of the Annunaki on Earth. Once the downloads were complete, nine mighty Annunaki stood in place of the fragile hybrid barons, muscular, lizard-fleshed humanoids whose skin was like armor. Little Quav was destined to be the tenth of those hybrids to ascend; when the time was ripe she would be transformed into the goddess Ninlil, wife and consort of the cruel Enlil. Reborn, Lord Enlil himself had made no secret of his desire to regain possession of his chattel, and so the hybrid girl had been hidden in this ghost town beneath the surface of the Earth, far from prying eyes.

That had been over two years ago, before Brigid had learned to see the truth. Now, as she looked at the delicate little girl who jogged along at Balam's side, she saw the snake goddess that she would become, that she had once been millennia ago. It was no hallucination, no double-image brought on by fever. This was more akin to knowledge, and how knowledge informs a viewer's eyes, like the comprehension of ink markings on a page as letters and words, paragraphs and chapters. Ultimately, the ink markings are still just ink markings; the reader only applies meaning by his participation, and then only through choice.

Brigid trotted on, following the diminutive Balam and his cheery charge.

ONCE THE LAST of his passengers had departed, Alfredo turned his boat around and began the arduous return trip through the winding chasm away from Bensalem.

On the island itself, the sixty-strong party followed Ullikummis as the stone giant strode silently up the winding path that trawled beside the dark and oppressive cliffs looming all around. The climb was steep and the path itself became narrower as they got higher, its edges dropping away in verticals that were absolute, sharp rocks waiting far below them like jagged incisors. Ullikummis never slowed his rapid pace, and nor did he address the party. He simply strode upward on his trunklike legs, trusting his visitors to follow. In their minds they had come to the house of god, and it would benefit them naught to yearn for encouragement now that they were in his presence.

There were occasional murmurings from the group, particularly the older folks, several of whom were well into their fifties and beyond. But for the most part, the people were silent as they followed in the footsteps of the divine, trekking up that unforgiving pathway of schist as if on a pilgrimage.

As they neared the top of the cliffs, a mighty structure came into view—a towering building carved from the rock. It stood there like some mighty castle, spiked towers jabbing upward into the overcast skies, some so high as to scrape at the low clouds as they passed. Though clearly a building, the structure looked rough and unfinished, much like Ullikummis himself. Mottled rock made up its walls, pitted with holes and thorny spikes where it had never been smoothed or sanded. Empty windows peered down at the approaching group, the sunlight lost in their depths, rendering them black as night. Beneath them, a single arched doorway loomed like a mouth, fifteen feet wide with stalactite spikes lunging down from its ceiling.

Several of the party stopped, marveling at the towering structure that overlooked the cliff in front of them, and a gasp ran through the group. A little lower down the path, one of the older men pushed forward, wanting to see what the fuss was about. As he did so, his foot slipped on the sandy pebbles that dotted the path and suddenly he was falling, tumbling from the path and down toward the jagged rocks below. He cried out as he fell, and the group turned at the scream, a sense of sudden terror rushing through them. The man's scream was cut abruptly short as he hit the sharp rocks and his body was pierced by one of them, killing him instantly in a burst of red.

"Come," Ullikummis said, speaking for the first time, his voice like millstones scraping together.

The crowd turned and followed their master toward his towering sanctuary at the summit of the cliff.

THERE IS AN oft-repeated phrase that goes, "It was so quiet you could hear a pin drop." As Brigid walked through the empty streets of Agartha beside Balam and Little Quav, that phrase might have occurred to her, and she might have smiled. Not now. The phrase was a human one, and Brigid's thinking had been subtly altered, shifted in such a way as to discard such whimsy as pins dropping. Instead she remained emotionless as she followed Balam of the First Folk through winding streets cluttered with black-walled buildings carved from basalt, crouching at the edges of the roads in some uncanny funereal procession, lamenting the loss of the ancient city's vibrancy. No one lived here anymore, other than Balam and the hybrid girl.

Once Balam had had two sons who had acted as sentries for the underground city, but like so much else down here beyond the gaze of the sun, they had departed, and no mark of them remained.

Balam's home, like most everything else in Agartha, was constructed of dark basalt, its black sheen highlighted with the distant glow of the cavern ceiling. In the time since Brigid had last been here, it seemed that Balam of the First Folk had developed an interest in gardening. A simple stone fence marked the boundary of the property, and a basic garden had been set to grow there, a tidy patch of grass lined at its edges by daffodils and roses.

"You've grown flowers," Brigid stated as her gaze swept over the garden.

Balam turned to her, nodding. "And vegetable plots in the back," he agreed. "With Quav here, I find myself in a curious conundrum, with both time on my hands yet trapped, never able to let her out of my sight. Growing things brings us both pleasure, and oftimes sustenance when we need it."

Brigid nodded, thinking of her arduous journey here and of her last meal; it had been the soup that had been brewing on the range of the late farmer and his wife, snatched away as she torched their farmhouse, their conversion either impossible or perhaps just too boring to accomplish. "It's nice," she stated, forcing a smile on her full lips.

Balam thanked her, ushering his way into the house. Little Quav still held his hand, and she checked behind her to make sure that Brigid would follow. The child should have no great bond with Brigid, and yet she had seen so few people other than Balam during her scant years alive that she had begun to place significance in all of those precious faces, believing each to be a friend in the way an innocent child will. In some obscure way, Brigid was the closest thing the child had to a mother figure.

Brigid entered the stone building, ducking her head beneath the low sill of the door. As she did so, she became instantly aware that Balam stood poised in front of her, and there was something shining in his hand. Shaped like a viper's head, Brigid recognized it instantly—it was an ASP emitter, a weapon capable of blasting a bolt of plasma that could rip Brigid in two.

"Now, why don't you tell me who you really are and what you're doing here?" Balam asked as he leveled the fearsome weapon at Brigid Haight.

Chapter 10

Kane lay on the sparse scrub grass between towering redwoods, his hands reaching once more to his face. His lips were pulled back from gritted teeth, and his whole body was trembling with agony. "My eyes," he grunted. "I can't see."

From somewhere nearby, a harsh bird cry echoed through the towering trees, its sound a piercing hostile note.

Leaning close to his partner, Grant reached out a steadying hand and pressed it solidly against the man's arm. "Okay, buddy," he said, keeping his voice low. "Let's try to keep calm." Over the course of their long relationship, Grant had known Kane to be many things, and the man certainly had an impetuous streak. But if there was one thing Kane was not prone to, it was panic. Even now, as the unshaved ex-Mag took a strained breath through gritted teeth, he managed to keep his movements quiet, resisting the urge to shout in his pain.

"What is it? What's happened to me?" Kane asked.

Grant held two fingers up in front of Kane's face. "Can you see anything at all?" he asked in response. "How many fingers am I holding up?"

"Just light an' color," Kane said after a moment. "I can't…dammit," he finished in frustration.

"Okay," Grant reassured him. "It's okay. Give yourself a minute. If you can see light at least there's something there. Maybe just a side effect of the interphaser or somethin'."

As Grant spoke, Rosalia came hurrying to the group with her scraggly dog in tow. "Area's clear," she summarized, "but there's a lot of noise coming from that way." At Grant's querulous face, she elaborated. "You ever hear parrots fight, Magistrate? Sounds kind of like that."

"And that's gonna be where Domi is," Grant concluded with a reluctant sigh.

"We need to keep moving," Kane muttered, straining to get up off the ground. "We have to go help Domi."

Grant pressed his palm against Kane's chest. "Not so fast, partner. You're in no state to…"

"We were sent here to help Domi," Kane reminded him. "We can't compromise that just because—"

"You're blind?" Rosalia finished. "You think me or Grant here want to be wet-nursing you? Use your head, Magistrate Man."

Slowly, Kane nodded. "Leave me here then and go find Domi."

Standing, Grant stared down at his partner, his obvious concern drawing lines across his newly hairless head. "You going to be okay?" he asked, realizing as he said it how stupid a question it really was.

Kane pushed himself to a sitting position, leaning far back with his elbows and forearms still pressed against the ground. "Just go," he instructed miserably.

Crouching for a moment, the beautiful Rosalia placed her hands to either side of her dog's head, forcing it to look at her. "You stay here and take care of Kane," she instructed. "You bark like a maniac if there's trouble, yes?"

The dog whined as it looked at Rosalia with its impossibly pale eyes before adopting a guard position at Kane's side.

"Goes double for you, Magistrate Man," Rosalia added, touching Kane's hand for just the scantest of moments.

An instant later Rosalia and Grant were off, and Kane heard their retreating footsteps as they hurried through the underbrush.

DOMI PUSHED herself backward, away from the bloody torso that lay in the center of the nest. Above her, its wings flapping like two great punkah fans, the mother bird hovered in place for a moment, beady eyes watching its home before it brought itself to a landing at the nest's edge, its scythelike talons clutching the rim. As quietly as she could, Domi shuffled backward, her eyes never leaving the bird's as she clambered over the fallen torso of the girl. The bird pecked at the wolf's body, tearing great hunks of flesh from it and swallowing them whole. After a moment Domi came up to something solid behind her, and she turned swiftly, looking to see what it was. As she did so, the great bird squawked, a loud and hideous sound this close to Domi's ears.

Domi found that she was standing beside the clutch of eggs, and realized it was one of these that she had backed straight into. Even as she watched, one of the eggs began to break open, and Domi looked on in terror as a sliver of its blue shell snapped off, dropping away to the bed of the nest at her bare feet. There was a hollow tapping and then another chunk of eggshell broke away, this one as large as a dinner plate as it slid down the side of the egg. A viscous mucus glistened on the underside of the broken shell, catching the sun for a moment as the plate-size chunk slipped away.

Behind her, Domi heard the bird twitter excitedly, watching the birth of its hulking progeny.

Then Domi saw something poke through the shell, a sharp line jabbing at the hole in its surface. The spike disappeared, and a moment later an eye appeared at the twelve-inch hole in the egg's surface, black iris in the center of a red-and-gold circle, the eye itself perfectly round. The eye was twice as large as a human's, and Domi shivered as she saw the thing blink, feeling faintly unsettled at being just five feet away from that alien orb.

With another tap, the shell broke wider and a face appeared at this makeshift window. The head was bald, a pointed beak jutting out three inches from its underside like a pair of garden shears. The baby bird squawked then, a sound like nails on a chalkboard, and Domi took several steps away. But as she did so, the mother bird cawed angrily above her, and Domi felt something prod against her back.

The albino girl turned to see that the mother was nudging her with its beak, knocking her back toward the opening shell as the baby made its way out into the world. Then the gigantic bird gave a single flap of its mighty wings, knocking Domi across the nest and off her feet. Domi fell to the bed of sticks and branches, and her head knocked against something hard and unforgiving. She looked up in time to see it was the blue eggshell, and the sharp face of the baby bird was lunging at her from a little way above.

"WHAT'S GOING ON with Kane?" Rosalia asked as she dashed through the trees at Grant's side. Beside her, the large ex-Mag had brought his Sin Eater back to his hand as they weaved through the trees, running in the direction of the bird squawks.

"I don't know yet," Grant admitted, "but I'll give you even odds it's nothing good. Trust me, it never is."

The sheathed sword slapped against Rosalia's butt as she vaulted over the fallen limb of a tree. Grant couldn't help but admire the woman's stamina. He was taller than her, longer of limb and a trained Magistrate to boot, yet she kept pace with him effortlessly, her breath coming steady and even. It was clear that this mysterious woman was at the peak of physical fitness. Grant had met her many months ago during an investigation into DNA smuggling out in the coastal village of Hope. Back then, the two had found themselves on opposing sides of a lawless operation, and Rosalia had proved herself to be a wily and capable foe. He had followed her across the vast Mojave Desert, he on a motorized wagon while she remained on foot, and yet she had seemed indomitable, outpacing him, her fierce spirit refusing to allow her to compromise. If she could be trusted, as Kane seemed to believe, then having her as an ally was doubtless an asset to the struggling Cerberus operation. That was, of course, one very big *if.*

Suddenly a dark shadow crossed their view overhead, and both Grant and Rosalia ducked their heads as something swept by. Overhead, amid the behemoth branches of the towering redwoods, a colossal bird raced through the air. Automatically, Grant had trained his Sin Eater on the bird as it passed by, and he watched with irritation as the thing hurtled upward in a sweep of mighty russet wings.

"Grant...?" Rosalia urged from just beside him.

Grant turned at her call, and a moment later he saw what it was she had spotted. There, between the hulking tree trunks, lay a corpse of one of the incredible birds, its shadow-dark feathers marred with a splash of congealing blood.

Keeping their heads down, Grant and Rosalia jogged toward the fallen bird. As they got closer they saw that its head lay at an awkward angle, beak open and a thin, sharp tongue sticking out. Its eye was open and unresponsive.

"Broken neck," Grant concluded.

From all around, the two Cerberus warriors could hear rustling from the trees, the sounds of nearby squawking and the swoop of mighty wings.

His pistol still in hand, Grant engaged the hidden Commtact he wore beneath the skin. "Domi?" he urged. "Can you see us?"

Barely had the words left Grant's mouth before Rosalia grabbed at his firm bicep, pulling him closer to the bole of the nearest tree. Grant looked at her irritably, then followed where she silently indicated, peering up into the air above. Three fearsome shadows were cutting through the trees at a rapidly increasing speed as a trio of the gigantic birds power-dived at the newcomers.

"What the flock...!" Grant growled as he jabbed at

the trigger of the Sin Eater, blasting a stream of 9 mm titanium-cased bullets at the approaching creatures.

In response, the birds opened their sharp beaks and unleashed a horrendous chorus of angry cries.

DOMI DROPPED BACKWARD, falling to the floor of the nest with a grunt as the hungry infant broke free of its egg and jabbed its sharp face at her. The infant unleashed a hideous shriek as its would-be meal dropped away, the noise so close to Domi's ear that she almost missed Grant's hail on her Commtact.

Behind her, the mother bird was ruffling its feathers, poking its melon-size head at Domi, nosing her back at her newly hatched child with the hook of her beak. Domi yelped as that sharp implement ripped through her flesh, tearing a strip of chalk-white skin from between her shoulder blades.

"Grant, you gorgeous, gorgeous man!" Domi shouted into the Commtact pickup. "Where the fuck are you?"

Grant's voice came back over the Commtact as Domi rolled out of the way of the baby bird's jabbing beak. "We're on the ground close to your transponder," he explained, "but we've run into some trouble of our own."

"Tell me about it," Domi responded irritably, her foot whipping out in a vicious snap-kick that knocked the baby bird's three-inch knifelike beak aside. "I'm in a nest and mommy bird is trying to make me dinner for her newborn boy."

"Where—? Shit, hang on," Grant said over the Commtact. There was a moment's silence, then Grant's voice came louder once more. "Whereabouts are you?" he asked.

Behind her, the mother bird clambered into the nest, lethal talons plucking at the bedding as Domi rolled frantically to one side. The second of the three eggs had begun to crack, and with a blurt of chirruping noise, another viciously sharp beak appeared, nudging the thick shell aside.

"I got a peek a few minutes back," Domi explained as she rolled out of the mother bird's way. "Gotta be thirty feet above ground in the branches of a redwood."

DOWN ON THE GROUND, Grant looked all around him as the trio of birds dived at him and Rosalia for a second pass. Beside Grant, Rosalia had drawn the *katana* that Shizuka's aide had loaned her, and she stood in a ready stance as the birds plummeted through the air.

"There's a shitload of forest here," Grant snarled over the Commtact as the Sin Eater bucked in his hand. "Are you able to give us an indicator which tree?"

"Will do," Domi assured him. "Stand by."

As Grant's Sin Eater drilled bullets into the lead bird's breast, Rosalia's blade swept through the air in a flash of steel, lopping off the creature's head with an explosion of blood. Split in two, the creature's decapitated head went sailing through the air past Grant's shoulder while the body tumbled over the leaf-strewn ground, churning up soil and grass in great clumps.

A half second behind, the bird's nest-mates seemed to balk as they witnessed the fate of their fellow. One of them swooped away, rolling its leathery wings and whipping around a hulking tree trunk, disengaging from its dive. The other wasn't so quick and, while it tried to change course, Rosalia was lunging ahead, driving twenty-five inches of razor steel through the monster's plumage and into its curving belly.

Grant watched in astonishment as the dark-haired woman's sword stuck fast in the bird's torso and she, still holding the sword tight, was carried up into the air with it. Rosalia wrenched at the sword as the wounded creature flapped its mighty wings, ascending into the branches with three fearsome strokes of those sail-like appendages.

As Rosalia was dragged off her feet, the other bird turned back and lunged for Grant, kicking up dust with vast sweeps of its heavy wings. Grant spun and crouched to protect his face as the thing's talons clawed for him, each pointed nail as wide as two fingers. The beast missed Grant's face by inches, and the ex-Mag felt a pummeling on his back and shoulders as the thing's talons clawed against the Kevlar of his coat.

Then Grant's hand snapped out, grabbing for the bird's ankle as it began its ascent just a few inches shy of hitting the ground. Despite his weight, Grant was pulled along for two paces before he found his foothold in the shifting soil with its smattering of dead leaves and moist grass. The bird flapped its wings, cawing in frustration as it tried to get free of its sudden burden.

"This is for the birds," Grant growled and, with a flex of his arm muscles, he swung the bird around his head like a hammer thrower, letting go at the zenith of the arc and watching as the bird careened away into a nearby tree with an almighty crash. As the bird struggled to right itself, Grant took several steps forward, blasting a stream of lead slugs from the Sin Eater in his other hand, drilling them through the creature's brain pan.

Up above, Rosalia was struggling with her newfound flight where the *katana* sword had lodged itself in her flying foe's belly.

"Stupid…" Rosalia muttered, and she pulled the sword free in a rush of blood and intestines. Then she was falling, spiraling through the air in a fifteen-foot drop as the hard ground hurried upward to meet her.

Above her, the wounded bird smashed through the upper branches of a poplar tree, cawing in pain as its large intestine unraveled around it.

At the last moment Rosalia twisted her body, meeting the ground with her feet and bending her knees to absorb the impact.

"You okay?" Grant asked from where he still stood, gun trained on the swooping birds above. He was fifteen feet from where Rosalia had landed.

"Fine," Rosalia grunted in response. "Just give me a second."

As she spoke, something came tumbling from the skies, a fuzzy down covering its body.

"Heads up!" Grant called.

The eye-catching mercenary leaped back as the flailing body of a baby chick wrapped in an egg—a baby almost three feet in height and with a vicious beak shaped like a scimitar—smashed into the ground in a shattering of blue shell and a crunch of newly formed bones. The thing flapped its useless wings for a moment as it lay on the soil, dazed and mortally wounded by the hard landing, the broken remains of the shell splayed all around its failing body.

Over the Commtact, Domi's straining voice came to Grant's ear. "You get that?" she asked.

DOMI PEERED OVER the side of the high nest at the egg-shell debris strewed far below where she had knocked the egg over the side. "Come on, Grant," she muttered under her breath, "get your ass up here already."

Behind her, the mother bird squawked angrily as it realized that Domi had killed one of its young before it had even properly hatched. As the hulking bird lunged at Domi, its beak snapping together like an oversize pair of scissors, Domi sidestepped. The beak snapped shut on empty air, but already the bird's head was twitching around to make another attempt at Domi's face.

Timing her move with perfection, Domi drove her fist up into the underside of the bird's mouth, ducking its snapping beak as she delivered the uppercut. The bird cried out in annoyance, and Domi disappeared beneath its round belly, rolling swiftly across the nest as the bird danced on the spot. This close, Domi could see the thudding of the bird's breast as its heart beat against its ribs.

A moment later Domi was behind the massive bird, bringing herself up in a fighting crouch. But as she readied her attack, something flitted across the cramped nest just behind the albino warrior. Domi turned to see a great slice of eggshell splinter against the nest floor, and then the oversize chick was flapping its fluffy wings as it struggled out of the remains of its egg.

"So that's how it is, huh?" Domi spit through clenched teeth. "Double your pleasure, double your fun."

Then the baby bird staggered across the nest as it sought its live prey—Domi.

The newborn was almost three feet tall, coming up to above the petite Domi's hip. It strutted across the nest on unsteady legs, struggling a little as it clambered over the broken torso of the teen girl in favor of Domi, her radiant form catching its eye.

A QUARTER OF A MILE away, Kane was trying to make sense of everything as he sat sprawled on the scrub grass. His face was burning, the left eye a source of incredible heat, and his vision remained just a blur of flickering light and color.

This had been building for a while, he knew. Several weeks ago, when he had been held as a prisoner in Life Camp Zero, he had been starved for several days and suffered sensory deprivation. His body had become one great mass of aches, the kind of bone-deep weariness that one felt with influenza. Even in that state, Kane had driven himself on, staging a dramatic jailbreak and releasing his Cerberus partners from the hands of the stone would-be god, Ullikummis. He had been pushing himself ever since, even as the world darkened around him.

But something must have triggered this, he knew. Amid the swirling colors in his vision, he saw something for just a moment, a sweltering desert, heat haze bucking and weaving beneath an unforgiving noonday sun. Kane concentrated, trying to make sense of the vision.

He seemed to be running, great powerful strides across the yellow sand. He could hear—what?—his own breathing, deep and even, his bare feet as they shushed against the swirling grains of sand. But it wasn't him; the strides were too long, the speed like an animal's, something superhuman.

Kane allowed himself to be swept up by the vision,

taking in the sights as a low, rocky outcropping budded into view on the horizon. The outcropping formed the mouth to a cave, beneath which—somehow he knew this—a network of underground tunnels and caverns formed the home of a wise Annunaki philosopher called Uppelluri. Uppelluri had taught him everything he needed to know, every guiding tenet that he would carry with him for that long journey into space, after his father imprisoned him.

No, Kane realized, *not him.* This wasn't his story; it was the story of Ullikummis, the Annunaki creature's life flashing before Kane's eyes as his true sight receded.

Beside him in the forest, Kane heard the dog growl with irritation.

"What is it?" Kane asked, turning to where he could detect the dog, unable to see anything at all. "Is someone coming?"

The dog padded closer, nuzzling Kane and sniffing at his face. Then the mutt whined in some imitation of a human response, before lying at Kane's side.

The dog sensed it, smelled it, this thing inside him. Something had become caught in Kane's eye, or just next to it, where the scar had formed at the top of his left cheek.

It was something Annunaki. Something evil.

Domi glanced up, checking that the mother bird was still tangling itself as it searched for Domi. Then she looked back at the hideous little bird chick. The baby bird let out a noise from its sharp beak that sounded like a cross between a shriek and a burp, and then it lunged at Domi, pecking at her with that pointed beak. The first peck caught Domi high on the left breast, and she staggered backward with the impact as a line of blood bloomed there.

When the fledgling went for her a second time, Domi weaved aside, bringing herself up and around the jabbing little neck before grasping it with both hands. Behind her, Domi could hear the fearsome mother bird squawk with irritation as it saw what the albino girl was doing. Securing the chick's throat in a firm grip, Domi employed a savage twist of both arms, breaking the creature's neck with an audible snap. The baby bird twitched in her grasp for a moment before shuddering itself to the bed of the nest.

Domi let go, turning her attention back to the mother even as, behind its immense form, the third egg began to hatch, a sharp-clawed foot poking out from its side.

"Dammit, come on, Grant," Domi muttered as she jumped aside even as the mother bird's pecking beak threatened to pierce her.

THIRTY FEET BELOW, Grant used his left hand to push the tails of his coat aside and reach for his belt as he watched the branch cover above him. Another of the man-size birds was plummeting down from the higher branches, cawing angrily as it hurtled toward these intruders in its territory. A second bird followed in its wake, this one appearing even larger as it detached itself from a lower branch.

"Any ideas?" Rosalia asked, raising the blade of the *katana* over her head in a two-handed grip.

"A couple," Grant told her as he found the belt pouch

he was searching for and pulled out a small metallic globule roughly the size of a ball bearing. The globule was called a flash-bang, a simple defensive weapon employed from time to time by the Cerberus personnel as a quick way to wrong-foot an opponent. Once deployed, a volatile mix of chemicals inside the flash-bang would cause it to explode in a bright burst of light and noise—literally a flash and a bang. Like the firecrackers employed by magicians, the explosion looked impressive but was largely for show, incapable of causing any noteworthy damage.

As the first bird came close to Grant, he flipped the flash-bang in the air toward it, shouting to Rosalia to close her eyes.

Rosalia looked away, but she couldn't help but hear the tumultuous detonation as the explosive went off. The fearsome bird of prey, unprepared for what was happening, shrieked and reared away from the crashing burst of light, temporarily blinded by its brightness. Grant turned back in time to see the bird hurtle off into the ground just a few yards from where he stood, the glistening fuse of the flash-bang charge hanging in the air for a moment before finally burning itself out.

However, the larger bird was still rushing groundward, its eyes locked on Grant. This creature had been behind the other as the flash-bang went off, and its companion's body had been enough to shield it from the full effect of the noisemaker. Grant whipped his Sin Eater around, but as he did so the blaster clicked on empty.

"Damn!" he said, skipping backward out of the bird's path.

Rosalia favored more of a hands-on approach than

that of her ex-Magistrate companions. As the bird closed in on the retreating Grant, she began to run, leaping into the air with a graceful swish of her tanned legs.

The hulking bird flinched, seeing Rosalia's shadow as she sprang from the ground. By then it was too late; the razor-keen *katana* cut through the monster's throat as easily as it cut the air, hacking a great chunk of flesh from the beast and spraying gore across the nearest tree trunks.

Rosalia landed with catlike grace, spreading her arms to retain her balance as the wounded bird struggled to take off again, a trail of blood spattering the air behind it.

Grant looked at her, his eyebrows raised with amazement. "Nice moves," he said simply.

"You know the best thing about a sword?" Rosalia replied as Grant pushed home another clip into the Sin Eater's loading port. "It never runs out of ammo."

WITH LONG-PRACTICED accuracy, Domi leaped aside as the mother bird's beak jabbed at her again. Just two feet away, the last remaining egg was splitting apart down a jagged line, and a trilling caw could be heard echoing from within.

The large bird's head twitched again as it jabbed its open beak at Domi, as if the full-grown woman was a worm. Domi spun but she wasn't quick enough. A line of red blood appeared in a slice along the top of her arm as she hurried to evade that sharp beak. She needed a weapon, something to force this feathered brute away from her.

Domi dived to the roughly weaved floor of the huge

nest as the bird flapped its wings, rolling out of the way as the bird squawked with irritation. As she dropped, Domi's ruby eyes searched the nest for something to arm herself with. The broken parts of eggshell were sharp, but they would likely break apart under any pressure; there were jagged bumps visible in the base of the nest, thorns or other simple protrusions, but none of them were at the surface where they might be reached for and snapped off.

Then, from behind, Domi heard the remaining egg break open and the chick hurry forth on short legs, cawing as it greeted the sunlight for the first time.

Another one, Domi thought with irritation, wondering how she'd deal with yet another of these ferocious monsters. She need not have worried. The chick paused for a moment, then hopped over to the bloody corpse of the teenage girl, pulling a strip of flesh from her face with a swift lunge.

Despite her strong stomach, Domi felt disgusted by the maneuver, seeing someone who had been alive less than an hour ago turned into food like that. As Domi tamped down the rising nausea in her stomach, the mother bird flapped its wings again, swiping at Domi and knocking her over. The albino girl slammed against the floor of the nest with a resounding thud, struggling to remain conscious as the world seemed to swim around her.

As Domi lay there, willing herself to just keep her eyes open, dammit all, she felt one of the larger bird's mighty feet press into her back, the sharpened talons cutting a line through the thin material of her dress.

"Come on, Grant," she muttered, her lips just barely moving. "Come on, Kane."

GRANT CHECKED the branches above them once more, scanning the area for any more of the fiendish birds. Satisfied that they were safe for the present, he sent his Sin Eater back to its hidden sheath. Then the formidable ex-Mag pulled a long coil of wire from the inside pocket of his coat, looping it five or six times over his hand with quick, easy twists. The wire was a monofilament as thin as fishing wire, yet it had the strength of tensile steel.

"Stand back," Grant instructed as he leaned down and plucked a mid-size stone from the forest floor. Then, attaching this weight to the other end of the monofilament, he whipped it around his head like a lasso. The rope spun faster and faster, and Grant added to its length, careful not to hit any of the nearby trees.

An instant later Grant slackened his grip and the weighted end of the monofilament went shooting up into the air, passing through the lower branches before wrapping itself around a tree limb about twenty-five feet above the ground. With the other end still wrapped around his hand, Grant tugged on the wire, making sure it was secure. Then he loosened the tautness around his hand and turned to Rosalia as the dark-eyed woman resheathed her sword.

"You any good at climbing?" Grant asked.

Rosalia nodded. "I'm lighter than you are. You need me to go first?"

"It'll take both our weights," Grant assured her, "but you have a point." Actually he was thinking that he still didn't entirely trust the olive-skinned woman, despite what he'd said to Shizuka. For now he would rather not turn his back on her if he didn't have to.

With two sharp tugs, Rosalia tested the wire for herself and then began clambering up it, using the trunk of the tree as a push-off point, walking up the trunk as she went hand-over-hand up the monofilament line.

Grant let her get ten feet up before he began to follow.

Chapter 11

Domi squirmed as the pressure on her back increased, crushing the air out of her lungs as the huge avian held her in place. She was blacking out, the black spots of hypoxia blossoming before her vision like raindrops. Above her, the enormous bird cawed again, yet the sound seemed more distant to Domi, as if she was suddenly hearing things from under the surface of a swimming pool.

Something brushed against Domi's side then, nuzzling at her, a tiny point like a pin being dragged along her arm. That was the chick, she realized, not large but still large enough—and hungry enough—to hurt her. Its own cry sounded like a scream this close to her ear, and yet she couldn't seem to locate it through the black wash that was painting itself over her vision.

I…need…to…breathe, Domi thought, each word taking an eternity to form in her mind.

By then, Domi had stopped struggling, her movements reduced to just the slightest of spasms in her leg muscles as she flinched away from the pressure on her spine. The newborn chick probed her with its pointed beak, peering at the albino girl as she ceased flailing beneath its mother's toe. Its head twitched up and it looked to its mother for confirmation, twittering an ugly little squawk before turning back to Domi's twitching form.

As the just-hatched bird opened its beak to take a bite from the warm flesh in front of it, the nest shook and Rosalia leaped over the ridged side, her *katana* blade cutting through the air in a wide arc. The blade cut through the young bird's neck, whipping its head from its body instantaneously.

Above, the looming form of the baby's mother cawed angrily, its feathers puffing out in an intimidating display.

Still moving, Rosalia's blade continued in its long arc, and the dark-haired woman directed it upward and into the upper mound of the mother's belly. A clutch of dark feathers burst free of the monstrous creature's torso as the sword sliced through them, and the mother bird squawked again, head lunging to peck at this intruder to her nest.

Rosalia ducked low, the bird's scimitar-like beak cutting the air just an inch above her, the sword still swinging in her hands. She turned on the spot, driving the kinetic energy of her momentum into the sword thrust as the blade swung around and at the bird once more. This time Rosalia aimed low, the sword cutting into the bird's ankles—both of them as thick as the branch of an oak—where it perched upon Domi's prone form.

The sword struck hard, but Rosalia hadn't enough power to drive it through the creature's limbs. Instead it stuck midway through the thing's left leg, and Rosalia rolled aside as the bird's fearsome jaw snapped at her.

The dark-haired woman kicked off, powering herself away from the creature's path, leaving the sword where it was, stuck fast in the monster's leg.

The bird flapped its wings as if to frighten away its

new foe, and Rosalia leaped for the nearest wall of the nest, grabbing its edge and flipping herself over the side. The bird took two steps forward after the dark-haired mercenary, trotting off of Domi's back in its haste to stop the murderer of its last child. Its beak darted ahead, but all the bird saw was the disappearing swish of Rosalia's skirt as she dropped down beneath the level of the nest, hurling herself under the branch that it was propped upon.

Rosalia waited there, hanging horizontally, facedown on the underside of the nest, arms and legs stretched wide to hold her there, her hands entwined in the interwoven branches that made up the nest. The bird's head appeared for a moment, upside down as the monster peered over the side of the nest, trying to locate its prey. Then, with equal suddenness, the bird's head snapped back and disappeared.

Rosalia couldn't know, but Grant had just reached the top of the monofilament line and, having assessed the situation in the space of an eyeblink, he had leaped from a nearby branch onto the back of the hulking bird. Grant's hard landing had caused the bird to rear up, and Grant whipped one of his powerful arms around the beast's neck, securing his grip like a rider taming some impetuous steed. The monstrous bird dipped and reared like a bucking bronco, wings flapping in place as it tried to shake the heavy and unwelcome passenger off its back.

With a practiced flinch of his wrist tendons, Grant called forth his Sin Eater pistol once more, the long-serving weapon of his Magistrate days, bringing the blaster around as the hulking bird tried urgently to fling him free. A moment later the muzzle of the fourteen-inch barrel was pressed flush against the bird's beady black eye and Grant pulled the trigger. A stream of 9 mm bullets burst from the handcannon at point-blank range, obliterating the creature's eyeball and driving half a dozen slugs into the thing's brain as it continued to strut around its nest in frustration.

It took four seconds, give or take, before the bird finally keeled over, sagging to the floor of the nest.

Grant leaped from the shifting carcass, the barrel of his Sin Eater still trained on the hideous thing, which had landed right on top of Domi. Grant spotted someone else's arm poking out from beneath the fallen creature, as well. Sending his blaster back to its holster, he placed both hands against the bird's flank and pushed, shoving the thing off of Domi and the other person who was trapped beneath.

To Grant's surprise, the other person turned out not to be a person at all, just a woman's torso, her pretty face caked with dried blood and only the one limb attached to her body. With no time to spare, Grant turned his attention back to Domi, studied her for a frantic moment to see if she was still breathing. Her summer dress was torn in places, and a handful of scratches decorated her arms and back, several of them quite deep.

"Domi?" Grant urged. "You okay?"

The unmoving figure of Domi gave no response.

I'M LIVING somebody else's life, Kane realized as he rested in the forest clearing. His left eye was still aching, but that terrible burning sensation seemed to finally be ebbing. For a moment there, it had felt like an acid touch, drilling through his optic nerve and burning into his brain. Even now, with the pain abating, he could still sense it, still recall that muscle memory as his eye had clenched upon itself, trying to escape the fearsome pain.

The vision in his right eye, meanwhile, seemed to be getting clearer, the play of light and shadow beginning to once more form shapes.

Kane blinked, squeezing his eyes shut tight for a moment to try to shift the feeling of discomfort that had overwhelmed him for several minutes. When he opened his eyes again, the left one remained dead, a dull ache around its edge. His right eye, however, flickered like a badly tuned television set, the picture finally righting itself in a misty, soft-focus way. Kane cupped one hand over his right eye, blinked repeatedly in quick succession, trying to properly clear whatever it was that had affected him. After a moment he took his hand away and looked around. Things seemed normal, albeit a little bright. He could see again.

He was in a grassy area surrounded by trees, many of them reaching two or three hundred feet into the air, their tops so high that it hurt Kane's neck to look at them. He was propped on his elbows on the soft grass, his legs out in front of him. Rosalia's charmless dog lay at his feet, and its ears twitched as it realized that Kane was stirring, turning its long muzzle toward him and sniffing at the air. Just beyond where the dog lay, Kane saw the interphaser unit poised beside its carry case, and as he looked further around him he detected the subtle ring of stones that marked the clearing. Some were missing but it was clear that this had once been some ancient site of worship. Yet again, the interphaser had used a site of forgotten mystic power as its focal point for transporting matter across the quantum ether.

With a yip, the scruffy-looking dog stood and trotted off into the trees, presumably, Kane thought, to take care of its toilet.

Whatever had been going on in Kane's head, it hadn't been his life. The life had belonged to the Annunaki called Ullikummis, who had been tortured and clad in stone from a young age, his very genetic makeup altered by the adept geneticists of the Annunaki race. Kane ran his hands over his face, pushing against the muscles as though to wake himself up. As he did so it became clear that his left eye remained utterly blind, no longer able to detect even the broadest of changes in light. His right eye, meanwhile, worked as it always had, and Kane deliberately changed his focus, checking that he could see both near and far, that nothing had been damaged.

His face felt different, too, a tightness against the skin by his left cheek. He probed his face, running his fingernail along the groove of the scar that ran alongside his left eye. It felt hard, not just the scar, but his whole face, the muscles fixed in one expression like a palsy.

There were a lot of things going on at once, Kane realized, but it didn't take much imagination to conclude that it was all connected. Something had cut him a while back, and had infiltrated his flesh, affecting his muscles and somehow replaying another being's life for him to watch as silent observer. The Annunaki were masters of organic technology, Kane knew. Most recently, he had chosen to have a living stone placed beneath the flesh of his wrist, a senseless thing that functioned in conjunction with other Annunaki tech to unlock doors and provide other basic functions. The sacrifice had been necessary for him to escape from Life Camp Zero, and Kane had had the so-called obedience stone removed at the earliest convenience, before it could fully take hold of his brain.

Kane's mind raced, trying to recall just where he had received the scar. There had been a running battle in the now abandoned Cerberus redoubt between his colleagues and the faithful agents of Ullikummis. Kane himself had taken on the great stone god, using guns and ultimately his own body to try to fell this monstrous creature. Grant, Domi and Brigid Baptiste had fought at his side then, Brigid employing acid to damage Ullikummis and give Kane a chance to battle him on fairer terms. But Kane had failed, awakening in a cramped prison cell carved out of the rock. It must have been then, he realized, after the acid had burned through sections of Ullikummis's stone face and chest, flecks of his stone cladding burning away like so much vapor. A tiny fleck, perhaps no bigger than a grain of sand, might have got caught in the cut in Kane's face, infecting it somehow with a tiny part of Ullikummis.

And now interphaser travel was affecting the thing, Kane realized. Each time he traveled via the unit, the pain in his eye had become worse, triggering the visions of this monster's early life. Since the interphaser utilized some form of molecular transfer, it was possible that in breaking down and remaking Kane numerous times a second, the unit had misread the infection, triggering it to grow. Kane was no scientist, but it was a theory at least, albeit a less than reassuring one. Yet, rather than pay heed to this warning sign, Kane had battled on, the urgency of things in light of Brigid's disappearance and the fall of Cerberus too great for him to pause and think.

And now? Now, Kane realized, may just be too late.

Slowly, like a man waking from a deep sleep, Kane pushed himself up onto his knees and crouch-walked over to where the interphaser waited.

"You and me are going to have some words," Kane snarled at the interphaser, "once all this is over."

Kane carefully placed the pyramidal unit in its padded travel case.

As he closed the seals on the interphaser's case, a sudden barking came from Kane's left and he looked up, turning his head far enough that his right eye could see what was happening. Rosalia's dog had returned, and it stared at Kane with infinitely pale eyes, moist tongue lolling out of its mouth and tail briskly wagging as it barked for attention.

"What's up with you?" Kane asked, hefting the interphaser in its case as he made his way toward the mutt.

As Kane got closer, the dog turned and, with just a brief look over its haunch to make sure that Kane was following, began jogging off into the thick cover of the forest.

"Great," Kane muttered with a shake of his head. "Now I'm taking orders from a dog." With a resigned sigh, the ex-Mag walked hurriedly past the trees after his furry companion, away from the direction Grant and Rosalia had gone.

UP IN THE NEST high in the redwood's branches, Grant peered up from Domi's still body, scanning the edge of the nest where his curvaceous partner had disappeared.

"Rosalia?" Grant called, his voice firm. "It's clear up here now."

Unlike the other members of the Cerberus crew, Rosalia had no Commtact surgically imbedded in her skull. Instead, the newcomer relied on a portable unit that she had to engage as required, a little like a cell phone. Sometimes, Grant reasoned, it was just easier to shout.

A moment later Rosalia reappeared at the bowl-like lip of the huge nest, climbing over its side with appreciable noiselessness. "How's your friend?" she asked, seeing Grant kneeling by the albino form of Domi, checking her for signs of life.

Domi's chalk-white skin felt warm to Grant's touch, at least, which was a relief. Placing two fingers beneath Domi's nose where she lay facedown on the nest, Grant stilled his thoughts. After a moment he felt the reassuringly warm pressure as Domi breathed out.

"She's alive anyway," Grant said, the sense of relief clear in his tone. He had known Domi a long time; losing her now after everything they'd been through with Brigid seemed unimaginable.

Rosalia nodded, turning her gaze upward as she scanned the higher branches of the trees. There were at least three more of the colossal nests up there. The occasional shriek of one of the monstrous birds echoed through the trees, and she spotted the shadow play of wings through the higher levels of the trees, call and response, call and response. "Do you have any idea what those things are?" she asked, keeping her voice low.

Grant peered up at Rosalia as he examined Domi. "Nothing I've seen before," he admitted. "Look kinda like eagles. Big eagles."

Rosalia nodded solemnly. "Rocs," she said.

Grant shot her a querulous look at the word, reminded automatically of Ullikummis. "Like stones?" he asked.

Rosalia smiled, her teeth bright against the olive tan of her skin. "No, it's spelled *R-O-C*—roc or rukh," she told him. "You ever hear of Sinbad the Sailor? It was a children's story from the Middle East, just entertainment. On his fifth voyage he encountered a great egg, which was the product of the gigantic bird called the roc. The story claimed that the roc had a colossal wingspan and would frequently snatch up full-grown elephants in its claws, spiriting them away to feast upon at its leisure."

Grant whistled with incredulity. "That's one big bird."

"It's just a story," Rosalia reminded him, "made to entertain. There's likely very little fact to be found there. I was just reminded of it."

Grant peered over at the corpse of the deceased mother bird, assessing its size for a few seconds, his mind racing. "These things weren't up to grabbing elephants," he said, "but they could no doubt lift a person. That's most likely how Domi ended up way up here without a line."

Then he looked at Rosalia appreciably, thinking over what she had said. "You're pretty knowledgeable, huh?" he said.

Rosalia smiled. "I paid attention in school," she told him.

With swift efficiency, Grant ran his hands over Domi's unconscious body, checking for broken bones or any wounds he might not have noticed by sight alone. She seemed okay, and Grant decided to move her, rolling her gently onto her side. As he did so, the albino girl began to groan, and Grant spoke to her quietly.

"It's all right," Grant assured her. "You're okay now."

Domi's eyes flickered open, two bloodred orbs appearing from behind those thin white shutters. "The birds…?" she asked.

"They're gone," Grant assured her. "For now."

"What happened?" Domi asked weakly, scrunching her eyes as she tried to recall. "I remember knocking the egg over the side, and then it all got kind of…hectic."

"You're fine," Grant said as he pulled a small med kit from his coat and removed a tiny antiseptic spray, the container no longer than his thumb. "Just a few cuts."

"What about the girl?" Domi asked, but as she said it she remembered how the pretty teenager had ended up. Even now, her boyfriend had likely suffered a similar fate in one of the other nests that littered the trees around them.

Grant made Domi sit up, then he applied a little of the antiseptic salve, spraying it on the lacerations that marked her back and shoulders. As he did so, his Commtact came to life.

"Grant, it's Kane," the familiar voice at the other end said. "How is everything?"

"We've found Domi," Grant replied. "She's a bit dinged up but she'll be fine. I'm just checking her out now. How 'bout you?"

"Still feeling kind of woozy," Kane said. "Whatever hit me really knocked me for a loop."

"Hang tight," Grant advised. "We'll be back with you soon as we can. Then we can jump outta here and get back home."

"No, something's spooked the mutt," Kane explained. "Could be important. I'm checking it out now."

"Wait a minute. I thought you couldn't see," Grant challenged, concern in his voice.

"I can see better," Kane told him vaguely. "You concentrate on getting Domi back on her feet."

With that, Kane broke off the Commtact link, and Grant muttered a curse beneath his breath. He was worried for his friend.

"What is it, Grant?" Domi asked.

Grant rolled his eyes. "Kane—what else?"

Domi winced as Grant applied more of the antiseptic salve, dragging her breath through clenched teeth as the spray froze her wounds. "They've built a new ville out there," Domi explained, "on the ruins of Snakefishville. They're calling it Luilekkerville.

"They have Magistrates guarding the gates," Domi continued, "but the gates themselves are left open. I used two of them, and they were easy to enter and exit—no fuss, no muss. The ville is very welcoming, the people are real friendly. It's kind of…weird." As an outlander, and a somewhat freakish-looking one at that, Domi had suffered her fair share of rejection by ville folk, Grant knew.

"And that's Ullikummis's influence?" Rosalia queried. "But he's warlike, aggressive."

"That's the weirdest part," Domi explained. "The people of Luilekkerville place an enormous emphasis on worship, their cathedral dominates the place, standing roughly where the old Admin Monolith used to be."

Grant nodded, knowing all too well the traditional layout of the villes.

"But they talk about Ullikummis as a force of love, like he's something mystical," Domi continued. "I snuck into the sermon and the preacher there didn't even use his name, just spoke about how love was a rock and a rock couldn't be broken."

"What about the stones?" Grant asked, recalling the way that the insidious things imbedded themselves in people and took control of their thoughts.

Domi shook her head. "They're not using them, not as far as I could see anyway," she said. "Maybe the Mags have got them under those hoods. I couldn't check that, but the people haven't been given obedience stones, so that part of the ritual wasn't evident anymore. They're just, I don't know, letting Ullikummis into their hearts. They believe in him, Grant, believe in this utopia his followers have promised."

Grant shifted in place uncomfortably. "Snakefishville was just a pile of rubble two months ago," he told Rosalia. "Easy to believe in utopia when your god comes along and rebuilds your home from the dust up, I guess."

Domi nodded in agreement. "He's bringing them what they want. Security, a home, order. He's doing exactly the same thing the barons did, before they evolved into their true forms as the Annunaki. It's the same old trick dressed up as something new."

"The Program of Unification all over again," Grant rumbled. "Only now we know where it's all going, and it's nowhere good. This shit ends with the extinction of free will, and with it the end of mankind as we know it."

"And you have to remember what happened in Tenth City," Domi said, worry in her tone.

Rosalia was bemused. "What happened in this Tenth City?" she asked. "I never heard of it."

"It was a combat training camp," Grant explained, fixing her with his steely gaze. "Ullikummis presided over about two dozen local farmers, hardening them and forcing them to fight one another in brutal bouts. Those who failed, he would kill—sending them to be cremated."

Rosalia nodded emotionlessly. "Sounds ghastly," she said.

"It was," Domi acknowledged, "but there was more to it than that. The whole ville did something to people's heads, gave them tanglebrain, tricked them into obeying Ullikummis's commands. Brigid believed it was something to do with the architecture, somehow enhancing subliminal suggestions made by the Annunaki overlord himself."

Grant smiled in irritation. "We closed Tenth City down," he told Rosalia, "used explosives to wipe it off the face of the Earth."

Rosalia nodded. "Sounds about right for you," she said. "Subtlety was never a Magistrate's strong suit."

Grant let the veiled insult pass.

"So now we know he doesn't even need to use the stones to make people obey him," Domi growled angrily. "Just a promise of something better is enough."

"It's as it has always been," Rosalia observed. "People wish to believe in a better future, to have hope even when there is none. This...religion that Ullikummis has created is a promise of a better tomorrow, a mind-set for a better way of living."

"But it's a lie," Grant snarled impatiently.

"Until everyone believes it," Rosalia suggested archly, "at which point it would supersede and so become the truth. That's the nature of religion, is it not?"

"All the more reason to put a stop to it," Grant growled, pushing himself up from the nest bed, his muscles tense.

Rosalia watched Grant with dark eyes, marveling at his building fury. As an ex-Magistrate, Grant naturally hid his emotions, but this growing cult seemed to wear at his patience, making his anger bubble just below the surface. Like Kane, he was frustrated, too, at the loss of Brigid Baptiste, and that frustration was expressing itself as rage.

"They no longer need the obedience stones—they've come to accept him now," Domi argued bleakly. "I don't know how we fight this anymore."

Rosalia turned to the petite albino girl, a catlike smile forming on her lips. "Don't give up too easily, Domi," she said. "Even belief systems can be rocked if you can find their weakest point."

Grant let out a low whistle. "That's asking a lot," he said. "Now, me and Kane, we've faced down aliens with tech far superior to our own before now, we've battled our way through alternate dimensions and we've even stopped an attack by angels from outside of space-time. Yeah, seriously. But turning back the tide of a whole fucking religion—that is asking a lot, even for us."

Rosalia's smile became wider. "You scared by a little challenge, Magistrate?"

Chapter 12

The dog wended its way between the trees and Kane followed at a jog, the carry case for the interphaser slung over one shoulder. He was edgy now, conscious that one half of his vision was missing and he could be literally blindsided if he didn't exercise caution. Kane had always displayed a remarkable talent he referred to as his point man sense, so named because he'd always taken point back in his days as a Magistrate. This point man sense made Kane seem almost preternaturally aware of possible threats around him and able to react with exceptional speed. As such it had saved his own life, and that of his partners, on numerous occasions. Though it seemed supernatural, Kane's point man sense was in fact a remarkable combination of his natural five senses, an exceptional focus of his mind so as to become somehow more aware of the environment around him. But with his vision compromised, Kane suddenly found himself relying on his other senses—and most especially his sense of hearing—more than ever before.

Up ahead, the dog hurried on, its feet padding against the soft underbrush of the forest as it made its way to whatever it had found in Kane's absence. Kane just hoped it wasn't a bitch in heat or some muddy pool that only a dog would think noteworthy.

He need not have worried.

As he hurried past a clutch of tightly bunched birches, their trunks so close that two had become wrapped together in their upper limbs, like silver-skinned Siamese twins, Kane saw the dog come to a halt. The mutt was standing at the edge of a hole that sank deep into the ground. The hole was wide in its center and followed a jagged stretch like a fault line, tapering off after about forty-five feet until finally it closed up. The line stretched off through the trees, curving a little as it snaked through the forest. Several of the trees along the quakelike line had fallen, and two poplars stuck out at diagonals where their roots had become entangled in the hole's walls. Occasional wisps of some light, amber-colored mist were drifting out of the hole, settling in pockets along its length.

The dog peered into the hole, sinking low on its haunches and sniffing at the air, getting its nose well into the gap. Kane sniffed, too, more warily and from a greater distance, scenting the air. It smelled a little like tangerines or some other pungent fruit, yet remained faint, enticingly out of reach. The smell was familiar, but he couldn't place it immediately, needed to think. The dog ceased sniffing at the hole, turned to Kane and barked once, seeking his approval.

Kane held his hand out for the dog as he approached the hole, still scenting the air for himself. His nose wrinkled. The smell was odd, and yet it was definitely something that Kane had smelled before. The broad-shouldered ex-Magistrate checked around him as the dog nuzzled against his hand, pushing itself against his palm affectionately. Over there, almost directly in front of where he stood, Kane could just make out the rebuilt towers of Snakefishville, or whatever the place was called now, through the trees.

The rent in the ground looked like the result of an earthquake. Kane realized almost immediately what would have caused it: the subterrene boring machine that had been used to destroy Snakefishville. Although this area had suffered from earthquake activity historically, this crack looked recent, had doubtless occurred sometime in the past few months. The subterrene was probably the catalyst.

Kane took another step closer, peering into the dark hole and letting the subtle fragrance drift around him, the amber mist playing at his booted feet. The nameless dog watched Kane, its head tilted at an angle wonderingly.

The gap looked dark within, the rough sides of the open soil like a wound falling away into the absolute darkness of shadow. Kane pulled a small tube from its storage place inside his jacket, unclipping the top of the xenon beam and letting the powerful, miniature flashlight illuminate the area at his feet. The xenon beam gave one-thousand candles of light, bathing the dark trench in artificial daylight. Even so, Kane could make out little other than various tree and plant roots, insects scurrying away from the light behind the drifting tendrils of mist. The trench itself seemed to be some kind of shelf arrangement, and at best Kane could see fifteen feet down before the remainder disappeared beneath the hooked lip of the surface.

The yellowish mist continued to drift around his boots, scenting the air with a faint, too-sweet smell like rotten fruit.

The dog seemed to watch Kane encouragingly for a moment. Then, with a shake of its head, the scruffy hound began to clamber down into the trench, making its way along a steep slope and into the pit beyond.

"Kane to Grant," Kane subvocalized, engaging his Commtact. "Definitely got me a little something that's worth taking a closer look-see."

Grant's basso voice rumbled back over the Commtact after a moment. "I read you, Kane. We're still patching up Domi here. Can join you in maybe five, ten minutes. You able to wait?"

Kane watched the dog traveling away down the hole, and he wondered how mad Rosalia would be if he lost the animal.

"How long have we been partners, Grant? Was I ever able to wait?" Kane teased.

"You be careful," Grant warned. "With that trick eye and whatever the hell's going on with the monster birds out here, this is all starting to get a little too screwy to go off half-cocked."

"Roger that," Kane confirmed. "I'm just going for a recce, nothing doing."

"ACKNOWLEDGED," Grant said, an irritated reluctance in his tone. He had known Kane too long to attempt to hinder the man's curiosity once something had piqued it. Up in the nest, the ebony-skinned ex-Magistrate was adding several strips of antiseptic gauze to Domi's arms and side while Rosalia kept watch.

"They're coming closer," Rosalia warned, her eyes on the network of branches all around them. "Naturally, a bird won't enter another's nest but they must sense that this one's been—" she looked down dismissively at the oversize bird corpses and dead wolf scattered across the nest "—vacated. We need to get out of here pretty soon."

"Yeah, and as long as we're up here Kane's off playing maverick Mag on his lonesome," Grant grumbled, winding another strip of gauze around Domi's scratched arm. "You have any idea where these bird things came from, Domi?" he asked. "Something to do with—what did you say it was called?—Luikk…"

"Luilekkerville," Domi corrected.

At the edge of the nest, Rosalia nodded knowingly. "From the Dutch," she said. "It was a fairy-tale utopia, a home for the idle."

Grant looked at her, eyebrows raised in surprise. "You sure know a lot," he said.

"You sure don't," Rosalia shot back.

For a moment they glared at one another, then Grant turned back to Domi. "Well? Any ideas?" he asked.

"I didn't see any birds in the ville itself," Domi recalled, "nor any of the kind of tech a person might use to mutate normal birds, assuming that's what they are."

"It's a reasonable assumption," Grant allowed. "They've either been enlarged through an unnatural growth agent, or there's some kind of genetic tinkering going on at a more basic level."

Rosalia spit with irritation. "Look at them, Magistrate," she said, "use your eyes. They're not any kind of bird I recognize. You?"

Grant took another look across to the man-size corpse of the mother bird. "Kind of reminds me of a falcon," he said, shaking his head a little with uncertainty.

"The beak's not right," Rosalia told him, "and the plumage is too dark. It's more like an eagle's coloring."

Domi winced once more as Grant placed the last of the adhesive strips on her arm. The strips would help prevent the wounds from becoming infected, but she would be wise to wash them thoroughly as soon as she got to a clear water source. "So what do you think they are, then, Rosalia?" Domi asked, nodding at the birds.

"Hybrids," Rosalia said, fixing Grant and Domi with her cold stare.

WARILY, Kane followed the ragged-looking dog as it trotted down the steep incline and into the trench that ran between the trees. After a few steps, the dog turned back to check that Kane was still there, before trotting on. The mangy thing continued to do this with every ten or so paces, making sure Kane didn't fall too far behind.

"Whatever you can smell down here," Kane muttered, "it sure has put a tick up your butt."

The dog padded on, watchful of the least-steep slope that would take them both down into the trench.

Kane switched off his xenon beam, allowing his eyes to adjust to the encroaching darkness as they continued on. He didn't want to alert anyone down here of his approach; for the moment he just wanted to figure out what it was he was approaching.

The strange-smelling, amber-colored mist continued to float close to Kane's feet, reminding him obliquely of the Annunaki but with no clear comprehension of why. He must have seen this mist before, perhaps while on the mother ship *Tiamat,* but he was damned if he could place where.

The mismatched pair continued downward, and when Kane looked up he could see that they had gone beneath the lip of the crack, the sunlight now filtered at an angle and directly lighting only the wall behind him. He continued to follow the dog, wondering what this canine had detected. It was a strange beast, to say the least—it seemed to be attracted to all things Annunaki, or at least to all things alien. Kane couldn't put his finger on it, but he was beginning to suspect there must be more to the scruffy dog than its appearance implied.

Abruptly, the dog halted, ducking low as it peered at something up ahead, its body held rigid, tail upright. Kane lowered to a crouch, following the dog's line of sight.

A vast underground cavern opened out in front of Kane, only slightly lit by the burning of three candles spaced at intervals around a wide circular pit. The pit was fifteen feet in diameter, and the amber mist seemed to gather over it like a blanket of gold, swirling in eddies as the breeze caught and toyed with it. Kane could just barely make out the glint of metal at the edge of the circle, marking it out more formally. The metal strip was inscribed all the way around its surface, a pattern of glyphs that Kane recognized as Annunaki but had no way of translating. If Brigid Baptiste had been here, she might have been able to figure them out, but left alone he had no chance of knowing what the writing said. A simple wooden jug waited by the far edge of the circle.

Kane was about to lead the way into the cavern when he sensed a movement. He waited for a moment until a woman paced into the lit area from the shadows, reading from a heavy-looking hide-bound book, its leathery pages whispering as she turned them. The woman was wearing a long dress of crimson and black that enshrouded her body, hem brushing at the ground as she moved. She wore a hood over her head like a wimple, covering her hair so that only her ears stuck out at the burgundy material's edge. Kane could see a few wisps of the woman's hair where it had broken free from the wimple, and it trailed in several black streaks like cats' tails that reached down past her shoulders, curling in on themselves to make spiraling patterns at her breast.

The woman walked around the wide circle in the ground as if marking her territory, before coming to a stop by a large rock, beside which a patchwork blanket had been lain, a simple cloth bag propped at its edge. As she turned, Kane saw her face properly for the first time; she was young and striking, perhaps thirty years of age. Furthermore, something glistened on her cheeks, reflections of the candle flames catching twin streaks that seemed to emanate from her eyes. Kane narrowed his own eyes, conscious that his left was still sightless, and tried to make out what it was that glistened on the woman's face. It moved down her face slowly, like liquid, and it glistened a red so dark as to be almost black as the candlelight caught it. It was blood, Kane realized with a start—the woman was crying tears of blood.

As Kane watched, the bloodstained woman bent with supple ease and placed her heavy book atop the blanket. Then, to Kane's surprise, the woman reached behind her and began to untie her dress, pulling at it until it fell away from her, pooling around her legs. Still wearing the hood, the woman stepped out of the dress, revealing her young, athletic body only slightly masked by her simple underwear, and a necklace with a pendant of smoky glass hanging between her breasts.

Beside him, the dog stood and issued the lightest of whimpers. Kane placed a firm hand on its back, settling the mutt before it could run to investigate.

In front of them, the woman bent to reach for the wooden jug that had been left at the edge of the circle, and Kane watched as she dipped the jug into the circle itself. It was a pool, Kane realized.

The woman with the bloody tears raised the jug and tipped its contents over one outstretched arm, laughing as the amber liquid sloshed over her. At that moment, Kane knew where he had seen a pit like this before. It looked like—

"HELL!" Grant said. "We've had more than our share of trouble with hybrids. The Annunaki hid among us as the barons, their hybrid DNA providing the ideal starting point for their ultimate rebirth. If these birds have been created by mixing DNA then it stinks of Annunaki involvement."

Rosalia herself had been a part of a group that traded in genetic material not so long ago, and she understood what Grant was referring to. "You're jumping to conclusions, you realize," she warned him.

"Get used to it," Grant shot back. "Unfortunately where we're concerned there's not always someone sitting at the far side of the room waiting to explain precisely what it is we're fighting."

Rosalia's eyes darted left and right, and her hand went to the hilt of her hip-mounted sword. "Speaking of which," she advised, "it's time we got moving. Whiteface, you okay to move or you need someone to carry you?"

Domi glared at Rosalia. "I can make it under my own steam," she said. Like Grant, Domi had tried to be welcoming to Kane's new recruit, but she had a history with Rosalia that was less than pleasant. Six months ago, while Rosalia had been in the employ of a gang of brigands, the dark-haired mercenary and her partner had cold-cocked Domi, leaving her wounded as they made a break for it. Domi had avenged herself on Rosalia's partner, severing the man's spinal column and leaving him for dead. Rosalia, however, had somehow escaped the woman's revenge—for now.

The three-strong party of warriors made its way to the edge of the nest, close to where Grant's microline still hung from the bole of a nearby branch.

"I had to guess which tree you were in," Grant explained as Domi spotted the line hanging from the neighboring tree just a few feet away.

"Good guess," Domi replied.

At that moment there was a hideous screech from nearby, and the three companions spun in time to see another of the gargantuan birds come swooping down through the leafy branches toward the nest. Rosalia pulled her sword in an instant, as two more of the squawking birds came into view behind the first. "I'll handle this," she assured the others.

"No, we're in this together," Grant said as he powered the Sin Eater back into his hand from its hidden wrist holster.

Seconds later the attack was upon them once more, and Rosalia's sword swept forth, hacking wildly at the first of the birds as it attempted to pierce her torso with its sharp talons. Rosalia dropped to one knee, leaning backward and letting the vicious bird swoop over her, its fearsome claws just three inches from the swelling of her breasts. Her flashing blade carved an arc through the air, and a clutch of fluttering feathers was snipped from the retreating bird's dark plumage.

Beside the swordswoman, Grant closed one eye as he targeted the next of their avian attackers. His Sin Eater spewed hot lead as the creature got closer, its huge wings beating at the air with the sound of thunder.

As the battle proceeded behind her, Domi carefully stepped out of the nest and walked with pigeon steps out onto the five-inch-wide branch, stretching her arms out to her sides as the tree limb trembled beneath her. The albino outlander had a remarkable sense of balance, preternaturally aware of her surroundings at some instinctual level. As the three mighty birds of prey swept down to attack the lurkers in the nest, Domi picked up her pace and hurried along the tapering branch, her feet becoming a white blur as she sped toward the hanging thread of the monofilament.

As Grant and Rosalia battled with the others, the last of the birds spied Domi with hawklike eyes, and it flapped its massive wings once, subtly altering direction and lunging at Domi as she scampered along the branch. Domi leaped into the air as the creature knifed toward her, flipping herself over it as its sharp beak snapped closed on the spot where she had been standing. Then she was rolling across one of its wings, using it to lever herself up and away from the nest where the other birds struggled with her companions. A moment later, as the bird hurried away with a graceful beating of its mighty wings, Domi began plummeting toward the ground, gravity taking hold. But the albino woman was not worried; her hand snapped out and in an instant she had grasped the dangling cord of Grant's climbing line, letting it play through her clamping fingers for a moment to expel her extra momentum. A second later Domi was rappelling down the monofilament line bare-handed, speeding toward the ground like a hailstone.

Meanwhile, in the nest above, Rosalia pulled back her sword in readiness as the giant birds regrouped for a second attack. Beside her, Grant was holding his blaster rock-steady, watching the patterns that the birds made as they swirled through the towering branches of the redwoods.

"You want to know something strange?" Grant said after a moment.

Rosalia kept her eyes on the birds as they turned and began to drop. "What?"

"They're keeping to a very tight area," Grant told her, "like they can't leave this part of the forest."

"Maybe," Rosalia mused. "You have any theories why?"

Grant pumped at the trigger of his Sin Eater as the birds closed in. "Not yet," he snarled, the weapon bucking in his hand as a stream of 9 mm bullets burst from its barrel at the swooping birds. "But I'll bet if we leave this forest we'll be safe—they won't follow."

At his side, Rosalia lanced the two-foot blade of her *katana* upward, driving it into the leathery wing of one of the birds as it lunged at her, squawking its irritated babble as the sword pieced its appendage. Then Rosalia ducked, dragging the blade out as the bird swooped away. Here's a meal that fights back, she thought bitterly.

Down below them, Domi was just reaching the ground. Grant risked a glance over the side of the nest.

"We need to keep moving," Grant opined as the birds turned away, already preparing for another try at the humans in their midst. "You want to go next or do you want me to?"

Rosalia didn't bother to look at him as she replied, "Whichever. It doesn't matter to me."

"Fine," Grant said. "I'm the one with the distance weapon. Get moving and I'll cover you."

Turning to Grant, Rosalia offered him a sly smile for just a second. "Such a gentleman," she teased. Then she was away, vaulting over the high side of the nest and sprinting along the grand tree's limb, the sword flashing in her hand as it caught the rays of sunlight filtering through the tree cover. The screaming sound of air passing over the birds' wings became louder as Rosalia ran across the branch toward the monofilament line that hung from the neighboring tree, but she couldn't look to see where they were—the tapering branch required all her attention or a deadly misstep would result in a thirty-foot drop and doubtless cost the mercenary woman her life. Instead, she had to trust Grant's aim as she heard his Sin Eater come to life once more, blasting shot after shot at the attacking birds.

A dark shadow crossed Rosalia's path as she reached the narrow end of the branch, and she leaped in the air, reaching out for the narrow thread that was the Cerberus teammate's only way back to the ground. As she leaped, something squawked just a few feet behind her, and she felt her body buffeted by the wind as heavy wings flapped close to her back. Then her fingers were entwined in the monofilament, doubling it over her hand and wrist as she caught hold.

"Rosalia," Grant yelled, "watch your six!"

With reactions honed to the level of instinct, Rosalia turned as she began to descend the thin rope, swinging the *katana* she still clutched in her right hand. Above her, the sounds of gunfire continued as Grant tried to kill or frighten the tenacious birds of prey.

In a flash, Rosalia's blade struck the attacking bird as it pecked at her, slicing a gash across its face as she began to descend the monofilament line. The bird cawed angrily, pulling itself up and away from this challenger even as Rosalia dropped away, the thin line playing through her fingers with practiced ease.

A half dozen feet above, Grant's Sin Eater was blasting a cacophonous stream of bullets at another of the birds, playing its lethal dispatch across the face and body of the grasping monstrosity. The bird's wings beat at the air as the bullets struck it, swirling in place as chunks of flesh and armorlike feathers burst from its body. As it struggled among the branches, Grant sprinted across the nest, leaping over the corpse of the baby bird and the teenager who had been intended as its first meal. Then he was at the edge of the nest, clambering up its bowl-like side as he prepared to rappel to the ground.

At that moment, the bird that had tried to attack Rosalia swooped upward with a mighty beat of its wings, clawing through the air toward the nest. As it passed the edge of the nest, Grant appeared, and with lightning-fast instincts honed from numerous battles, the ex-Magistrate kicked outward with a booted foot. Grant's foot connected with the enormous bird's head with a solid, bone-crunching blow, causing the bird to shudder as it struggled up toward the branch.

Grant, however, was knocked backward by the force of his own blow, and suddenly he was falling, dropping over the side of the nest toward the ground.

"Crap!" Grant snarled as he toppled past the careening bird.

KANE KNELT SILENTLY beside Rosalia's scruffy dog at the edge of the underground shelter, watching as the mysterious, striking woman poured something from the circular pool over her arms and body. It looked like liquid gold as it spilled over her curvaceous form, arching and dipping around her as it clung to each line, each curve. The contents of the pit misted as they touched her form, not quite liquid but not yet gas. And as he watched, Kane now recognized just what that pit was.

He thought back, recalled seeing an identical pool about a year ago, when Grant's companion Shizuka had been wounded. At that point, the Cerberus team had found themselves in the clutches of the Annunaki, trusting a female hybrid called Rhea who owed her allegiance to Overlord Lilitu. The pit had been used to revive Shizuka, reknitting a vicious wound that had been inflicted on her midriff.

Kane thought for a moment, trying to remember how Brigid Baptiste had described the thing. She'd concluded by the markings on the metal circle that it was Tuatha de Danaan tech, acquired by the Annunaki as a part of their millennia-old pact. The Tuatha de Danaan were a humanoid race who had arrived on Earth after the Great Flood. More considerate than the Annunaki, the Tuatha de Danaan were characterized as scientists and poets, as well as warriors. They had settled in isolated Ireland, and had struck a pact with the Annunaki to oversee human development until the Annunaki were ready to return. Some considered the Tuatha de Danaan technologically superior to the Annunaki, and their more pacific approach to life had characterized them in legend as more beneficial than the Annunaki, whose own legends spoke of mainly blood and thunder.

The circular pit itself had been known in legend as the Cauldron of Bran, or the Chalice of Rebirth, and it had been said to have the property to revive the dead, bringing fallen warriors back to life. Brigid had theorized that the cauldron's mistlike contents actually contained nanomachines, introducing them to a bather and thus employed to heal wounds.

Finding this particular Chalice of Rebirth so far away from the Tuatha de Danaan's traditional stomping grounds did not surprise Kane. These alien infiltrators, be they Annunaki or Danaan, seemed to have seeded the face of the Earth with their technology, often misinterpreted as magic by the primitive locals.

A network of caverns splayed out from the main chamber here, ill-lit in the flickering fires of the three candles, and Kane realized that this might once have been a major meeting point for the secret races that hid in Earth's shadows. For whatever reason, the chambers had remained hidden for perhaps a thousand years, but the recent artificial earthquakes generated by the sub-terrene had opened a rent in the earth, uncovering this Chalice of Rebirth for the first time in a millennium.

The woman stepped into the pool then, its glistening essence playing across her legs, rippling reflections shimmering on her near naked body. Kane watched as the woman reached for something that had been contained in her discarded dress, pulling free a tiny bird's egg, no bigger than a silver dollar. Standing knee-deep in the Chalice of Rebirth, the woman ran her hand over the egg in the sweeping gesture of a conjurer, sprinkling some powder on the egg's oval shell. Then, to Kane's bafflement, she leaned down and placed the egg in the mists of the pit, muttering words that he could not hear. The egg seemed to spark with energy as it sunk out of sight.

"What th—?" Kane muttered.

He was still watching as the woman strode across the circle of the pit and reached for her cloth bag where it lay on the colorful blanket. She searched there for a moment, those eerie blood tears dribbling slowly down her face, before pulling out a small glass vial. The vial fit neatly into the palm of her small hand, just two inches in height. As Kane watched, the woman twisted the cork free and sniffed at the contents of the vial, closing her eyes in delight, the trace of a smile crossing her features for just a moment. Then, to Kane's surprise, the woman tipped the bottle until a single drop of liquid fell from its mouth, disappearing beneath the amber mist that curled around the surface of the pit. When the drop of liquid hit, a fiery spume of red shot from the hidden pool, blasting up toward the roof of the cavern.

"This ain't getting any better," Kane muttered as the dog beside him yelped loudly and leaped to its feet.

At the sound of the dog's bark, the blood-teared woman turned, fixing Kane and the dog with her piercing gaze. "Welcome, my darlings," she whispered.

They'd been rumbled.

Chapter 13

In the simple stone shack in the hidden city of Agartha, the black-garbed figure of Brigid Haight stared at the golden weapon that Balam pointed uncomfortably at her, his six long fingers poised to pull the trigger. The device, called an ASP emitter, was the favored weapon of the Nephilim—the muscle of the Annunaki and, according to myth, the wandering souls of fallen angels. The weapon was shaped like a coiling snake that reached down to the wrist, an open viper's head forming the muzzle from which a fearsome beam of plasma could be emitted. That beam was powerful enough to cut a human being in two, Brigid knew, for she had faced the weapons before, when they were in use by the Nephilim themselves. To see the normally peaceable Balam using such a weapon, however, surprised Brigid.

"What are you doing, Balam?" she asked innocently. "What's the joke?"

Balam stared at Brigid with baleful eyes, their dark pools shaped like great ovals on his bulbous head. "I think that perhaps you should explain how you got here and just what brings you to Agartha."

"I came to see you," Brigid explained, "and Little Quav, of course."

"For what reason, Brigid Baptiste?" Balam probed, the ASP emitter never wavering in his hand. It seemed incongruous, seeing such a weapon in the environs of this ordinary dwelling, with its simple wooden dining table and chairs, its potted plant and scattering of children's playthings in one corner of the floor. "You made a pact, Cerberus and the Annunaki, that you would not endeavor to impinge upon the child's development, that you would allow us our privacy until such time as she came of age. The child is not yet three annums old. So I ask again, why have you come?"

Brigid's emerald eyes narrowed as she watched the strange-looking creature of the First Folk, studied the ASP emitter in his hand. Although not averse to the reality of his world, Balam was a pacifist at heart, content to advise rather than sully his hands in combat. Brigid wondered where he had obtained the ASP emitter, presumed he had acquired it among other treasures that remained ensconced in the vast underground city. Even so, it was remarkable that Balam had armed himself like this, storing such a dangerous device in the home he shared with the hybrid child. "You're not yourself," Brigid said solicitously. "Put the weapon down, Balam. No good can come of its use."

Balam's pale six-fingered hand held steady, the gleaming blaster aimed at his visitor's belly. From behind him, Little Quav's light voice spoke up, a tremble in her tone. "Unca Bal-bal? What's happening?"

"Stay behind me, precious one," Balam instructed, not turning his head as he spoke to his ward.

"But hasn't Briggly come to play?" Quav asked in a sorrowful tone, taking a step closer to reach for the carved wooden building blocks that sat on a table beside Brigid's hip.

"I don't think this person we see before us is Brigid," Balam opined. "Not entirely.

"Well, Miss Baptiste? You've closed your mind up but still you read differently—I can sense that much merely standing this close to you."

"You've been down here too long, Balam," Brigid responded, taking a step to her left, then another. "You're jumping at shadows."

Balam shook his head ever so slightly. "I am not entirely unaware of what has been occurring on the surface," he told her. "When I approached Cerberus to check into disruptions in the Ontic Library, I was aware that there had been a fundamental shift in the nature of the war. The very rules themselves were rewritten that day, and I realized at that moment that hiding was not enough. I knew that someone would come for the child Ninlil," he said, referring to Little Quav by her formal Annunaki name, "and that she would be a key player in the final war of the gods. But I did not expect that caller to be you, Brigid Baptiste."

Brigid's eyes were fixed on the ASP emitter, a timer ticking down in her brain like a metronome. "You talk too much," she growled.

And then Brigid moved, her left arm jabbing out and knocking over the stack of child's building blocks, sweeping them toward Balam even as he flinched his trigger finger and unleashed a screaming blast of plasma from the nozzle of the ASP. The pale green burst of light zapped from the weapon's snakelike head, vaporizing one of the wooden blocks as it lanced across the room toward Balam and the child. Brigid ducked as the tail of the beam shot by overhead, her hand grasping for the TP-9 semiautomatic secured at her hip. Her quick-thinking maneuver had worked—but only just—as the blocks had distracted the untrained Balam, throwing his aim barely enough that she could evade the path of the lethal beam of energy.

Then Brigid was leaping aside as Balam fired a second blast from the ASP emitter, this one more carefully aimed as her fur cloak splayed out behind her. Brigid cartwheeled across the small interior of the stone shack, snagging the grip of her TP-9 and pulling it free from her hip holster. The compact semiautomatic was a bulky hand pistol with a covered targeting scope across the top and was finished in molded, matte black. The grip was set just off-center beneath the barrel and, in the user's hand, the unit seemed to form a lopsided square, hand and wrist making the final side and corner.

Behind Balam, Little Quav began wailing, terrified by the shrieking sounds and bright light cast by the ASP emitter.

"Quav," Balam instructed swiftly, "stay behind me."

Little Quav nodded, placing both hands over her ears as Balam unleashed another plasma blast from the snakelike weapon's mouth.

Diving aside as the plasma beam cut through the air, the smell of ozone filling her nostrils, Brigid lifted her semiautomatic and snapped off a burst of bullets. Three shots fired from the weapon's barrel, 9 mm bullets racing toward their target.

Balam clipped off another blast from his plasma weapon and the pale green beam emanated like a sudden wall of light in the confines of the stone-walled room.

Brigid watched incredulously as the beam cut her

bullets from the air, melting them within the ferocity of its hard light. Then her leather-clad form was vaulting over the simple dining table, legs swinging around to kick aside the chair waiting at its far side. The chair fell, crashing to the floor just a foot from where Balam stood protecting the girl. Quav screamed then turned away, running from the room into the back part of the simple stone dwelling. Balam took no notice, concentrating on getting a bead on this interloper who had presented herself as his old ally.

Something behind Brigid caught light, a set of drapes catching fire as Balam's plasma blast went wide. Brigid rolled across the floor as another burst of plasma cut through the room, bringing herself up into a crouch and whipping the TP-9 around once more, training it on Balam. Despite his actions, Balam's face remained impassive, conveying no sense of anger or animosity. He was simply doing a job, defending the hybrid child as he had promised to do. He bore Brigid no malice.

Squeezing the trigger of her blaster, Brigid sent a stream of bullets at the pale-skinned, slender alien. Balam dipped his head as if praying, and Brigid's bullets cut through the air above him, pounding against the wall behind him with a triple burst of ruined masonry. Then Balam took a step forward, blocking the doorway through which the girl had disappeared. "Leave us, Brigid," he pleaded. "Before someone is hurt."

Brigid bit back a curse, kicking over the table and ducking behind it as Balam reeled off another plasma blast. "I'm just here for the girl," she shouted over the sound of the flames licking the other side of the table. "I mean her no harm."

Balam leveled the ASP at the table that Brigid had chosen for a shield. "She's safe here, Brigid," he advised her. "You must leave. Whatever it is you think you're doing, it's wrong—wrong for you and of no benefit to Cerberus or to Little Quav."

"No, it's not," Brigid snapped. "Quav won't be hurt. It's time the child met with her destiny."

"Whatever that destiny may be," Balam said evenly, "it's at least a decade from now. Depart while you still can, Brigid. Truly, I would not wish to hurt you."

Hurt as in kill, Brigid realized. The ASP emitter would cause a lot of damage if just one bolt hit her. Even as she thought it, the ASP shrieked again and Brigid saw a glowing circle begin to form on the underside of the table she crouched behind. Balam was burning through it, focusing his plasma beam at the one obstruction in his path to ejecting Brigid Haight from his home. The circle glowed brighter and brighter, turning from red to orange to yellow in a matter of moments, an intense whiteness growing at its center.

On the isle of Bensalem, the faithful trudged into the castle of their master, hunkering down as the harsh sea breeze whipped all around the castle walls. The castle itself was made up of many smaller structures, and as they came closer Ullikummis's devotees saw that it followed a familiar pattern, the towering central pillar surrounded by lower buildings, each one contained within a roughly hewn wall of rock. The structures, too, were carved from rock—no, not so much carved as bashed, broken, *assaulted* by the elements until they had taken their present configuration.

Ullikummis strode onward on his powerful legs, their rock surface dark in the silvery light from the overcast sky. Fifty-nine people followed this stone-shod god, determined to show him that their devotion was absolute.

The main arm of the building tapered high into the air, ending in that spike that dominated the structure's center. The faithful looked around them, admiring the bleakness, the austerity of the building outside and in. It was a conglomeration of rock, rough walls on all sides, low barricades pitted along the main arteries like some perverted hurdling course. There were irregular hollows in the rock like doorways, opening out into rooms like warrens, big and small, each as harsh and unforgiving as the one before it. Besides the sound of Ullikummis's stone stumps slamming against the rock floor as he walked, there came no sound from the castlelike dwelling, only the light sounds of the faithful as they followed their master to imagined salvation.

Within, it was hard to tell quite where they were in that sprawling castle. The floor was uneven, inclines here and there like little hillocks on the floor, twists in the main artery that turned them around like a man gripped by fever dream, his bedclothes wrapping around him as he slept.

As they paced through the vast castle, one of the faithful stopped, mouth agog. "It's massive," he said. "Just…massive."

Suddenly Ullikummis halted, and the legion of the faithful stopped behind him, waiting for him to address them. They had walked through the whole of that central spear, and just ten paces ahead they could see a grand window overlooking the stormy ocean. The window towered twenty feet into the air, its sides spiked as if with thorns made of rock, reminding a few of the group of the inside of an iron maiden. Outside, the waves crashed against one another in furious battle as they fought for supremacy.

With the window and its angry ocean vista behind him, Ullikummis turned, his magma-bright eyes burning as he looked at the recruits who had entered his self-made home, until he found the one who had spoken. "My house has many rooms," Ullikummis said in a voice that sounded like two slabs of granite crashing together.

Then with softly spoken words, Ullikummis commanded those people who had become entranced with him to prepare themselves. "What follows will alter you forever, and only the strongest will survive," he rumbled.

"Wh-what will it be?" one of the group of pilgrims asked, a woman in her forties with white streaks appearing in her wavy chestnut hair.

"The future needs your strength," Ullikummis explained, "if it is to be kept on the correct path. Even a god cannot be everywhere, and there comes a time when I must rely on my most loyal subjects to help usher in paradise."

The group of almost sixty people seemed to take in a single breath, astounded that their god would trust them to bring heaven to Earth.

"When the world looks back on these dark times," Ullikummis said as he lined them against one of the walls, "they will remember this moment, speak of it with reverence, pen songs in your name, as well as mine.

You will be my Nephilim, my angels, my will incarnate."

Then Ullikummis raised one of his powerful arms, stretching the stony fingers of his hand out in front of him, his lava eyes and veins glowing more fiercely than before as his power welled. There came a rumbling all around him, shaking the walls of the castle like the passage of a supersonic jet plane. The shaking emanated from below as something burrowed up from the ground beneath the castle, drilling through the rocky structure of Bensalem. And, for just a moment, the acolytes of the new tomorrow felt fear.

"Now is the time to make peace with yourselves," Ullikummis told them, "for not all of you will survive the necessary process.

"Close your eyes."

As instructed, Ullikummis's devotees closed their eyes and waited for the future to take hold. One such devotee—a six-foot-tall, ruddy-faced cobbler by the name of Gregory Samms who had turned fifty just a few weeks before and was tiring of his hard life toiling over leather night and day—felt the change in air pressure within the chamber of the oppressive castle. Samms's feet seemed to tremble beneath him, a quaking feeling rumbling through the bones of his legs and up into his chest. Samms had given himself over to the burgeoning belief that had taken hold in pockets across North America, walking away from his life of toil and hardship to go on this fabled pilgrimage, to meet the one true future god. Now, as he stood with eyes closed, the floor rumbling beneath his exquisitely clad feet, Gregory Samms felt the pounding of his heart in his chest, drumming faster and faster, thumping louder and louder against his rib cage.

Gregory Samms tried to relax, willing the tension away from his body as he stood in the dark cocoon behind his own eyelids. In that instant, something pushed against the heel of his shoe, brushed along the length of the sole that Samms had spent many hours working on so that it would give him the most comfort for the long walk to the coast and to Alfredo's fishing boat, which in turn had brought him here. The hard thing brushed against his left sole again, pressing against the ball of his foot.

Beside him, Gregory Samms heard someone cry out in surprise—or perhaps it was pain?—and he fought back the urge to open his eyes, to find out what it was that had made his fellow pilgrim scream.

And then it had him, drilling through his shoe, splitting the hard leather as it pushed itself up into his foot. Gregory yelped with pain, but before he had finished his cry he felt a second spike, this one drilling up through the base of his right foot like a lance, driving through shoe and flesh and bone.

The thing had been called by Ullikummis, whose psionic bond with the rocks allowed him to speak to them, to command them as easily as he did the simple-minded apekin that covered this planet like a rash. The stone-clad Annunaki stood there, willing the rocks to burst from beneath the surface, to push themselves into the humans and create new life-forms, in much the way his Annunaki forefathers had created their Nephilim, forging them from the human forms.

Ullikummis could control the rocks in an alchemical way, altering their properties and making them into something semisentient. He had need of warriors, had quested for them since his return to Earth less than four months ago. He had tried the weak flesh of the apekin, making human fight human as they struggled to prove themselves to him in the most brutal manner imaginable. And all that had served to do was bore him, proving once and for all that the Annunaki were far superior to anything this pathetic race of jumped-up monkeys could ever achieve. He had waited then, seeding the world with his thoughts, letting the story change and drift, the promise emanate in words the humans were drawn to. When they came to him again, after these scant months, they came willingly, with newly conquered hearts and minds.

Fifty-nine worthless human shells writhed in agony in front of Ullikummis now, eliciting a chorus of pain as the rocks bore into their useless, fragile bodies, driving into their flesh without mercy. Ullikummis watched emotionlessly and if he made any connection to the genetic tortures that his father and Ningishzidda had bestowed upon him millennia ago, he did not acknowledge it.

Standing stock-still, Gregory Samms felt needles of shooting pain drive up his legs, and he swayed for a moment, wanting to fall over just to take the pressure off his legs. But he could not fall; savage stone spikes now held him in place, emerging out of the floor and driving up through his legs like nails.

This is the future, he told himself. God is merciless.

Then the stone splints climbed up his legs, tearing his flesh apart as they drilled through his fragile human body, reknitting torn muscles and ligaments into something new. Samms screamed as the stone writhed within his erect body, twisting, burrowing lances erupting inside his legs with white-hot pain. The old cobbler rocked in place, held upright purely by the stone shards that had pierced him, driving through him with infinite delicacy. Already he was in so much pain that he could not hear anything other than his own shrill cry, and he was no longer aware that he was just one voice in a chorus of agony that echoed through the lengthy corridors of the Castle of Bensalem.

Then, just when Gregory Samms thought the pain could not get any worse, the stone growths reached up into his groin, entwining themselves with his testicles, clutching and solidifying wherever they touched as they drilled down the shaft of his penis.

Samms's mouth was stretched wide, his scream a shrill and rising note as the stone growths continued upward, wrenching his nervous system apart with jagged spines, ripping through his body like nails through wood. He felt the stone tree within him, running up his legs, his groin, into his abdomen. Then he felt it wrench at his guts, piercing his intestines and colon, ripping up through his belly with icy fingers. He shrieked again, trying to remember how beautiful the future would be, how he would be a part of that brave new world.

By then, the growing stone had reached the cavity of his chest, and Gregory Samms felt it deflate his lungs, crushing his breath from within as it filled the capacity there. It was as if concrete was being poured down his throat; he could feel it mass and solidify within him, crushing the breath and the life out of him. He screamed once more as the forming stone tugged at his upper arms, oozing through the flesh of his forearms, his hands and fingers, filling them from the inside out. Suddenly his hands felt cold, all sensation leaving him as the stone took the place of his flesh, ossifying him from deep within.

Gregory Samms was still screaming as the coiling stone clawed its way up his throat, driving spikes through his neck and filling his mouth with its solid coldness. Abruptly, his scream ceased, the noise cut short by a voice box now changed beyond comprehension.

The cobbler felt the stone move onward, rising up into his brain, oozing behind his eyes like liquid as it took control of his sight. At that moment, for just a second or two, Gregory Samms lost consciousness, blacking out as the pain of the alien invasion finally became too much.

When Gregory Samms woke up, he found himself changed where he stood into a monstrous creature of the glorious future god. As he stood there, Gregory felt the stones still shifting within him, but it was less forceful now; they seemed just to be settling into their final places. He stood hunched over, his back bowed as if in supplication to his new master. His skeleton had been altered, and so had those of the people around him, the bones and flesh ossified, entwined with the penetrating semisentient stone that Ullikummis had commanded to change these people. Because of the bent-over manner in which he stood, Gregory Samms was just five feet tall now, but his limbs had stretched, becoming long and rangy, the hands now far ahead of his body. His jaw had changed, too, its stone parts clacking together in an elongated muzzle that bore little similarity to that of a human.

His mind was gone, just the slightest vestige of what he had been before remained, nagging at him like a distant candle flame in the darkness. He had been overcome by the entheogen, the beautiful sense of the god within.

Abruptly, the stone shafts that had penetrated his feet pulled from the floor, emerging and locking in his body, no more stone needed to complete the alchemical task of altering his form. As they disconnected from the floor, Gregory Samms sank to his knees, his long arms sagging forward to prop himself up. All around him, others of the loyal acolytes were sinking to the floor, as well, adopting the same pose as he did. They looked more like dogs now than men.

Ullikummis looked at his war dogs, their loyalty unquestioned. A combination of thinking creature and solid stone, they were more like statues than men, living statues, waiting for him to give them their orders.

Of the fifty-nine applicants, just fourteen had survived the horrendous metamorphosis; the others had lost too much blood in the transformation. It mattered nothing to Ullikummis. Humans were a cheap commodity, more could be found as he needed. These creatures would be his final gift to the world, and they would serve him in his ultimate pursuit of his father, Enlil.

BRIGID LEAPED ASIDE as the upturned table in front of her suddenly split. A lance of plasma shot through it and zapped across the room in a line of yellow-green light.

She could smell burning, and when she looked, Brigid saw that her cloak was on fire, flames licking at its hem.

Brigid reached for the neck clasp of the cloak with her left hand, and in an instant she had shirked the heavy cloak from her shoulders, letting it smolder as it sank to the floor behind her.

Up ahead, another plasma beam cut across the eight-by-twelve room, cutting through a shelf of ancient carvings that Balam had carefully arranged along one of the cold stone walls. As the artifacts clattered to the floor, Brigid brought her TP-9 semiautomatic up once more, caressing the trigger and snapping off another burst of gunfire. She gritted her teeth as the shots went wide, cutting through the loose indigo-colored robes that Balam wore around his slender form.

In the back room, Little Quav crouched beside the heavy stone range, hugging her rag doll tightly as she pulled one hand over her ear. The cacophony of the shots in the next room terrified the little girl, who had never had to witness violence before. She had never seen Balam lose his temper, never seen him strike out for any reason, and her contact with other people had been negligible at best. Having a vicious firefight suddenly erupt like this in her own home left the girl shocked and quivering with fear.

There came another brilliant burst of plasma as Balam attempted to cut Brigid down as she sprang toward him. Brigid felt the burning heat of the beam play across her back, cutting through her leather armor and atomizing it where it had covered her right shoulder blade. The red-haired woman grunted as she tumbled to the floor in a tangle of limbs, her exposed back raw from that horrendous blast of heat.

The slender figure of Brigid Haight lay still on the floor, her face against the stone, her chest rising and falling as she drew breath. Balam held the ASP emitter on her for almost a minute, watching carefully as the woman quietly breathed, the exposed flesh of her back turning an angry red where the plasma beam had side-swiped her, the edges of her leather armor still smolder-ing around the wound.

After a minute Balam lowered his weapon, keeping it ready in his long-fingered grasp.

"Uncle Bal-bal?" Little Quav asked, calling from her hiding place where she cowered in the kitchen. "Is ev-erything all right now?"

"Stay where you are, Quav," Balam instructed, pacing toward the fallen form of their red-haired at-tacker. As Balam came near, Brigid moved, her right arm pumping out like a boxer delivering a knockout punch, the TP-9 she held bursting to angry life. A burst of bullets struck Balam, slicing through his dark robe and cutting into his side.

Balam stumbled a single step before crashing to the floor, the ASP emitter clutched uselessly in his grasp. Brigid lifted herself off the floor, gazing down at the fallen alien form, a wisp of gun smoke drifting from the barrel of her TP-9. In a moment, the flame-haired woman had ejected the used ammo clip of the semiauto-matic, tossing it aside as Balam lay on the floor in front of her, then slapping another into its vacated breech.

"Come out, Quav my darling," Brigid said as she

approached the open door to the kitchen. "It's time to leave."

The terrified girl looked up at Brigid as she entered the kitchen, her feathery blond hair in disarray around her face, salty tears glistening on her cheeks.

"It's okay," Brigid said, extending a black-gloved hand to the hybrid girl. "Everything's going to be all right now."

Slowly, tentatively, Little Quav reached her hand for Brigid's, taking the hand of the only person left to take care of her in the underground city of Agartha.

Chapter 14

Watching from the ground, Domi and Rosalia gasped as Grant's bulky form came sailing over the edge of the nest. The ex-Magistrate toppled over the side and began hurtling through the air, his arms windmilling as he struggled to find something to grab on to. To Grant's right, the knocked bird went sailing away with the force of his brutal kick, its own wings flapping hopelessly as it struggled to prevent itself falling to earth along with its attacker.

"Stupid Magistrate." Rosalia spit. "He'll get us all killed."

Hearing Rosalia's disparaging comment from where she sat against one of the trees, Domi shot a fierce look at the dark-haired woman. But Rosalia was already moving, running back to the monofilament line that hung from the neighboring tree and using it to pull herself upward, running up the tree trunk at an angle.

Up above, Grant's arms batted against the smaller branches as he fell through the tree cover. Automatically, he had commanded his Sin Eater back to its hidden holster, freeing both hands to make a grab for something—*anything*. But his hands merely brushed through twigs and leaves, his speeding weight snapping even the larger branches as he whipped past them.

He was a dozen feet from the fast-approaching ground when Rosalia called out to him.

"Go limp!"

Without a thought, Grant did as instructed, letting his muscles relax as the dark-eyed beauty kicked off from the tree and barreled toward him through the air. Then Rosalia's swinging form slammed into Grant's, the force of his momentum knocking the breath from her body in an angry burst. Grant felt the woman's arm grasp around his chest as they swung on the monofilament, sailing through the air between the towering tree trunks. Then her hand loosened its grip on the wire, and together they began to sink gradually earthward, swinging back and forth like a pendulum.

Nearby, the woozy bird of prey slapped into the earth, a clump of leafy branches tumbling in its wake.

In another second it was all over and Rosalia let go of Grant as his feet touched the ground.

"Nice move," he acknowledged, brushing his right index finger to his nose for a moment. The gesture was a private code between himself and Kane known as the one-percent salute, something they had developed during their years as hard-contact Mags and referred to missions with marginal chances of success. Quite why Grant had used the gesture with Rosalia, who had no clue what it meant, he couldn't say, but afterward he would realize it marked a sea change in their relationship, the first instant when he had felt that just maybe he could trust her with his life.

Domi looked up at the two of them from where she rested with her back pressed against a tree. "You guys okay?" she asked.

"Yeah." Grant nodded.

"I'm just talking to Lakesh," Domi continued, gesturing to her ear where the Commtact was buried. "Trying to get a bead on Kane's transponder now."

"Good idea," Grant agreed, engaging his own Commtact and hailing Kane. He tried for a few attempts, but there was no response. "Guess he's busy," he muttered lightheartedly, but he was clearly concerned.

"Busy isn't good when you're talking about Kane," Rosalia observed.

"You're right," Grant agreed. "Domi? What do we have?"

"Lakesh is working out our relative coordinates now," Domi replied.

THE AMBER MIST swished around her legs as the semiclad woman in the Chalice of Rebirth took a step toward Kane, her supple fingers playing through the air enticingly. "Come, come," she said, her voice little more than a whisper, "out of the shadows with you, blind man."

Kane almost started at the words, but he managed to maintain his poise at the edge of the vast cavern. The dog, however, scrambled forward, rushing to get closer to the mysterious woman and the circular pit she stood within, sniffing at the vapors swirling around her body. Slowly, easing himself off the rock shelf, the broad-shouldered ex-Mag following the dog as it hurried around the cavern, hefting the compact carry case that contained the precious interphaser. As he did so, Grant's voice came to his ear via his hidden Commtact, but Kane tuned it out; he didn't want to give this mysterious woman any hint that he might not be here alone.

As he got closer to the familiar Chalice of Rebirth, Kane saw that its amber surface was mottled with other colors, colors that had been hidden by the floating mist. A circle of blood red drifted in one corner, a streak of blue close to the center, a shuddering splash of green shaped like a flatfish. Something had infected the healing chemicals there, changed them in some way that Kane could not yet comprehend. Then he saw that the near-naked woman was staring at him, watching him carefully with haunting eyes.

"I'm not blind," Kane said by way of greeting.

The woman peered up at his face, studying his eyes for a few moments, the twin streaks of blood glistening on her cheeks as the flickering candlelight caught them. "No, not yet," she agreed. "But soon."

The hairs on the back of Kane's neck rose. "What do you know about it?" he demanded.

"I can see it, see *you*," the woman said. "You've lost something very dear to you and you wear that loss like a shirt."

Kane glared at the woman, wondering what she was talking about.

"A friend," the mysterious woman elaborated in her hiss of a voice, "a woman. A soul mate, I think."

"Soul *friend*," Kane corrected irritably. The woman was talking about Baptiste, his *anam-chara*, and dammit all if Kane didn't want to find out how. "My name's Kane. You have a name?" he asked, struggling to keep the rage from his tone.

The strange woman looked at him, and Kane watched those streaks of red glistening on her cheeks like twin tears, as if she had been crying her own life's blood.

"They've taken to calling me Maria, but I've had other names before that," she told him, "as have you. You and the woman—this soul friend as you call her—you fit together like lock and key. You feel lost without her."

Kane began shaking his head, stopped himself. "Look, what the hell?" he growled in frustration.

"Take a seat, Kane," the woman who had called herself Maria said, indicating where the blanket lay beside the rocks. "I'll be with you in a moment, and then we can talk."

Reluctantly, Kane shrugged his shoulders and made his way across to the blanket, feeling that strange weight behind his blind eye. "Come on, boy," Kane called to the dog, encouraging it over to his side with a pat on his thigh.

Maria stood in the glowing pit, washing herself with its mistlike contents and uncapping and placing the contents of several vials into places in its surface. As she did so, Kane saw the amber color wash away, replaced by a new color, a new chemical. Whatever this woman was, she seemed to perform the operation by sense alone, adding a few drops here and there like a chef preparing a meal.

After a couple of minutes the woman seemed to be done, and she stepped from the circular pit, reaching for her dress as Kane watched. She seemed shameless, unbothered by his eyes playing across her supple, youthful form. She looked to be perhaps thirty years of age, her skin tight and exceptionally pale. Kane watched distrustfully as she dressed, making no secret of his interest in her.

"So, Kane," Maria began as she retied the clasp at the

nape of her neck, hiding away the pendant that dangled there, "what brings you here, to my realm?"

"Your realm?" Kane asked. "Huh. I thought it was just a big ol' crack in the ground, didn't realize someone owned it."

"Don't be supercilious." The woman berated him. "Nobody owns the Earth, Kane."

Kane laughed irritably, thinking of the Annunaki and their master plan for world domination. "Know a whole load of people who might disagree," he said. "One of them probably owned that puddle of goop before you came along, matter of fact."

Maria gave Kane an indulgent smile as she bent her knees and crouched in front of him. "Your eye looks bad," she said.

"It's okay," Kane told her. "Hurts a little but—"

"No," Maria interrupted, shaking her head. "It looks bad—*evil*. You feel it, too."

Kane shook his head, trying to clear it. "My thoughts," he began, "they've been getting confused. I'm seeing stuff that didn't really happen to me. I can't really explain."

Maria reached for Kane, placing one of her hands gently on his. "An evil thing is inside you," she told him.

Kane wondered then why he was talking to this stranger, how she could possibly know so much about him. "Just who are you anyhow?" he asked.

Before she answered, Maria pushed a stray lock of hair back under the hood she wore. "My name is Maria Halloween. Many years ago, I witnessed the bright lights in the sky that heralded the nukecaust, far away to the north. I lived through that, just a girl, saw the way it altered the world."

Kane studied the woman, looked at her unlined face for a long moment. "That would make you over two hundred years old," he said, ridicule in his tone. "It's not possible, not for a human." Of course, even as he spoke Kane thought of Lakesh, who had, with organ transplant and scientific trickery, lived more than 250 years.

Maria Halloween stood, taking a few paces away from Kane and the dog that knelt at his side. "You and your companion—this soul friend—you have lived numerous lives, worn numerous faces. Your soul lives on after each death, meeting and entwining with hers in the next life. It gives you strength and pulls you forward, Kane, and now you find yourself weakening devoid of her support."

Kane glared at her. "What's your point, you old witch?"

Halloween visibly started at the epithet. "Many are the ways to keep a person alive—many are the deaths we avoid," she told him. "This pool is one way, but there have been others before it. Once I was old, now I am young, crone become maiden like the phases of the moon."

Kane gestured to the pit. "This here is alien tech," he said. "If you're tinkering with it, that ain't going to end real well, take it from me."

The woman with the blood tears fixed Kane with her gaze. "You're scared," she said. "Lonely and scared."

NEARBY, in the forest above the hidden cavern, Grant, Domi and Rosalia were making their way through the dense cover of the trees to where Grant had left their interphaser. To his annoyance, the unit was not there and he had to trust that Kane had taken it with him.

"So," Grant asked, scanning the branches above, "where did those birds come from?"

Domi shrugged. "I don't know," she admitted. "I got here before dawn, didn't see anything too weird on my way to Luilekkerville."

Rosalia perked up. "You mean, they've not reached the ville?"

"How do you mean?" Domi asked, wincing as she turned to the dark-haired woman.

"Those…things are big," Rosalia explained. "A normal bird maybe has a hunting ground of a few miles, more for a bird of prey. Based on their size, those things should be traveling—I don't know—sixty, eighty miles daily in search of food."

"They didn't come near the ville," Domi assured her. "At least, I didn't notice any of them in the skies, and they're pretty hard to miss."

Domi and Rosalia waited while Grant spoke to Lakesh in quiet tones, double-checking the coordinates with Lakesh via their Commtact link. Once he was done, Grant looked at them, concern etched on his brow. "You think it's strange that the birds won't leave the forest?" he asked Rosalia.

"Seems like an odd quirk," she mused. "They're not natural, and I think someone's breeding them and keeping them here."

"Someone?" Domi asked with surprise. "There are still a few muties out there, lady, throwbacks to the dark times. You live in the Outlands long enough and you'd see—"

Rosalia fixed Domi with a look. "Yes, I know. I didn't come down in the last shower."

"Well," Grant said, stepping between the two women as they stared one another down, "if there is some kind of artificial force behind these creatures, then I guess we're looking for a 'monster maker,' as well as Kane."

"He didn't answer your Commtact call earlier, did he?" Rosalia pointed out. "You thinking the two might be related?"

Grant sneered in annoyance. "I'm trying not to," he growled as he moved off into the forest, following the directions Lakesh was giving over the Commtact.

Grant led the way from the stone-circled clearing that had served as a parallax point, with Domi and Rosalia following. Lakesh was still feeding Grant information over the Commtact, triangulating the location of Kane's transponder.

As they made their way through the trees, Domi spit a curse. "Wish I still had my knife," she grumbled.

Rosalia turned to the albino girl, and Domi saw something glinting in her hand. It was a dagger, its blade six inches in length, and the dark-haired woman was offering it to her.

Domi took it, muttering a brief word of thanks.

"*De nada.* I always carry a spare," Rosalia told her, patting her wrist.

Just then, Grant noticed the ripped-up shear in the earth, zigzagging between the trees. "Look," he said, keeping his own voice low.

"Any ideas how that got here?" Rosalia asked.

Grant nodded, briefly explaining about the subterrene and how it had all but destroyed Snakefishville the last time he had been here.

"So, what do you think?" Rosalia pressed.

"Crack like that probably leads somewhere," Grant mused. "Lakesh is picking up Kane's signal right about here, so since he ain't above us, I'm guessing he's underground."

The three Cerberus warriors split up in a show of practicality, checking the area until they found a wider crack that led down into the caverns below the earth. Within a minute, they had regrouped at the steep entrance to the underworld.

"We don't really know what's down there," Grant reminded them, pulling a pair of dark-tinted glasses from his inside pocket. The glasses featured electrochemical polymer lenses that gathered all available light to give Grant a limited form of night vision in the darkness below. "Either of you have night vision?" he asked.

Domi shook her head no, and Rosalia did likewise.

"Typical Magistrate," Rosalia teased Grant, "always so prepared."

He wasn't entirely convinced that she admired him for that quality. "We'll just have to wing it, then," Grant told his companions. "Since he ain't answering, I don't want to use a flash beam and scare any locals who might be holding Kane."

Grant led the way down the steep earth slope. It was almost vertical in places, with the curling roots of trees and bushes sticking out like the fingers of accusing jurors at an execution. They were not to know it, but Grant and his party had entered the network of caverns via a different crack to the one Kane had found, and that difference would cost them dearly.

THE DARK-EYED Maria Halloween reached her hand out to Kane, brushing her fingers along his cheek as they stood by the pit. "This soul friend—your *anam-chara*—gives you great strength," she whispered. "It makes your soul powerful."

"Yeah," Kane said, feeling his skin prickle with the touch. Beside him, Rosalia's unnamed dog slinked away from the witch woman, scampering off into the shadows with a fretful whine.

"Like all forms of energy, this power can be tapped, Kane," the bloodstained witch reasoned. "Drawn from you and utilized in oh so many ways."

Kane's hand moved in a lightning-quick gesture, grabbing the woman's wrist. "I don't think you should start messing with that," he warned her, holding her arm tightly as he pulled her hand away from his face.

"Well," she said and shrugged laconically, "you really don't get a say."

And then Kane felt his knees buckling, and his grasp slipped from the woman's wrist as he sank to the floor of the cave. Even as he succumbed to the blackness, Kane realized that there had been something on the woman's touch, something that paralyzed him in just three beats of the heart. Whatever else she was, Maria Halloween was an herbalist par excellence.

GRANT LED THE WAY into the cavern, his boot slipping on a chunk of loose soil as he hurried to reach lower ground. Domi reached out, grabbing Grant's wrist as he stumbled, steadying him with effort. The hulking ex-Mag was almost twice her weight, and it took Domi a moment to secure her grip.

Grant turned to her, his eyes obscured by the polymer lenses. "Thanks."

Rosalia was finding it increasingly difficult to see as they got farther into the rent in the earth. The sunlight still stroked against the soil above her, but its rays were struggling to reach way down here, this far away from the earth's surface. It's remarkable, Rosalia thought, how much of the earth remains out of sunlight. Like another world hiding in plain sight.

While Rosalia struggled to see, beside her Domi seemed to be coping better. There was something strange about the albino woman, Rosalia knew, though she could not put her finger on quite what it was. Like her, the pale-skinned warrior seemed to be very conscious of her surroundings, but with her it was more instinctive, a kind of innate combat sense that kicked in whenever she was in danger. And, for Domi, it seemed that every occurrence was potential danger; she was like a wild animal, ever alert to predators.

The three-strong party continued onward, all three of them walking with appreciable stealth now as they dropped into the near absolute darkness of the caverns. Through the electrochemical filter of the lenses, Grant saw everything as if through a greenish light, the occasional edges of the deepest roots appearing white like flashes of lightning. The shelf had become a ceiling above them now, and Grant had to duck to make forward progress.

They turned a corner in the tight, tunnel-like gap beneath the earth, finding themselves in a space so narrow that two people would no longer be able to pass. Grant heard a noise coming from up ahead, and he held his arm up, blocking Domi's path.

Unable to see, Rosalia stumbled into Domi's back before she could stop. "Damn, I can't see shit back here," she said.

Grant waited, peering into the eerie green-lit world through the night vision of the polymer lenses. He could hear the thing, whatever it was, snuffling as it moved, its scrabbling feet brushing against loose soil.

Suddenly a set of pointed jaws appeared from out of the darkness, lit in Grant's lenses like white sticks of lightning on green.

"Shit!" Grant thundered as he brought his Sin Eater up to blast the thing hurtling toward him.

Chapter 15

Though paralyzed, Kane could still sense the things around him. Whatever the Halloween woman had used on him, it had knocked him out almost immediately. He wasn't sure, but he had a pretty good idea that the woman was a mutie. He hadn't seen many of those in recent years, but back when he was a Magistrate in Cobaltville, a grim part of Kane's duties had been to patrol the surrounding area close to the ville walls to ensure none of the Outland reprobates snuck into the city. Among those reprobates, now and again, he and Grant had come across a mutie. Usually they were some kind of human, uglified by radiation so that their calloused skin looked like scales or their eczema had become spiked like a porcupine's back. But there were other muties, too, doomsayers who could predict the future, for instance, and even some who looked normal other than a little something extra—a sixth toe or prehensile hair that reacted to their emotional mood.

Kane was pretty sure that this woman with her blood tears and her ancient wisdom was a mutie. But as he reached that conclusion, any sense of conscious reasoning left Kane, and his paralyzed body turned itself to sleep.

Down in the caverns beneath the earth, Grant brought the dark muzzle of the Sin Eater up into play, targeting the feral-looking creature that bounded toward him. The thing's wide jaws slobbered, sharp canine teeth shining like bright knife blades in the green lighting of the night lenses. Grant's index finger was clenched, and as the Sin Eater slapped into his palm it depressed the trigger, snapping off a series of shots even as something struck him from behind. The shots blasted wide as whatever hit him knocked his arm, and the bullets burrowed into the earth wall beside him with dull thuds.

"You dumb ass," Rosalia hissed right beside Grant's ear. "It's my dog." It had been her arm that had thrown his aim.

Grant turned, staring at the mongrel as it nuzzled against Rosalia's leg, conscious that his heart was pounding against his chest. "I thought you couldn't see down here," Grant said.

Rosalia looked up at Grant and smiled, a bright green line of teeth materializing in his night-vision lenses. "He's not had a bath in a month," she told Grant. "I recognized his smell."

Shaking his head, Grant sent his pistol back into its hidden holster with a practiced flinch of his wrist tendons. "Three shots. Bet somebody would have heard that," he said. "Let's get moving. If we weren't on the clock before, we sure as heck are now."

THE WOMAN with the tears of blood looked up from her busywork at the edge of the resuscitation pit where her cloth bag lay. There had been a noise, a triple thudding as of a distant drum being banged.

Maria Halloween let her eyes lose focus as her mind

reached out, and the flickering candle flames seemed to become a light show across her blurring vision.

Years ago, when she had begun her long trek from Sao Paulo, when she had been a young woman the first time over, she had been idealistic. The nukecaust was a part of her childhood, and the broken United States presented a land of opportunity like never before. A woman with her talents could truly shape this infant country as it clambered out of its cot. *Bruja* they called her—*witch*. And yes, she was a witch. She was a witch as her mother had been and her mother's mother, and her grandmother's mother and on through the maternal line.

Her ability to read people went deeper than that of her forebears, though, augmented by the radiation that had swept across the globe in the wake of the nuclear nightmare, igniting something deep inside her. And it was not just people that she could read, the *bruja* had the ability to look deep into nonliving things, too, discerning their purpose and seeing new applications for them in a flash of inspiration. She sought out these points of rebirth, utilizing them and their ilk to re-create herself, her old face made young once more. And, too, she saw how to use them, to add things and so change them, altering their purpose, renewing their worth.

Her vision lost focus now as she searched the immediate area, sensing and searching for the source of the drumbeats. In her mind, it felt like the ocean, where the ocean meets the shore. But already the drumbeats had halted, and without them it became harder to locate their source.

Maria reached her hand out toward the Chalice of Rebirth once more, producing a clutch of tiny eggs with a simple sleight of hand. The eggs were colored a creamy yellow-white, small and glistening as the candlelight flickered across their surfaces. There was red swirling in the amber mist of the chalice pit, life-giving blood that the *bruja* had had spilled there and nurtured for many weeks.

The woman with the blood tears hissed two words to the silent cavern then, old words but good words, a rhyme. "Hinx minx."

Then she tipped her hand, dropping the first of the eggs and letting it fall into the pool where it disappeared amid the misting curlicues of amber and red. As the egg immersed itself in the life-giving concoction of the Chalice of Rebirth, Maria turned away, for she never liked to see the things that came forth once she cast her spells. The nanomachines in the pit were melding with the thing in the egg, the lifeblood tinkering with the mixture in a way that perhaps only the *bruja* herself could really understand.

A moment later something stepped forth, clambering out of the pool on four abbreviated legs, its long snout raised. It moved toward Maria for a moment, sniffing at her. She in turn stood perfectly still, her arms crossed over her breasts, hands touched to their opposing shoulders, her eyelids closed. The newborn thing twitched, sniffing at her for a couple of seconds before moving on. She was a null thing, dead or not really there; she smelled of nothing. The thing's reptilian legs scampered across the metal ring surrounding the Chalice of Rebirth, waddling at a swift clip into the darkness, its long snout turning this way and that as it sought its prey.

As the monstrous thing disappeared into the shadows of one of the surrounding tunnel-like caverns, Maria Halloween dropped the second and third of the eggs into the pit.

"Hinx minx..."

"You hear that?" Grant asked, motioning down the gloomy dirt-walled tunnel that led beneath the earth.

It was distant, the sound of scrabbling claws against loose soil.

"What is it?" Domi whispered.

"I don't know," Grant admitted. "Rosie girl? You got a second dog I never noticed?"

"No," Rosalia said, unimpressed with Grant's attempt at levity.

"Then get down!" Grant snarled, even as the sound of the scrabbling claws became louder in the darkness.

Grant was a wide-shouldered man, and he swiftly took stock of his surroundings as the scrabbling sound became louder—closer. There was a hard-packed wall of earth and rock looming by his left shoulder, and he had taken to occasionally scraping against it where the path had narrowed more than before. That had become necessary as the right side of the path opened off into a vast drop, a tumbling cliff face that fell farther than Grant's night-vision lenses could discern. Wherever it led, he figured it for a sheer drop.

As he mentally prepared himself, Grant saw it through the night lenses of his glasses, drawn in green and black like a photographic negative. He would maybe call it a crocodile, because that's what it reminded him most of. But it was long, its tail stretching a good eight feet behind it, its flattened jaws three feet or more ahead of its eyes where twin vertical slits had opened wide to absorb whatever nominal light still ebbed into the cavern. It was reptilian; that much was clear. Leathery scales ran down its flanks, a glistering sheen to their surface as if they were still wet, and mist clouded from its back. It raced along toward Grant and his companions, two stubby forelegs pulling it forward at the speed a grown man might sprint, the tail swishing at the ground behind it. Given its fantastic size, Grant could be forgiven for calling it a dinosaur, something from a child's book come to life.

Without conscious thought, Grant powered the Sin Eater back into his palm, rattling off a half dozen shots at the monster as it arrowed toward him along the narrow dirt tunnel. The 9 mm bullets pinged off the creature's leathery hide, scraping against it before falling aside, clattering against the rock wall. Then the monster was upon him, its massive jaws opening wide as it lunged at his legs. Behind it, through the medium of the night lenses, Grant detected a second of the monstrous things hurrying down the tunnel.

The powerful ex-Mag sidestepped as the first of the monster's jaws snapped shut like a trap, missing dismemberment by a matter of inches rather than feet.

"Stay sharp," Grant shouted as he weaved out of the path of the first creature. "This one's got a friend."

"But what is it?" Rosalia returned, seeing little more than shapes in the darkened tunnel.

Grant had no time to explain. The monstrous reptile lifted itself from the ground on its powerful back legs, its body rising as its wicked jaws snapped for Grant.

Suddenly the ex-Magistrate found himself pushed back against the wall of the narrow tunnel, his left arm coming up to ward off the creature as its jaws snapped at the air. Mouth open, the beast's teeth were like scimitars, and Grant guessed that each sharpened tooth was close to a foot long. He rolled his shoulders, moving his head aside as the monster took another bite, jaws clacking shut on empty air.

Domi, whose night vision was superior to Rosalia's, leaped onto the monstrous creature's back, wrapping her hands around its thick neck where it widened into its torso. "Hang on, Grant!"

Even as she spoke, Domi was pulling out the knife that the Mexican had given her and, in a powerful swoop of her arm, drove the six-inch blade into the monster's flesh between two ridged scales. The reptile reacted with irritation, rolling in place, trying to shake its attacker from its back.

Behind them, Rosalia could not see much in the darkness of the tunnel, but she felt Domi pass her, and could make out the albino girl's pale skin as she flipped and flopped ahead. But, while she couldn't see, Rosalia could hear the creature—whatever it was—as it snarled and sniffled, the slick mucus noise coming from the back of its throat as it breathed. She unsheathed the *katana* with a swift arcing of her arm, drawing the glinting blade in a single, graceful movement and placing both hands on the grip as she held it poised in front of her.

It was too dark to see properly, and attacking the first creature while it struggled with Domi and Grant would be folly, threatening to put their lives in danger as much as it might help them. Rosalia glanced behind her, saw where the sunlight still trickled into the caverns, stray rays glinting from the polished metal of her sword as it moved. In a flash, Rosalia angled the blade, twisting it in her grip so that it caught the sunlight, reflecting it down the corridor in a narrow beam. Magically, the tight cavern was lit with a thin shaft of weak light, enough that its edges became clear.

To the left, a rough rocky wall loomed, its highest edge little more than six feet above them, forcing Grant to duck as he wrestled with the creature who had attacked them. To the right, that sheer drop opened up, the ground falling away into blackness. And there, behind where Domi and Grant struggled with the first monster, came two more, bolting through the tunnels like bullets, one after the other.

Committing what she had briefly glimpsed to memory, Rosalia turned her sword, plunging the tunnel once more into blackness as she sprinted for the next of the creatures, her ragged-looking dog at her side. "Come on, boy," she encouraged as she leaped on the flipping tail of the nearest. "Fetch!"

KANE WAS NO longer conscious, not in any traditional sense. Yet something inside him was awake, and it flashed visions before his eyes, burning from the left-hand edge of his face as it swept across the theater screen of his mind.

The stone god was clambering up a mountainside, his breath floating away in clouds of mist in the chilling temperatures of the Semien Range. Ullikummis was fleetingly irritated at how long it was taking, climbing this towering edifice this way when he could have taken a skimmer craft or one of the graceful Mantas to reach his vertiginous destination. But he tamped down his impatience, reminding himself how this was a mission of stealth and how the use of a machine to get here would be tantamount to announcing his presence and admitting his father's involvement in the scheme to kill Lord Teshub.

Kane felt all this, the thoughts and the history behind them, like some silent observer lurking in the princeling's soul. Though fully formed and clad in the stone plate that would ever be his skin, Ullikummis was perhaps sixteen, maybe a little older, certainly still a teenager.

The Annunaki prince climbed onward until he lurked just below a plateau, clutching its underside with strong fingers as his legs swung free beneath him. Hanging there, Ullikummis stilled his thoughts, listening for any hint of life above him. Icy winds from the east played around the mountains, stroking cold fingers against the crevices and freezing Ullikummis as he hung. He remained, enduring their cold caress as he listened for movement.

This area should be heavily guarded. Teshub was bacchanalian in his excesses, but he had chosen this remote hideaway for a reason—he feared the wrath of Enlil. Up here, in the Semien Range, Teshub had been titled the Lord of Heaven, and stories of his fearsome thunderbolts had spread throughout the apekin humans who worshiped the Annunaki and all the wonder they brought. Ullikummis feared no lightning bolts, for what could lightning do to a thing made of stone?

Eight minutes passed, with the formidable form of Ullikummis simply hanging there in silence, like another part of the mountain grown into the shape of a living thing. Then he heard it, the faintest scraping against the rocks above as a booted foot moved on the path directly above him.

Effortlessly, Ullikummis shifted his weight, causing his eight-foot-tall body to swing like a pendulum, faster and faster as he dangled beneath the jutting outcropping of the mountain's side. In an instant he was over the side, swinging up and around, appearing on the path that had been above him just two seconds before, poised behind the guard there. Despite his bulk, Ullikummis landed with almost complete silence, any slight sound of his feet landing hidden by the banshee wail of the winds as they circled through the mountain range.

Standing with his back to Ullikummis, the guard was one of the Nephilim. The humanoid creature was dressed in plate armor and had covered this with a fur cloak that served as protection against the bitter cold. Nephilim warriors were a hybrid of DNA created in *Tiamat*'s bubbling vats, and they possessed qualities of both the local humans and the Annunaki. They were utterly hairless, with dark, scaled skin over their thick hides, high cheekbones and craggy brow ridges over their blank, soulless eyes. They were completely subservient to their Annunaki master, and would gladly give their lives for Lord Teshub if only they were capable of such an emotion as gladness.

Ullikummis stepped forward, stone hands as large as plates slapping against either side of the Nephilim warrior's head and whipping it around. Then Ullikummis stepped away, letting the Nephilim drop to the ground, his neck broken. The body fell into the snow with a light shushing sound like grain.

Ullikummis turned instantly, preternaturally aware of the second warrior, who had chanced upon the scene without warning. Dressed like the other though in a fur cloak of a much darker brown, the Nephilim pulled a huge blade from its sheath at his waist even as he saw Ullikummis standing over the dead body of his colleague. Ullikummis met the blade—a golden scimitar that flashed in the morning sunlight—with his own arm, letting it cleave into his stony flesh for a moment before flicking it aside.

The Nephilim grunted as the blade left his hand, spinning across the pathway before clattering against the rough wall beside them. Ullikummis needed to keep this quiet, and sound carried far too quickly in the icy climes of the mountains, he knew. The mighty Annunaki prince stepped forward and reached for the Nephilim, grabbing the creature's outstretched arm before he could react.

With a single movement Ullikummis wrenched the Nephilim warrior off his feet, dragging him on stumbling legs and knees across the five feet separating them before letting go. Still moving, the Nephilim sagged forward, his face smashing against the ground with a clack of his jaws as they were forced together by the brutal impact.

Ullikummis took a step forward, driving his foot into the center of the Nephilim's back and pressing down with all his weight. The Nephilim gagged, struggling to free himself like some trapped butterfly on a pin, arms and legs flapping, yet unable to get away.

Beneath the weight of Ullikummis, the Nephilim soldier choked, his metal armor buckling under the incredible pressure. Ullikummis drove his heel deeper into the creature's back, forcing the last vestige of breath out of his struggling lungs. Blank, soulless eyes widened with fear as the effort to take another breath became too much. Ullikummis relentlessly forced his weight against the helpless creature's lungs. Beneath the breastplate of the armor, something snapped, the noise filtering to Ullikummis's keen hearing despite the muffling effect of the creature's fur cloak. No emotion showed on the stone god's face; his mouth remained a grim slash. But he pushed again, pushed harder, hearing the second rib crack, then a third and fourth.

A viscous drool began to seep from the Nephilim's open mouth then, and Ullikummis watched as the yellowish liquid oozed out, dark spots of red coming more and more frequently as it stained the snow.

Finally, once the Nephilim had stopped shaking and was still, Ullikummis removed his great stone foot from the warrior's back. He remained standing over the body for two silent minutes, watching for any sign of movement, of life. Satisfied that there was none, Ullikummis buried the two bodies beneath a shallow covering of snow before making his way up the mountain pathway, his body crouched low, snow settling on his broad shoulders and the vicious spikes that grew from them like a stag's antlers.

And Kane saw all of this, confused and uncertain, wondering if it was his history, his memories that were playing out.

I am living somebody else's life, Kane realized again

as the visions swelled within his mind's eye. And whatever it was, whatever was really happening, he was slowly but surely losing his identity in the mix.

Chapter 16

Rosalia rolled as the nearest of the two monsters lunged at her in the darkness. She could barely see anything in this gloom, relying on occasional glimpses as a rogue shaft of sunlight glinted from the creature's shiny scales or fearsome teeth.

Spinning in a crouch, Rosalia jabbed the sword at the monster as it came for her, cuffing it across the snout. The beast reared back for a moment, unleashing a hideous noise that sounded somewhere between a growl and a hiss. Then it came at her again, lumbering through the darkness on admirably powerful legs.

A few feet away Rosalia's dog was tackling the remaining creature, barking and snarling as the creature prowled toward it. Suddenly the monstrous croc darted forward, jaws snapping as it grasped for the dog's flank. Agile as a coyote, the dog scampered backward, maneuvering itself just barely out of reach of the monster's crushing jaws. But then the dog's feet slipped on loose earth, and for a moment it found itself sliding backward over the sheer drop to the right-hand side of the narrow path. Its hind legs wheeled in empty air before finding purchase on the hard rock face of the cliff, balancing there like a cantilever with its forepaws on the path.

The vicious reptile attacker saw its struggling prey through nocturnal eyes and bounded forward, its huge jaws opening wide to reveal a pointed tongue and set of daggerlike teeth that could doubtless shear a man—or dog—in two.

The dog bounded up and away, scrambling with belly low to the ground as it ducked beneath the monster's gaping mouth. Unable to stop, the hulking creature found itself suddenly out of path, its leathery feet swishing against nothing but empty air.

Rosalia's dog barked triumphantly as the monstrous alligator-like beast went hurtling from the cliff path in a scramble of flailing limbs, its huge tail swishing through the air as it dropped from sight. For a long moment the creature's bellowing sounded like a scream that gradually became quieter, echoing back at them from the caverns.

Pressed right up against the wall, Grant ducked and weaved as a set of monstrous jaws came at him in the darkness, even as Domi struggled with the beast itself. Domi jabbed with the knife in her hand, plunging it into the beast's head as it writhed beneath her, trying to shake her off.

Trapped, the back of his coat rubbing against the wall, Grant struggled to avoid another attempt from the creature to bite off his head. The beast reared back, spittle washing over Grant's face, congealing against the lenses of his polymer glasses as he pulled desperately aside. Then Grant's right fist came up in a vicious uppercut, driving through the air at the monster's lower jaw. Within that fist, Grant still held his Sin Eater and he depressed the trigger, powering shot after shot into the calloused skin of the creature's mouth.

Domi felt the monstrous lizard writhe and flip beneath her as Grant's shots drilled into its jaw at point-blank range, and then she lost her grip around its throat. Suddenly the petite albino warrior was hurtling backward, falling from the creature's back and rolling across the dirt path.

The Sin Eater blasted, firing bullets into the monster's hide as it flailed in front of Grant. With a flick of its massive eight-foot-long tail, the reptilian nightmare whacked Domi across the chest as she struggled to regain her footing behind it, and the pixielike woman went sailing through the air, the knife spinning out of her grasp.

Suddenly, Domi was falling, plummeting over the side of the precipice. She spit out a curse as she reached out, her arms lunging through the darkness as she tried to grasp for a handhold—any handhold—lest she fall to her death. For a moment it seemed impossible, and Domi's heart skipped a beat as her hands met with nothing but empty air. Then relief came as her left arm scraped against something hard and rough—the rock face. Still falling, Domi clawed against that rock, feeling the sharp edges bite at her, breaking three fingernails as she frantically tried to slow her descent.

She had fallen perhaps a dozen feet before she finally came to a stop, clinging there to the side of the cliff. There was no time to think, no time to catch her breath. Immediately, Domi began scrambling back up the rocky wall, urging speed to her muscles as she rushed to return to battle and help her comrades. But the cliff wasn't as vertical as it appeared—in actuality, it dropped away in a bowl-like acute angle, forcing Domi to climb both up and back as she took up a more horizontal position with her ascent.

"Grant?" she called, her voice echoing in the cavern. "I'm gonna need some help here."

Up above, Grant heard Domi's call even as he unleashed another burst of fire at the creature that had him pinned to the wall. Grant found his bullets spraying in all directions as he tried to blast the monster, and he grunted as one of them pinged off the Kevlar plating of his coat. His shadow suit would help redistribute the kinetic impact of the bullet, but he was sure he'd end up with a bruise there tomorrow...that is, if he made it through to tomorrow.

The creature's jaws snapped shut again, closing just inches from Grant's head, the shearing power of its mighty incisors tearing for his face. In that second, Grant urged his Sin Eater back to its holster and grabbed the monstrous beast around its torso, close to where its shoulders should be. Then, with an almighty effort, Grant pushed against the monster, driving it away from him even as its vicious jaw opened once more to snap at him. Grant ducked his head and body, letting the jaw snap on empty air. Then, with his body still low, he pushed with all his might, his boots struggling for purchase as he shoved the mighty dinosaur-like beast back. The thing reared up on hind legs and tail, its short arms—each of them still longer than a man's forearm—waggling in the air as it struggled to reach for its opponent.

Grant cursed as one of those short forelegs snapped against him, the clawed limb shredding a chunk from his coat as it pushed at him. But still the ex-Magistrate would not yield.

Grant was away from the wall now, the monstrous gator held in a wrestling grip, shoving it against itself, forcing it to lose ground. Grant pushed harder, demanding more from his incredible muscles as, inch by torturous inch, he shunted the reptilian beast away from him. Those lethal jaws clamped shut once again, teeth gnashing just two inches above the top of Grant's head. And then the monster lost its footing as Grant pushed even harder. Its back legs left the ground and wagged pathetically in the air, just its massive tail holding it in place as Grant shoved its body up to a near vertical angle.

Almost directly below, Domi found herself running out of options. She hung almost horizontal, trying to climb up the bowl-like cliff spider-fashion. "Grant?" she called. "Rosalia? Someone?"

Grant took another agonized pace forward, his right foot stamping down against the rough earth of the path. As he did so, he pushed himself lower, getting better leverage for what he planned to do. Above him, the monster's jaws snapped at the air with frustration, and it unleashed a fearsome growl of rage. Grant dipped his body, pushing his left shoulder against the underside of the writhing creature, shoving it against the monster's leathery belly. His boots slipped a little against the ground as Grant gave one last, almighty push. As he did so, he stepped back, letting go of the reptilian creature that he had appeared to be wrestling. The beast flipped away from Grant, its snout scraping against the ceiling as it fell over onto its back. The path was narrow and the monster had fallen in such a way that half of its bulk was now positioned with legs in the air, poised over the edge of the cliff. Gravity did the rest.

Hurrying up the cliff side, Domi pulled herself tighter against the wall as the dark shape of the monster went sailing by, plummeting to its doom far, far below. "That's two down," she muttered.

A moment later Grant's head appeared over the ledge, a dark blob of shadow in the darkness as he reached down for Domi.

"You okay, kiddo?" Grant asked as he helped Domi clamber the last few feet onto the cliff path once more.

"Define 'okay,'" Domi snapped, irritation in her voice.

But there was no time for celebration. The snarling sounds of battle came from just a little way ahead as Grant and Domi hurried to help Rosalia, who was struggling with the last of the crocodile-like creatures. Grant's hands brushed the spittle from his polymer lenses as he ran, and when his vision cleared he saw something he could not quite believe. Sure enough, there was the slender form of Rosalia, ducking and weaving with all the grace of a ballerina as she drove the blade of the *katana* at the creature's hide, piercing it multiple times in quick succession. But that was not the unbelievable part. Rather, as Grant watched, arms and legs pumping to meet with this lizardlike foe, he saw Rosalia's dog suddenly lunge at the creature's exposed neck. Perhaps something had become damaged in the polymer lenses during his own struggle, or perhaps the night vision had confused Grant's brain for a moment, making him hallucinate something that wasn't quite there. But what he saw was the dog double and triple, turning into a pack of ghostly images, each dog wrapped in the one beside it, insubstantial and yet whole and complete unto itself. The multi-image blurred and enlarged, a multitude of wolflike hounds lunging at the exact same point on the beast's throat, tearing at it with a thousand savage teeth.

"The hell?" Grant muttered, stopping so suddenly in his tracks that Domi slammed against his back.

"Grant?" Domi asked urgently.

For a moment Grant said nothing. Instead he simply stood there, watching in astonishment as Rosalia and the dog attacked the monstrous croc with untold brutality. Its scales tore away and chunks of its flesh sailed from its body as the dog—or dogs?—dug teeth and claws into its throat. Rosalia continued slashing at the thing with her *katana,* cutting hunks out of the sinewy muscles of its forelegs and torso.

It was over in a matter of seconds. The slithering form of the reptile was pulled apart, flaps of flesh flopping from its torso, throat and limbs, its tail writhing as it was pulled apart by its relentless attackers. Rosalia stepped back, breathing hard, her blade dripping with blood, and a moment later the dog scrambled to her side, looking up at its mistress for approval, just one dog once more. Where ten seconds before a fierce reptilian monstrosity had lurked in the tunnel, battling savagely with the dark-haired woman, now there was just a splatter of ruined flesh, the contents of an upturned butcher's stall attached to the still-writhing remains of the swishing tail.

"Grant," Domi asked again, her voice coming from just behind him, "what is it?"

"I don't know," Grant admitted. "Just—" He stopped, unable to explain what he thought he had seen through the night lenses, already unsure if he had really seen it.

Wiping the bloody sword on her skirt, Rosalia leaned down and stroked her dog behind the ears. "Good dog," she soothed. "Good boy." The dog yipped happily, enjoying the attention as it chewed on a morsel of flesh.

Grant and Domi joined Rosalia amid the blood and gore that lined the tunnel, Grant's eyes flicking to the croc's tail as it continued to spasm against the ground despite no longer being connected to anything that could be termed a body.

"What did—" Grant began, but he stopped himself as Rosalia looked up.

"What was that?" Rosalia asked, not catching his first words.

"Just wanted to say that you did good there, girl," Grant told her. Whatever he had seen or not seen, now was not the time to discuss it—not while Kane's life may be at stake.

As that thought struck him, Grant reengaged his Commtact unit, calling on Lakesh for advice. "Lakesh, how close are we to our man?" Grant asked.

For a moment the connection was silent while Lakesh refreshed and triangulated the transponder signals being picked up by satellite and relayed to his computer laptop over a hundred miles away. "By my reckoning you're almost on top of him now, Grant," Lakesh informed his friend. "You should be able to see him. He's less than two hundred yards ahead of you—to the west of your current position."

Grant looked around, grinding his teeth in irritation.

"We're in darkness and we've got a wall on one side of us and a sheer drop on the other," he explained.

"Can you go forward?" Lakesh suggested.

Grant peered into the darkness through his night lenses, seeing the path continue into a tunnel cutting through a towering rock face. "Looks like that's about all we *can* do," he said.

"Good luck," Lakesh said and signed off.

Within seconds the trio was hurrying down the path toward the tunnel with Rosalia's scruffy dog running alongside them.

MARIA HALLOWEEN crouched on the floor where she had left her cloth bag, glancing up as Kane muttered something in his disturbed sleep. She had sensed him so long ago, heard rumors of the *anam-chara,* the joined souls, before then. But she could only dream of the power they might bring.

It was a world of hidden forces, of gods walking the Earth. The woman had heard the story told several times, of how the hybrid barons had changed, physically and mentally altering to become some ancient tribe of gods. Their tech was all over; King Jack had shown her some of the strange devices that he had amassed while she stayed with him in his own hidden barony.

In theory, by channeling the soul power through her, Maria could cease her ongoing dance with time, turning young-then-old-then-young-again in her dangerous quest for survival, and finally lock herself and her pattern.

Carefully, the woman with blood tears on her cheeks unfolded the bag, pulling at this tab and that tie until suddenly the whole thing flopped open like a tablecloth. Brushing the contents aside, she assessed Kane's position once again before moving the bag-turned-sheet to a position near the back of the Chalice of Rebirth. She had remained here for the sake of her aging, utilizing the pool's effects to pull her back to youth, but the process was flawed; it could not hold forever. She had needed to dip into the pit over and over to keep her limbs supple. Otherwise, in just a few weeks she found that her old aches came back, old-woman pains hiding beneath the lustrous skin of her false youth. But, by converting the energy of the *anam-chara,* the soul bond that linked Kane to Brigid Baptiste, the *bruja* would ascend, altering her own genetic structure to something closer to the Annunaki themselves.

The sheet that had been a bag lay on the floor of the underground cavern, its pattern revealed. The pattern was surprisingly simple, just a series of concentric circles stitched into the fabric like the orbits of the planets. She paced out the space between Kane and the sheet, flattening one rumpled corner with her foot before finally being satisfied with the arrangement.

Then something began whining in the pile of belongings that had come from her bag, an alarm going off.

It was time.

GRANT WAS FORCED to duck several low-reaching stalactites as he led the way through the narrow tunnel beneath the earth with Domi and Rosalia following right behind him. Rosalia's dog panted and snuffled as it looked around, then weaved through the ex-Mag's legs and trotted on ahead of the three humans it accompanied.

"Guess he knows where he's going," Grant muttered as he watched the dog through the night lenses.

Grant was feeling increasingly wary as the tunnel narrowed and they came to a point in the natural hollow where he had to walk sideways like a crab to actually get through. "Tight squeeze," he advised his companions as his back scraped against the rough wall.

Domi had less trouble, thanks to her smaller frame and natural litheness. Even so, she was getting uncomfortable with the claustrophobic feeling the tunnels elicited, finding the warm darkness oppressive.

In the rear, Rosalia trekked on, thinking nothing of the passageways or the discomfort they brought. Like Domi, Rosalia was small enough to weave through the narrow passageway fairly easily, keeping her hands spread and running them along the walls so she could "see" after a fashion, feeling her way like a blind person. When the dog hurried off, she found her mind soothed—the mutt had been her companion for more than half a year, and she had never yet known it to go headlong into danger of its own accord. Though no guarantee, the dog's hurrying ahead suggested that there was no immediate danger to be met.

The passageway turned a sharp corner—sharp in more ways than one, Grant thought, given the way the pointed rock walls jabbed at his clothing. Then, as quickly as it had narrowed, the path flared out again and Grant realized that they had entered a vast cavern even as his night lenses blossomed with a brilliance that threatened to blind him. Grant closed his eyes, letting the electrochemical adjust to the increased light in the room, holding up a hand to warn the others to absolute stillness. They could see him now, for the cavern ahead was lit by three wide-spaced candles that stood at the edges of a circular pit. When Grant opened his eyes, the room was painted in lime and chartreuse via the night lenses, but it was brighter, more details clear in the picture. Grant recognized the pit instantly as a Chalice of Rebirth like the one that Shizuka had used all those months ago.

His eyes roved the darkness, spying the woman leaning over the blanket, her long dress brushing against the floor, a wimple over her head. Slumped beside her, Grant recognized the unconscious figure of Kane.

"Hello," Grant mumbled. "What have we here?"

As he spoke, a strange glowing seemed to form above the blanket where the woman was standing, twin cones exploding above and below the blanket like blossoming water lilies. For a moment, baffled by the night lenses, Grant didn't realize what he was looking at. Then Domi's voice came from behind him.

"Grant," she whispered. "It's an interphaser gateway."

Grant pushed back his night-vision lenses, looking at the glowing swirl of colors with his own eyes unencumbered. His breath caught in his throat as he realized that they were positioned above a parallax point that had opened a rip in space and was drawing something to it like a magnet.

"Just what the hell have we stumbled on?" Grant muttered as the lotus blossom of color became brighter and two solid figures began to form in its center.

Chapter 17

The hollow echo of her boot heels resounded through the empty streets as Brigid Haight hurried Little Quav out of Balam's home and into the underground city of Agartha. Behind them, the pale form of Balam lay in a heap next to the smoldering remains of Brigid's cloak, the ASP emitter sprawled across the black basalt floor. Little Quav's short legs stumbled as she hurried to keep up with the fierce pace that Brigid set. Outside, past the little garden that surrounded Balam's home, a street of similar buildings stretched off toward the towering core of the city. Each of the buildings looked the same, and despite being unoccupied, Balam had clearly made some effort to tend to their gardens, making this deserted city more homely for himself and his precious charge.

As they ran, Little Quav clutched at her rag doll's arm, and the doll swung from her hand, its legs dragging along the ground. "Why...are we...running, ...Briggly?" Quav asked, her voice stuttered and breathless.

"We need to get help for Uncle Balam—he's hurt himself," Brigid told the girl, glancing down at her for just a moment. In reality, Brigid was very conscious that they needed to get away from Balam's dwelling in case the bulbous-headed alien recovered. Brigid was pretty sure she had shot him dead, but she had no idea how his alien physiology worked. What she did know was that

Balam was ancient, and she concluded that he had to be pretty tough to have lasted so long.

As they turned a corner, skirting past the towering center of the underground city, Brigid heard a scraping movement from behind her. She stopped, flattening herself against the nearest wall and indicating for Little Quav to stay quiet.

Quav looked at Brigid with imploring eyes, fear making her shake. "What is it?" she whispered.

Brigid placed a finger to the girl's lips, warning her again to remain silent. Then the flame-haired ex-archivist silently stepped to the edge of the building and peered out, trying to locate the noise. Something was moving back there, scraping noises against the basalt rock from which the city was carved. A row of buildings lined the street on both sides, old abandoned dwellings that had once housed the citizens of Agartha. Brigid held her breath, counting the buildings in her head to work out which was Balam's. She need not have bothered; after a few seconds she saw the figure moving in the doorway, stepping out warily into the pseudo sunlight of the street.

Balam was swaying unsteadily, his large head rocking on his shoulders as if a rock teetering in a landslide. A smudge dusted his forehead on the right side, blood from where he had crashed into his floor. Just then Brigid saw something glint in Balam's long-fingered hand, and she recognized the ASP emitter immediately. She doubted that Balam would fire on the girl, of course, but if he could get a clear shot at her then all bets were off.

Conscious of the burning sensation on her back

where she had been hit before, Brigid leaned down and spoke quickly to Quav, keeping her voice just a whisper. "We're going to play a game," she explained. "We're going to keep moving, but we have to keep really quiet so that the monster doesn't get us."

"Monster?" the blond-haired girl giggled, but she looked a little worried.

"Quietly," Brigid reminded.

Together the flame-haired woman and the little hybrid girl made their way through the empty side streets, passing more of the black rock buildings as they made their way toward the incline that led to the outside world.

As they got closer, Brigid found herself having to remind the child to keep quiet, and the girl laughed and chastised both herself and her dolly, much to Brigid's irritation. Then they were at the street that opened onto the incline itself, Brigid recalled, and she unconsciously kept to the shadows, eyes constantly flicking left and right as she searched for any other presence.

Balam was waiting there. His familiar, squat form was hiding, albeit badly, in the space between two buildings, watching the street as he waited for Brigid to appear at the only entrance and exit she knew to this secret world. Brigid cursed. She had been lucky to knock Balam down while the child was not looking, but to shoot him in front of Little Quav's eyes—well, the girl would not be so trusting of her actions if she saw that.

Brigid's mind raced, trying to recall alternate routes in and out of Agartha. It took a moment, but when it came, the solution was obvious. Rather than walk out of here with the girl, trekking through the Himalayas until they reached the parallax point that Brigid had used to get close to Agartha, she would use Agartha's own parallax point. She had the interphaser with her in the leather satchel on her back, and using the parallax point as an escape window was the most graceful—and obvious—solution to her quandary.

IN THE STREET beyond, Balam was still waiting, swaying gently in place as he tried to remain conscious. Brigid's attack had seriously wounded him and he was losing blood from his chest, as well as from a grisly damp patch that streaked the curve of his collarbone. He watched the street from his hiding place, the ASP emitter hooked over his wrist and hand like an extension of his arm. He was not used to involving himself in physical combat. Only recently, with the breakdown of the Ontic Library and the implications of that occurrence, had Balam chosen to arm himself, pulling an ASP emitter out of storage where it had been preserved in Agartha's Museum of Artifacts. Even so, he felt awkward using the weapon, conscious of its lethal power and the consequences that a rogue shot could easily bring.

But his suspicions had been right. The hybrid child, Quavell's daughter, was in trouble. Often seen as a prize in the ongoing war between humanity and the Annunaki, Little Quav held the key to the Annunaki royal dynasty in her DNA. It was imperative that she not fall into either group's hands—for the humans could be as pernicious as the sadistic Annunaki, a fact Balam knew from firsthand experience when he had been held prisoner by a military group.

He had drifted in and out of consciousness for several minutes while Brigid had gathered up the girl, calming her before they exited his home. His head throbbed where his skull had smashed against the floor, and the wound in his side felt like an acid burn. He took a deep, steadying breath through his flat nares, feeling the threat of his own weakness as it tried to overwhelm him. He must remain strong, recover the girl-who-would-be-queen-of-the-Annunaki, and get to safety. But if Cerberus had turned on him like this, where could he go?

A telepath by nature, Balam had detected something out of sorts with Brigid from the moment he saw her. She held herself differently from the Brigid Baptiste he knew, a swagger to her hips that had not been there before, no longer exhibiting that playful manner he had noticed in their previous meetings. He had not needed his telepathy to realize she was mentally altered; his psychic abilities had merely confirmed the change. He had been unable to read her fully, finding prying on her thoughts impossible, but he had detected the dark cloud that had taken hold of her mind even at his most subtle reading. She was thinking differently, he saw, and that made her unpredictable. He concentrated, trying to guess where Brigid would go if she did not use the fixed exit. There were a number of hidden ways in and out of Agartha, but Brigid had been unaware of these so far as Balam knew, and each of them was treacherous, especially for the child Brigid was now traveling with. No, there had to be a more obvious reason that she had not appeared here.

Balam dipped his head like an upturned bulb, checking the street again for signs of Brigid and the girl, but they weren't there. He was certain he had arrived in time. Even with their slight head start Little Quav would slow the woman down and, besides, Balam would have seen them if they had made it to the rising slope before him; it was too open an area to miss their retreating forms.

No, there had to be another way. Either Brigid was hiding with the child somewhere in the city itself or—

It struck Balam like a lightning bolt. She would use Agartha's parallax point, escaping via interphaser. In a second Balam waddled out of his hiding place, scurrying along the street on his ungainly legs.

HER BLACK leather-clad legs moving like pistons, Brigid dragged the tousle-haired girl along as she made her way to the parallax point via Agartha's empty back alleys. The interphaser was in its carry case, strapped across her back. The parallax point was located right in the center of the underground city. Brigid couldn't help but feel disappointed at the obviousness of it all. Agartha's street design all but pointed to the location of the gateway, as if the settlement itself had actually grown up around it. That was probably true, she realized—as early human settlements frequently grew up close to rivers and other water courses because of their use in crop irrigation and transport, so, too, would this Archon city have grown up around its own primary means of transport.

Like the rest of the ghost city, the towering structure waited in front of her in silence, dust and dirt marking its black basalt sides. Brigid slammed aside the door with an angry sweep of her hand, dragging Little Quav

inside and peering around her. A long corridor stretched
through the interior of the building, dark walls made
dull by the absolute lack of interior light. There had been
a stone here once, Brigid remembered—had it been here
or somewhere else? A black-hued stone with a surface
like glass that, when you looked into it, would show you
possible futures, different worlds. The stone had gone
by many names—Lucifer's Stone, the kala, the Kaa'ba,
the Chintamani Stone, the Shining Trapezohedron—as
different human cultures had convinced themselves its
visions unlocked enlightenment or madness. But it had
been shattered, its shards lost across the planet's surface.
The broken stone had shown a lot of things, but it had
never shown Brigid this truth, that she would emerge
from her own unsuspected chrysalis state into what she
was now, a creature of the Annunaki, a being driven
solely by contempt.

Little Quav looked at the woman who dragged her
along. After spending so much time with Balam, the
woman seemed to tower in Quav's presence. The little
girl liked her, though she couldn't really comprehend
why. To Quav, Brigid was the closest thing she had ever
had to a mother. She had met the woman a grand total of
twice, and the first of those times had been at her own
birth, which Quav could not possibly remember. Little
Quav's mother had died in childbirth, and the daughter
had been whisked away by Balam shortly thereafter. Not
yet three years old, Quav was beginning to recognize
her own body and to appreciate how it differed from that
of her foster parent. Balam was strange, alien, his six-
fingered hands long and gangly, his head shaped like a

hot-air balloon. He was not like Quav, not of her kind, and yet the girl had no one else to turn to.

Balam had become aware of this shortcoming, and he had covered the mirrors within the house, hiding Little Quav from herself. But there were other places, glass and polished wood where Quav would see her reflection, the metal implements she would use to eat with sometimes. Quav was a child and, like all children, she was curious.

After they had visited the Cerberus redoubt eight weeks ago, Quav had begun asking Balam questions. She had seen people in the redoubt, people like her or at least more like her than he was. For all intents and purposes she looked like a human child after all, perhaps more graceful, more ethereal, but still her hybrid qualities only added to her human nature. So she had understood the people at Cerberus as *her people,* different from Balam, who was *the other.*

It was inevitable really, that the girl would be attracted to humans, that she would trust them over Balam despite all of his kindness and selflessness in raising her.

Balam had told her about the humans but he had been evasive, refusing to answer the girl's half-formed questions, promising to explain more when she was older, when she was better equipped to understand. That had only made it worse. Little Quav loved Balam, but she wanted to be with humans now, now that she had seen them.

Little Quav remembered seeing Brigid in the redoubt, as well as another woman, a mothering figure who had taken care of her and placed a cold metal disc to her chest as she listened to Quav's breathing. Little Quav recalled most clearly Brigid's bright hair, for Quav had never seen hair on another person before. Balam was hairless; he didn't even have eyebrows with which to enhance his expressions. The woman with the sunset hair was called Briggly, or that's how Little Quav remembered it, and she had friends. There had been a giant man who smiled at her a lot like a big friendly monster. That man had dark skin as if he had been dipped in the shadows, but he had played with her a little, and his voice made Quav's insides rumble when he spoke. That man had been called Grant.

And there had been another, too, a man with dark hair and alert eyes, a man who seemed almost afraid of Quav. He had been called Kane, and Balam had explained that he was Briggly's best friend. Quav tried to picture him as she ran with Brigid through the towering power plant.

So it was, in one sense, Balam's own fault that Quav had been so easily abducted by Brigid. In protecting her he had hidden her from the world's pain, and so she had grown up ignorant of the dangers that world might present.

Standing beside the girl, Brigid turned around and around until she found herself facing the looming corridor again. She noticed a doorway, almost hidden by the dark shadows of the building.

"Briggly?" Little Quav urged. She sounded frightened.

"Quiet, child," Brigid urged, motioning to the doorway. "Monsters."

Then Brigid and the girl disappeared into the doorway, finding themselves on a spiraling staircase carved from the rock. The staircase went down and down, disappearing into the gloom. There was no light switch on the wall, no system to light the stairwell that Brigid could see. But even as she stepped onto the first step, a soft glow ebbed into existence along the sides of the steps, turning a warm orange as Brigid urged the little girl down them.

"Where does this go?" Little Quav asked as Brigid hurried her down the stairs.

"Just keep going," Brigid replied, firmly pushing the girl's shoulders.

After twenty stairs or so, the staircase changed, becoming narrower and switching to a coiling design made of beautifully tooled metal that shone as the orange glow touched it. The metal clattered as Brigid and the girl hurried down it, each step echoing in the vastness of an unseen room beneath them, reverberating back to them long after they had taken the steps themselves, so that the sound doubled and redoubled, over and over like a round robin chorus.

It took almost two minutes—Brigid could have done it in half that had she been alone—until the two of them reached the bottom rung of the swirling stairs. They stood in a vast chamber that stretched on for as far as Brigid could see in the minimal light. As with the staircase and the main parts of the building itself, the chamber was lit sporadically or not at all, faint specks of green and orange dotted around the walls as Brigid led the child, holding her hand. Perhaps there was a trick to operating the lights, Brigid thought, or maybe the Archons could simply see a wider range of the spectrum and so such concerns had never occurred to them. Whatever it was, it left much of the vast chamber in shadow.

They were in an underground room beneath an underground city, and the ludicrous thought struck Brigid that they must surely be getting close to the center of the Earth. The coldness of the room coupled with its size made it seem more like they were outside, however, up on the surface at nighttime.

Brigid peered around her. The chamber appeared empty, and its high ceiling gave one the impression of a vast open space, as if walking in a park at night. With no frame of reference, Brigid could not begin to guess the true size of the room.

There was machinery in the room, little clumps of it scattered here and there like conversational groups at a party, the spaces between them irregular. Brigid looked around her, singularly failing to recognize any of the alien tech on show in the shadowy gloom.

"Where are we?" Quav asked in her little girl's voice. "It's cold. Is Kane here?"

Brigid looked down at the girl, her brow furrowed. Of course, Little Quav had been born at the Cerberus redoubt and she had come to associate Brigid with her old companions, Kane, Grant and the others. Though the girl had only visited Cerberus once since her birth, she was perceptive. Furthermore, there was every chance that Balam had spoken to the girl about the Cerberus people; perhaps Quav had asked about them after her visit, for she had seen so few people in her short and sheltered life.

"Not Kane," Brigid replied. "Not today."

Brigid continued scanning the room for a moment,

searching for some reference point, a sign of where the parallax point might be hidden. Then there came a voice from above, clattering footsteps as someone stepped onto the metallic stairwell. Brigid glanced over her shoulder, narrowing her eyes as she tried to make out who it was in the darkness. But already she knew; after all, it could only be one person—Balam.

"Come on, Little Quav," Brigid said, her voice an encouraging whisper. "Don't look at the monster or he'll get you and eat you up."

Scared, Quav hurried beside the flame-haired woman, clutching her doll close to her chest as Brigid led them through the main artery between stacks of waiting tech, searching for the parallax point from which the interphaser could launch. All around the chamber, the echoing clanks of Balam's footsteps rolled from wall to wall, repeating themselves over and over so as to sound more like an approaching army hidden by the gloom.

Parallax points came in many forms, often disguised as ancient places of worship or even the simplest markings on a wall, Brigid knew. But this parallax point wasn't some rocky hole, a scratching in a wall or a simple statue. Brigid was left speechless by the sight of the vast metallic disc, stretching fifteen feet across the floor, constructed from concentric circles of silver and gold. Strip lighting winked into life on its surface, curving lines of green and red. As they came to life, Brigid saw the carvings in the metal discs, cuneiform patterns running their complete lengths, cup-and-spiral symbols mixed with the archaic glyphs. The juxtaposition of modern lighting and ancient design took Brigid's breath away.

Brigid strode across the area to the dark center of the circle, the interphaser unit balanced carefully in her hands. As she walked, the green-and-red strips glistened across the black sheath of her leather armor, painting her in stripes like some strange, insectile camouflage. When she had reached the center of those concentric circles, she bent, spying the square slot that had been inset in the floor there. It was little surprise to find that the interphaser fitted it perfectly, slipping into the space like the final piece of a jigsaw.

Little Quav was still standing at the edge of the broad circular pattern, watching as Brigid engaged the interphaser.

"Come, Quav," Brigid urged the hybrid girl. "Quickly now."

As BALAM REACHED the bottom of the stairwell, Brigid tapped the destination coordinates into the interphaser, even as Little Quav hurried to her side. Balam pushed himself to go faster, hurrying past the moth-balled heaps of ancient tech, old nullifiers, liquidizers, storage batteries.

Balam's legs ached and his chest burned as he ran across the vast room toward the fiercely lit area of the parallax point. He was unused to chasing people, and his need for medical attention was growing by the minute, the sticky blood of his chest wound congealing with the dark fabric of his robe. The bright markings of the parallax point formed a beacon in the darkness of the underground holding area, and Balam watched as Little Quav waited at Brigid's side.

"Quav, no," Balam called, but his voice was soft now, his breathing shallow.

He raised the ASP emitter, lining up his shot carefully, determined to knock Brigid out without harming his hybrid charge. But already the familiar lotus blossom of color was emerging from the interphaser, its swirling pattern dominating the room in a cone shape, lightning flashes playing in its midst. Downward, too, the interphaser's glow grew, drawing a pattern into the floor.

A single plasma bolt blasted from the ASP emitter on Balam's wrist. But he was sure he saw Brigid dip her head to him, a sadistic smile on her lips as she disappeared, the bolt itself cutting through the space where she had been with a stench of ozone. They were already gone.

Balam stared at the space where his quarry had been, gazing at it with the sorrowful pools of his dark eyes as the lit circle of the parallax point powered down, returning to darkness.

"No," he said to that darkness. "I deny this."

Even as he spoke the words, the pale-skinned humanoid was running to one of the nearby storage blocks, his deft fingers grasping through their seemingly haphazard grouping. In a moment Balam had produced an interphaser unit of his own from the mishmash of stuff, its triangular shape glistening as the last ebbing light of the parallax point played across its metallic surface.

"Now, where would you go, Brigid Baptiste?" Balam mused as he hurried back to the parallax point that Brigid's interphaser had just vacated less than a minute before. As realization dawned, Balam powered up the interphaser and input the Destination Zero code.

THE RELENTLESS colorburst faded. Chest heaving, Balam found himself standing in the surrounds of a man-made mat-trans unit, its tiled ceiling and armaglass walls all too familiar. Overhead lights winked on automatically as motion sensors detected his presence in the small chamber. There was a faint vibration all around as hidden fans began to ventilate the mat-trans cubicle, clearing any gaseous debris caused by the journey.

Balam took an unsteady step forward. He had quite forgotten how traumatic matter transfer could be and, in his weakened state, he had been ill-prepared for the disorientation it caused. Balam was surprised that no one had come to meet him—normally a detail of guards would be waiting on the far side of the antechamber, guns ready for any intruder.

Balam exited the mat-trans unit, stepped past the brown-tinted armaglass walls and out into the main operations room of the Cerberus redoubt. He had used this interphaser to travel here just eight weeks ago, when he had brought news of the Ontic Library's destruction. This was where Brigid and her friends were based; Balam congratulated himself on his deft application of logic in following her.

Except, as he stepped out of the mat-trans unit, Balam realized his mistake. The familiar operations room had changed almost beyond recognition. Where Balam expected to see the sleek lines of computer machinery, the smooth walls of the thriving ops center, he instead found rough rock walls and plinths, the oppressive spines of thick stalactites spiking downward from the ceiling, making it lower than he remembered. The room was no longer lit by a system of bright overhead lights and desk lamps; now, thin traces of orange lava glowed within the rock walls, lighting the whole space insouciantly.

But the most significant change of all was that the room was utterly silent, with not even the suggestion that anyone had ever been here. There was certainly no indication that Brigid and the kidnapped child had passed through. But if she hadn't returned to Cerberus, then where had she gone?

Balam felt the fiery pain increase in his chest. He staggered a step backward, placing a steadying hand on the armaglass wall where strips of rock cobwebbed across its once-smooth surface like the reaching tendrils of a vine.

There, amid the silent halls of the abandoned redoubt that had once been called Bravo, Balam slid down the wall. Then, collapsing to the floor, the pale-skinned figure clutched at the handful of oozing bullet wounds that littered his chest, coughing weakly into his clenched hand, a loose, rib-shaking wheeze as he slumped on the floor.

Chapter 18

Brigid Haight placed her hands on Little Quav's shoulders, pulling the hybrid girl close to her as the multicolored lotus blossom of her activated interphaser expanded around them, plucking them from the underground city of Agartha even as Balam blasted a single plasma bolt at them from the bottom of the stairwell. Brigid smiled, her eyes locking with Balam's as the interphase gateway took her and the girl out of the path of his plasma beam.

Travel by interphaser was instantaneous and it was something that Brigid had experienced countless times before. And yet this time it seemed somehow different. The familiar rainbow of light swirled in front of Brigid's eyes, sparks of witch fire flashing in its depths, but something else appeared there, too. It seemed to be a geometric pattern, made up of concentric golden circles and interlocking squares. Originating from the focal point of Brigid's vision, the golden shapes appeared to be dancing upon a sky-blue background. Brigid was conscious of other colors at the edges, blurring from her view, regular spots highlighting themselves in different shades of green and red. For a moment the colors seemed to taunt her, swirling in front of her eyes, and Brigid Haight wondered what it all meant.

And then she was back in reality, her hands still resting on the girl's shoulders. Relief washed over Brigid as she prepared to step out into the hallways of Bensalem Keep.

Except this wasn't Bensalem, wasn't the island fortress of her master Ullikummis.

Instead she saw a cavern's rocky walls, a glistening pit of amber in the cavern's center surrounded by a metal circle decorated with ancient runes. She recognized the pit immediately, knew it was a Chalice of Rebirth.

Still clutching Little Quav close to her, Brigid used her free hand to unholster her TP-9 semiautomatic as the swirl of the interphaser faded from view. But as she did so, she found herself locked in place as if held in some kind of stasis beam. Brigid's back arched as searing pain played across her form, her muscles tautening.

There, poised in front of the amber pool with arms outstretched, stood the slender figure of a woman, the long swish of her skirts a funereal black stained with lines of scarlet like bloody veins. Two mirrored spots glistened on the woman's cheeks, shining drips of blood like tears. The woman's arms were outstretched, and a sparking beam of energy like lightning seemed to be emanating from her right hand or being drawn into it, Brigid could not tell which. A second beam of crackling yellow-white energy connected the woman's left hand to a slumped figure lying on the ground beside her, making the still form dance on the spot. Even with his back to her, Brigid recognized the fallen figure—it was her longtime colleague Kane.

ACROSS THE CAVERN, hiding in the mouth of an offshoot tunnel, Grant, Domi and Rosalia had watched as the multicolored light coalesced into the familiar form of Brigid Baptiste standing beside Little Quav.

"That's Brigid," Domi whispered. "What is she doing here?"

Grant felt an increasing sense of disquiet as he watched the scene unfold. "I don't know," he said, "but I don't like it."

"Who's the girl?" Rosalia asked, tapping Grant on his muscular bicep.

"Shit," Grant said. "That's Quav. What the heck is going down here?"

Domi engaged her Commtact, placing her hand to her ear to drown out the increasing sounds of crackling energy that echoed through the vast cavern. "I'm calling up Lakesh, right now," she insisted.

IN THE BEACH HOUSE overlooking the Pacific, Lakesh Singh was just enjoying a refreshing glass of iced tea when his Commtact earpiece came to life with Domi's voice.

"Lakesh, we've found Brigid," she said.

Lakesh was so surprised he swallowed a mammoth mouthful of the drink and began to choke, coughing and spluttering before he was finally able to respond.

"Lakesh?" Domi asked.

"I'm here, dearest one," Lakesh croaked. "Please repeat—it sounded like you said you'd found Brigid."

"We have," Domi said, doing nothing to hide the joy in her voice. "Or maybe she kind of found us. She just appeared via interphaser gateway, but she's trapped in a…I don't know…energy prison of some kind."

Lakesh's fingers were already tapping at the keyboard

of his laptop computer, bringing up a refreshed feed of the satellite imagery, topographical map and transponder beacons of the Cerberus personnel in the area around Snakefishville. His hands moved at such a rate that his forearm nudged the desk, and his nearly empty glass of iced tea went sailing across the desk before clattering against the floor. He ignored it.

"I'm bringing up the transponder signals now," Lakesh said, his eyes scanning the screen in front of him. Three blips glowed with readings from the transponders—one each for Kane, Grant and Domi herself. But there were no others in the immediate area. "Domi dear, are you sure that Brigid is with you?"

"She's right in front of us," Domi said. "I'm looking at her now. She's twenty feet away."

The satellite surveillance was useless, of course. With Domi's team currently in a subterranean locale, there was no way that Lakesh could access a visual of them. His fingers jabbed at the refresh button with irritation, willing for Brigid's transponder signal to appear. But it singularly failed to do so.

"Domi," Lakesh mused, "I'm receiving no signal from Brigid's transponder. If that is her, then her transponder is deactivated."

SPEAKING QUICKLY, Domi related Lakesh's words to Grant and Rosalia. Their fiery-haired colleague had been missing for over a month with no indication whether she was even alive.

"Bottom line is that Lakesh can't track her transponder," Domi summarized. "Either it's offline or it's been removed somehow."

"Then we're just gonna have to make sure we don't lose sight of her," Grant growled, his eyes fixed on the scene playing out in front of him, "as well as rescuing her, Quav and Kane."

"WELCOME, *ANAM-CHARA*," Maria Halloween said as the power of the combined souls flooded into her. Her voice trembled now, shuddering as her body came alive with the power it was drawing from the two figures to either side of her.

The hybrid girl known as Little Quav had stepped away from Brigid and she stood just an arm's length away, watching as the lightninglike energy jangled across the woman's leather-clad form, swamping and trapping her like the fast-flowing torrent of a waterfall.

Brigid's mouth stretched wider as if to scream and her muscles were aflame as something deep inside was drawn out of her. On the floor beside the witch with tears of blood, Kane's body was flipping and flopping like a beached fish as similar energies cascaded over and through him, blasting him against the ground like a continuous stream of lightning bolts while leeching his very essence from his body.

Though Kane was still unconscious, Brigid struggled to fight it off, but it took every ounce of strength just to move her head. Brigid looked down to where the interphaser waited at her feet, wondering if she might still be able to somehow activate it and escape. Brigid saw the Annunaki child standing obediently there watching as her body glowed with power. They were standing on some kind of blanket, and Brigid recognized the nature of the symbols stitched there, her fierce intellect realizing immediately their significance.

"You…" Brigid struggled to speak, the word coming malformed through a mouth that would not close fully. "Explain what…is happening…to…"

"I disrupted the interphase flow," Maria said, almost casually. "Brought you here. It was quite simple, just a matter of timing."

ON THE FLOOR beside the witch woman, Kane's body was shaking and pulsing as the power was drawn from him. Suddenly his eyes snapped open, his fists clenched.

"Baptiste?" Kane muttered through thick tongue, feeling the field of energy cracking across his lips and teeth as he opened his mouth. Her voice sounded far away, yet he was sure he had heard her.

Tentatively, the searing pain pulling at every muscle in his body, Kane turned his head, trying to locate where the voices were coming from. It took a moment. His left eye was completely blind and it felt as if there was a weight there, inside his head, a density to his skull that he had never felt before.

He recognized the slender feet beside him wrapped in simple sandals that laced up past the ankles. That was the witch woman, Maria, and she was standing on tiptoe as fierce spurs of energy zapped across her skin. No, not standing—drawn upward, her body tensing like a violin string.

Kane looked further, adjusting his vision to try to see past the bright lances of energy that played over the *bruja*'s flesh. There was another woman there, trapped in a pillar of lightning as a small blond girl watched.

Kane's heart leaped—the woman was Brigid Baptiste, and the girl was Quavell.

With a colossal effort, Kane tried to push himself from the ground, his shuddering muscles fighting against him as the electricity snapped and bit at them. He had to get up, to free Brigid and stop whatever the hell this psycho witch was doing to them. Which was easier said than done.

BRIGID COULD SEE Kane's form struggling to move behind the witch woman as electricity played across him, his body shuddering. She wondered if she must look the same now as the energy caromed over her in fiery waves.

"H-how?" Brigid demanded angrily, tears pouring unbidden from her eyes as the energy washed over her, through her. "How c-c-could you…break into…th-th-the jump?"

"While you're in the quantum ether," Maria told her, "any parallax point can snatch you out, the same way that a whirlpool can drag a ship from its ocean path. As I said, it's just a matter of timing.

"I felt you calling across the void. I felt the power emanating from your linked souls," the old-young witch continued, gesturing to the prone form of Kane with a subtle incline of her glowing head. "That's power that can be tapped, taken, drawn from you. That's power that can shift Heaven and Earth. I called you both here, set the birds in flight knowing that sooner or later they'd bring you or one of your squadron of do-gooders. And now you get to fulfil your dream—now you get to really do good."

"Birds?" Brigid asked, bemused, straining to speak as shooting pains lanced deep within her bones. "What are you talking about?"

In front of Brigid's eyes, the woman with the blood tears closed her eyes in a long blink and began to ascend, every part of her body straining upward as if she could take off. A halo of energy glowed around her head, her hair flowing around her face as the wimple seared away, as if she had touched her palms against a Van de Graaff generator in an old physics class. When she opened her eyes again to look at Brigid, her eyes seemed somehow fuller, the pupils widening within the hollows, obscuring the whites.

"Your friend came to see my pretty birds," Maria told her, energy crackling across her teeth as her mouth moved. "And, in turn, I brought you here to join him. Reunited at last."

HIDING ON THE LEDGE that overlooked the cavern, Domi prodded Grant gently in the ribs. "She made the birds," she whispered.

"Yeah," Grant replied. "I got that."

"That would explain why they didn't attack the ville," Rosalia pointed out. "She's been keeping them on a very short leash so they'd act as a pointer, a beacon for Cerberus to investigate. Probably programmed them that way."

"Programmed?" Domi repeated, confused.

"When you train a bird you instil a homing instinct within it," Rosalia explained, her voice low. "You do that, the bird won't even leave its cage without being encouraged to do so."

"Enough chitchat," Grant snarled. "Kane's down there and so is Brigid. I don't know what the heck that woman's doing, but I've seen enough. We need to put a stop to it right now."

But before Grant could move, he saw Kane pull himself up from the floor and leap for the glowing woman standing between himself and Brigid.

"What th—?"

IN A STUMBLING flail of limbs, Kane half leaped, half staggered at the glowing form of Maria Halloween, crashing into her with all the grace of an avalanche. Halloween just stood there on tiptoe, shuddering ever so slightly at Kane's attack; it was as if he had batted against a wall.

Kane struggled to focus on his aim of trying to topple the woman, even as he bounced off the crackling bubble around her and slumped back to the floor. It was becoming harder to keep straight who he was now; these other memories kept bursting across his subconscious, threatening to overwhelm him.

As he slammed into the cavern floor, Kane seemed to see an ornately decorated palanquin finished in rose and gold looming in front of him, its curtain drawn against the hot sun. The goddess Ninlil stood at the foot of the palanquin, head bowed in contrition as he approached in his mind's eye.

Kane shouted a curse, willing the vision to leave him alone. It wasn't his life; it was the life of that monster, of the god prince Ullikummis.

The *bruja* turned at Kane's shriek, inclining her head in pity as he writhed on the floor, his body shuddering amid the sparking energy licking at his flesh. When she turned, she saw the movement from far back in the cave as a dark-skinned, muscular man with shaved head and tightly trimmed beard came hurrying out of the shadows, raising the unmistakable shape of a gun gripped in his right hand. The *bruja* watched, feeling the energy of twinned souls coursing in her veins, running through her body, as Grant pulled the trigger of the Sin Eater and launched a clutch of bullets at her.

"Eat this, bitch," Grant snarled as the Sin Eater rocked in his hand.

Behind him, Domi and Rosalia were rushing out from their hiding place, and Rosalia's dog barked joyfully as it saw its mistress.

Then the bullets struck the sparking energy that played across the *bruja*'s body, melting before they could carve a path through it to reach her. The energy—whatever it was—was acting as a shield for the woman within.

"Damn." Grant depressed the trigger of the Sin Eater a second time.

With the simplest of movements, Maria Halloween dipped beneath the bullets, running on the pointed tips of her toes at the ex-Magistrate, the cascading energy enveloping her body. Twin beams of energy ripped from her hands, joining her in crackling arcs to Kane and Brigid where they remained shuddering in place. Grant was astonished at the woman's speed; she seemed almost outside of time as she lunged at him. Before he could counter, the woman's arm swished through the air, slapping him across the underside of his chin and knocking him off his feet.

Domi watched in amazement as Grant went sailing across the cavern. Without hesitation, the brave albino warrior ran at the glowing form who was still pulling energy from her friends, the thin shaft of a knife in her hand. The *bruja* held up a hand in defence as Domi slashed at her with the knife, and the blade was repelled by the intense energy surrounding her, shooting up into the air and taking Domi with it, forcing the albino girl to stagger backward.

"Don't you understand?" Maria said, her words coming amid the rising crackle of the energy all around her. "I have multiple souls now. I'm ascending. I am becoming unto a god."

Then she came at Domi, her hand outstretched, palm open. Instinctively, Domi reared back, avoiding the blow by a fraction of an inch, the energy that surrounded her foe warming her flesh by its close proximity.

Domi drove the knife through the air once more, jabbing it at the woman's face with all her might, hoping to pierce the strange bubble of glistening energy that seemed to shield her. The blade pierced through the ever-changing lightninglike surface of the shield, but already the woman within was turning, driving her left palm at Domi's torso where the summer dress left her décolletage exposed. Domi felt the blow like a freight train slamming into her breastbone, and she went caroming backward, her feet sliding across the loose earth floor as she receded from the glowing woman. A moment later Domi's trip ended as she crashed into one of the rough rock walls, her head meeting with it with a resounding clunk.

Maria Halloween was glowing like a star now, the

entwined power of the shared *anam-chara* bond drawn into her, plucking the life from Kane and the woman once known as Brigid Baptiste. She could feel the incredible power running through her veins, feel her whole body changing, becoming something different and strong—becoming a god. The souls were drawing into her being, prostrating themselves to her.

At one side of the cavern, Rosalia's dog whined, sensing the incredible shift of uncanny forces beyond its ken. Beside the hound, Rosalia stood in the shadows by the wall, watching as Domi slumped into unconsciousness much as Grant had moments before. Gritting her teeth, Rosalia pulled her *katana* blade, wondering what she could possibly do.

Chapter 19

The tech was alien and very old. Beyond that, the *bruja* knew very little about it.

It was some kind of precious stone, dark in color, like a shard of smoked glass, and it stood no bigger than a woman's fingernail. It had been on Earth for at least a thousand years, and doubtless more, and time and again it had been said to bring about a sensation of strength and often of queasiness in its bearer. On occasion, it had been mistakenly called "evil eye" or "moonstone" or a hundred other simpleton names, the callers unaware of the stone's more esoteric origins and purpose.

The first written record of its existence could be found in the Domesday Book, where it was said to be owned by a parish in Suffolk, England. No record exists of how the parish had ended up with the item, described simply in the weighty survey as "an objet of peculy'r Glass-smithery, attach'd to a band of brass ringlets." Its value had been considered negligible, and more attention was paid to the worth of the brass alloy that it was attached to than the stone itself. Whether it had exhibited any unusual properties, the record had not showed.

The item had then disappeared, with several possible references of it appearing in jewellers' logs over a seven-hundred-year period. One possible—and more intriguing—sighting of the mysterious jewel during this era was as a part of an ostentatious belt that Sir Francis Drake could be seen wearing in a painting dated circa 1592, that ultimately resided in the National Portrait Gallery, London, England, prior to the nukecaust. However, said painting had endured some significant amendments during restoration over the intervening years, with several of the more objectionable pictorial mementoes removed while others were painted in their place, as was common practice at the time. Thus, it remained unknown whether the jewel itself was in fact a part of the original sitter's costume or was added at a later date. Furthermore, whether Drake, also known as Draco or "the Dragon", ever owned the gem, or indeed the belt, was unknown.

Discounting its anecdotal appearance in the Drake painting, the first truly definitive record of its existence could be found as a part of the belongings of a French noblewoman, the black glass hanging as a pendant on a necklace. The woman in question was renowned for her clairvoyance, but the necklace disappeared during the Terror when its owner was beheaded by Madame Guillotine in 1793, something she sadly had not foreseen in her scrying. Rumors had it that the removed necklace reappeared two years later around the neck of a maiden at one of the *bals des victimes,* although the veracity of this report, and of the occurrence of the *bals* themselves, remained somewhat contentious.

The gem had next appeared in the records of a count's family in Eastern Europe. The tales that had grown up around his castle were fanciful, speculations of vampirism based on the pale skin of the family who lived within. There again, perhaps it was the stone itself that had been sucking the life out of visitors, informing the tall stories that would be whispered in the local taverns on cold winter nights.

In subsequent years, hazy records suggested that the gem had been removed from the necklace to become a brooch worn by a fortune teller in the latter part of the Georgian era, before finally being incorporated into a charm bracelet when Queen Victoria had popularized the wearing of such ornaments throughout the British Empire. That bracelet, in turn, ended up as part of a collection given over to the Musée des Arts Décoratifs, Paris, but the eerily colored gemstone itself was removed, either prior to the donation or at some point shortly thereafter.

The *bruja,* Maria Halloween, had acquired it a hundred years ago under circumstances best left undisclosed. She could feel its succubus power throbbing at her breast as she hid it in a pocket, and she had carried it with her or around her ever since. Realizing that it could leech the power of souls, seeing it draw at the essence of another many years ago, the woman had waited those subsequent years to employ it, waiting for something truly special before she tapped its power again. The presence of *anam-charas,* the "soul friends" conjoined throughout history, promised the very jolt she was seeking, and even then she had had to take an enormous effort to bring them here in the same place.

Engaged, the soul stone began to suck energy, molding it so that it might be imbibed by the bearer of the gem. In essence, the gem turned its bearer into a dynamo, able to take and convert energy.

EVEN UNCONSCIOUS, Kane felt the pulling at his essence and bore the incredible strain of losing himself to another. He was a strong man, mentally and physically, and he should have been able to fight this. But the thing that lurked behind his eye, the *otherness,* the fleck of evil that had physically embedded itself in him, infected his thoughts, blasting the memory and the experiences of another across his own.

He felt four millennia pass as he sat hunched up in the pitch-black room inside the rock, the only light the light of his own veins, glowing like magma in the darkness. It was cold, the bone cold of the void, of space. The prison-cell asteroid had been sent on a long orbit of the Milky Way, designed to never return, and Ullikummis—the thing that was now in Kane's memory in place of himself—had been trapped inside, banished from the kingdom of Ka, the Earth.

To be lonely loses all meaning after four thousand years alone. Every day Kane—which is to say Ullikummis—uttered just one word, that he would remember its sound, remember how much he hated it: Enlil. It was the name of his own father.

Kane grasped for his own memories, feeling consciousness return. Vaguely the ex-Magistrate was aware of the noise in the cavern, aware of how it didn't fit with the vision that was playing itself out in front of his senses. He needed to shift it aside, to see past it and bring himself back into the picture. But as he reached for his own self, for his soul, he felt it being snatched from him, pulled further and further from his reach. Kane was renowned for his point man sense, his uncanny ability to detect things around him by the smallest of clues. Right now, only his point man sense gave any hint that the things he seemed to be experiencing within the asteroid were not real, that he was still in a cavern beneath the earth where a battle for his very soul was being fought. And Kane could not possibly know that he appeared to have already lost that battle, that his own soul was being absorbed by the woman called Maria Halloween, doubling her power.

I'm living somebody else's life here, Kane told himself as the vision of the interior of the stone prison filled his mind, yet I can't make it go away.

WITHIN THE CAVERN, the raven-haired form of Maria Halloween was glowing with fearsome power, sparking like a loose wire shot through with ten thousand volts.

Rosalia shielded her eyes with her raised left arm. In her right hand she clutched the *katana* sword, twenty-five inches of tempered steel glinting wildly as the sparkling form of the *bruja* reflected in its surface. Beside her, the scruffy dog peered up at Rosalia with its eerily pale eyes, head cocked as if in query. "I don't know," Rosalia admitted. "I don't know what we ought to do, dammit."

Two bright shafts of energy were blasting across the cavern, lighting the whole underground space like twin rivers of lightning, drawn to the witch woman from the withering bodies of Kane and Brigid. Kane lay slumped on the hard floor, his face dirty from where he had fallen against the earth there, his cheeks sinking as the very flesh of his body seemed to melt away. Across the cave, still standing on the blanket that the *bruja* had laid out, the familiar form of Brigid Baptiste was wrenched in pain, energy coursing over her strained form as it began to thin, becoming less of a woman and more just a skeleton. A wispy-haired blond girl was standing beside Brigid, her face displaying the same combination of puzzlement and obedience as Rosalia's dog as she stared up at her companion struggling within the pillar of cascading energy.

Rosalia looked across the cave, the whole area becoming a stark contrast of light and shadow as the fierce glow from the *bruja* woman lit it. Other than Kane and Brigid, there were two more people in the wide cavern, both of whom were unconscious. The chalk-skinned form of Domi lay close to the edge of the amber-misted pit, her head slumped against the cool metal ring that surrounded the pit itself. Grant was also slumped over, posed at an awkward angle where he had been tossed against one of the rough rock walls, the Sin Eater still clutched in his right hand, a bloody cut glistening at his left temple.

They're not going to be any help, Rosalia realized with irritation. So what now?

Attacking the witch was no use. She'd already shrugged off both Domi's and Grant's attacks, as well as Kane's, and she'd proved herself impervious to knife and bullet while her body was cocooned inside that cascading blister of energy. Even as her mind raced, Rosalia was aware that the woman was amassing more power while both Brigid and Kane seemed to be withering, their skin becoming taut on their emaciating frames.

Which means, Rosalia realized, that it has to be now. She glanced down at the dog, her lips pulling back from her teeth. "Come on, useless," she instructed, "let's go show this witch how it's going down."

With that, Rosalia began sprinting toward the witch woman with the ragged-looking dog hurrying along at her side. Sword raised, Rosalia dashed toward the woman standing between the wild beams of energy, and Maria Halloween seemed to become abruptly aware of her, turning her head to pierce Rosalia with a fearsome look.

Casually, Maria raised her left hand in a flicking gesture and sparks of the tremendous energy that had enwrapped her body burst forth, zapping across the cave toward the hurrying form of her new foe. Still sprinting, Rosalia ducked, letting the blast of energy rocket over her head, singeing several strands of her long hair as it shot toward the far wall. Rosalia didn't bother to look at where the blast hit, but she heard it racking across the rocky wall like a lightning strike, stinging against the earth that clumped there and leaving a puff of inky-black smoke in its wake.

There was twenty feet between Rosalia and the glowing woman now, and Rosalia's slender legs kicked out and ate the space at a distance-humbling sprint.

The *bruja* raised her hand again, fingers weaving in the air as she seemed to flick another of the lightning bolts at the woman with the sword. There was no escaping it—not at this proximity—and Rosalia raised her sword to deflect it. The blast hit the sword with the force of a jackhammer, knocking Rosalia back off her feet in a rolling crouch. For a moment trails of black energy continued to play across the twenty-five-inch blade, a plume of smoke emanating from its tip.

Rosalia righted herself, her eyes widening as the glowing woman seemed to become physically bigger. Halloween's proportions became larger, more like a statue than a woman, her limbs thickening to the width of the branches of the redwoods outside her secret underground lair. At the same time, Kane and Brigid seemed to wither to little more than shades, thin shadowy things in the shape of human bodies, like a stretched photograph, an illusory thinness of body that could surely not possibly be real.

Before Rosalia could pull herself off the floor of the cave, another blast shot at her from the witch's hand, a casual flick of the fingers launching that incredible burst of power. Rosalia raised the sword to try to deflect the blast, and she instinctively closed her eyes as the bolt of energy shot its blistering path toward her. At that very second, her scruffy-looking mongrel leaped straight into the jolt of energy, taking the full impact of the blast across its flank. Rosalia heard the dog whine with pain, and when she opened her eyes she saw the hound crash to the floor, the energy from the lightning-like bolt playing across its dark fur in fizzling white streaks.

"Good dog," Rosalia encouraged as she pushed herself to her feet and began hurrying across the cavern once more, finally knowing what she must do. Behind her, the dog was whimpering as the energy of that blast pulsed through its body, and a strange double image seemed to appear, a second ghost dog expanding from the flesh of the first for a fraction of a second.

The *bruja* flicked her wrist once more as Rosalia charged, unleashing another bolt of that fearsome energy. But the dog was already on its feet, and it seemed to attract the soul-draining blast like a lightning rod. The bolt that had been meant for Rosalia forked to an angle, missing her by perhaps six inches as it grasped for the dog behind her. The dog stood there and took it, vibrating as those incredible energies played across its body. Once again, it seemed to double—and then triple as another ghost image expanded from within it.

Then Rosalia swung her *katana* blade, cutting into one of the streams of uncanny energy where it had snagged the fallen form of Kane. It was like striking rubber. Rosalia's blade hit the lightninglike streak and bounced off, propelling her backward in a staggering, three-step dance. Gritting her teeth, she jabbed at the unfathomable stream of energy with her sword again, plunging the tip into the sparking line as it formed and re-formed in jagged stripes of yellow-white. This time her blade cut the stream, and the energies diverted, racing up Rosalia's blade like a rushing river. The blast hit her with the force of a hurricane when it touched. Rosalia had her feet widespread as she felt the energy cascade down the blade and through her body, and she stood there, fighting against that exceptional force for almost three entire seconds. Then her feet slipped and, with a cry of agony, Rosalia was flung backward, hurtling up and over as she was launched ten feet into the air by the energy's savage touch.

Nearby the *bruja* gasped. "No."

Kane was lying on the ground where Rosalia had been standing moments before. Even in his delirious state, he felt the energy stop its relentless assault on his body as the woman's sword cut into its stream, diverting it for three precious seconds and relieving him of its attack. His body seemed to fill out once more, its withered muscles inflating as the stream stopped pulling out his essence.

For Rosalia, however, it felt as if she had been struck by lightning as the energy was conducted by the sword and into her hands. Her whole body screamed with fire as she sailed through the air before crashing back to the ground, the sword still sparking in her grip. Witch fire licked across the sword's shining surface, and when it had played out the blade had lost its luster, the jolt of energy turning the once-mirrored steel to the color of charcoal. Rosalia looked up as the sparking sword pulsed and shook in her hand, using all of her energy just to raise her weary head. And then she saw Kane rising as the darkness of exhaustion encroached on her vision, and she could only hope that what she had done had been enough.

WITH AN ANGRY SNARL, Kane raised himself off the ground as one of the fantastical streams of energy tried to target him again, emanating from the *bruja*'s expanding body. Kane sidestepped and the bolt blasted past him, lashing against one of the rough walls of the cavern. The *bruja* seemed now to stand fourteen feet tall, her edges blurring like some weird spirit, a vision from beyond. An expression of confusion turned to irritation as she saw Kane avoid the energy sucker that had been leeching his soul out of his frame.

Kane himself was still trying to recover from his own strange visions. He had lived four millennia in the space of two minutes, hurtling through space within a meteor, trapped as Ullikummis, the shamed Annunaki prince. With the draining fingers of energy removed, Kane began to return to himself, clinging to the last scraps of his own personality even as the fractured memories of Ullikummis played in the fields of his mind.

"Get the hell out of my head," Kane grunted, struggling to see through the miasma of visions whirling in front of his eyes.

For a brief moment Kane assessed the area as his vision popped and shook, spying Brigid's own emaciated form on the far side of the cavern and seeing the way the lightninglike chains of energy connected her to the woman who called herself Maria Halloween. Then he remembered, and then he clenched his fist and began to run, legs pumping, booted feet slapping against the packed soil of the ground as he hurried toward the fiercely glowing form of the *bruja*.

Maria Halloween turned her head to watch Kane, and it was an eerie thing to behold, like a stained-glass window come to life, multicolored rays of light bursting from her glowing form as she drained soul energy from Brigid Haight. Another streak of lightning emanated from the necklace at her breast, cutting through the air as it strove to reach for Kane's essence. Kane leaped it, bringing his fist around to strike the woman in her gut—as high as he could reach on her expanding form. There came a blinding burst of energy as Kane's fist connected, and the jewel that the woman wore at her neck let out a quiet sound like a sigh, a wisp of vapor spiraling from its apex. The *bruja* rocked back with Kane's blow, the crackling shield of energy humming all around her as it blinked off then back on again.

Kane's hand throbbed, and he felt the skin rip from his knuckles where he had struck the witch with all his might. Spots of blood bloomed across his knuckles, and at the same time something deep inside Kane swelled and something returned to him that he had been missing just seconds before.

Kane stepped back, weaving on buoyant feet like a boxer in the ring, his steel-gray eyes fixed on the spirit-like colossus in front of him. As he watched, the *bruja* seemed to shrink just a little, fourteen feet becoming twelve in height, the fierce glow surrounding her losing some of its magnificence, its heavenly luster. Kane himself seemed to grow bigger at the same time, his muscles filling out once more, the flesh swelling back over his ribs, filling the skintight material of the shadow suit.

Without pausing, Kane ran at the *bruja* again, striking her at the base of her rib cage with a left cross, a right, another left. The energy shield around her flashed and failed, and the woman known as Maria Halloween stumbled back, her body shrinking, returning to its normal proportions. Something was glowing beneath her dress, a flame sparking between her breasts where the pendant of her necklace dangled.

"You fool," Maria cried. "You've disrupted the flow, cut my link to your soul."

Spots blurring across his eyes, Kane kicked out at the woman, striking a savage blow to her gut, just below that glowing speck on her dress. The witch woman seemed to fold over the toe of Kane's boot, blurting out a gasp of breath as she tumbled backward to the cavern floor, coming to rest at the edge of the blanket concealing the parallax point. Kane commanded his Sin

Eater to his palm and watched her as she reached a hand to her breast even as the spark turned to a flame. The strange succubus gemstone was burning, its eerie procedure halted with a violent abruptness it had not been designed to endure.

The cavern shook as transtemporal energies washed through it, hurtling from the smoky glass of the gem and batting at the fragile structure of the caverns. All around Kane, the sounds of tumbling earth echoed as the place began to cave in, the fragile crack in the earth collapsing in on itself, sealing this wide bank of caverns once more out of sight of the surface dwellers.

Shuddering on the cavern floor, Maria Halloween pulled at the stone that she wore, snapping the necklace. But it was too late—her flesh seared with flames and she lay there, a pillar of fire in human form. Exhausted, all Kane could do was watch as oily black smoke poured from her body and the stench of burning flesh filled the crumbling cavern. He was an ex-Mag; it was his job to save people. Yet, at that moment, his weary essence bruised and battered, it was all he could do to stand, the torn skin of his knuckles bleeding.

All around Kane, hunks of moist earth came crashing down, sealing the last of the passageways that led into this cave, cutting it off from any further interference by man.

Within moments, Maria Halloween's body became ashes, rising and flaking away amid the oily black smoke that plumed from her flesh. The strange soul stone had been associated with vampirism before now, sucking at the essence of people until they had no will of their own. Here, too, the old myths of vampires seemed to echo, the bearer of the gem turned to ashes when the procedure to gain power failed.

And, as suddenly as it had started, it was over—the twin lances of energy that had fired from Maria's body disappeared. The energy cage that held Brigid Haight winked out of existence, and the redhead took a single half step back onto the heels of her boots, relief painting across her pale face as the flesh returned to her bones.

"Briggly?" Little Quav asked timidly. "Is the monster gone?"

Whatever it was that the witch woman had planned, Kane couldn't be sure it was actually evil. She had spoken of doing good, of employing change, even if her means of getting power—by stealing the *anam-chara* souls—seemed destructive. Perhaps it hadn't been—perhaps it had been the reason that the connected souls existed in the first place, to be funneled together and thus create a god of man.

Breathless, Kane swayed in place as he assessed everything around him. His partners were out of it, but there at last was Brigid Baptiste, standing beside Quavell's daughter. "Baptiste," Kane gasped, "I can't believe you're here. I thought I'd lost you forev—"

But before Kane could finish his exclamation, Brigid moved her body and he saw that she had released her TP-9 semiautomatic from its hip holster, shifting her body to reveal it. Kane could only watch as Brigid raised the weapon in one slender, black-gloved hand, pointing it directly at him. She had to be confused, he realized. The trip here, the attack by the *bruja*—all of it had messed up her mind; she was probably still half delirious just as he had been.

"Baptiste," Kane began softly, "it's me. It's Kane. Everything's okay now. It's okay. The good guys won."

Brigid's emerald eyes fixed on his and Kane saw them narrow infinitesimally just before she pulled the trigger of her blaster, unleashing a stream of 9 mm bullets at his chest. Kane cried out as the bullets struck him, and he staggered backward and slipped into the Chalice of Rebirth as Brigid emptied the clip in his chest.

"Didn't you get the memo, Kane?" Brigid snarled as her gun clicked on empty. "All the heroes are dead."

Kane felt himself sink into unconsciousness as the amber mists of the Chalice of Rebirth wafted around him, obscuring his vision even as Brigid Haight fired up her interphaser and made ready to depart with Little Quav at her side.

Chapter 20

"Kane, wake up."

"—is going on? Please exp—"

There were two voices in Kane's head now, and he struggled to make out which was which. After a moment he realized one—deep as rumbling thunder—was urging him to wake up, even as hands pulled at him, dragging him up. The second voice was higher and it sounded more urgent, if such was possible, as it asked if Brigid was still with them. That was Lakesh, talking over the Commtact, piping his request to all of the field team.

"I can't see," Kane muttered, the words coming loosely, half formed as if he had not quite woken up. His mouth seemed sore, not responding to his instructions, and his head felt heavy. The buzzing of the Commtact wasn't helping his temperament, either. Kane put a hand up to his ear, urging everyone to stop talking at once.

"Come on, Kane." Grant's rumbling thunder voice accompanied the sensation of being lifted. "We should get moving."

"What's going on?" Kane muttered through thick, swollen lips. He could smell burned flesh, and it made him feel suddenly hungry and nauseous at the same time.

"I don't know," Grant told his partner as he pulled

him from the Chalice of Rebirth, tendrils of amber mist playing across Kane's face and aching body. "I was out of it."

"Everyone was," Domi elaborated, her harsh voice grating on Kane's ears.

Kane felt something brush at his chest, pushing at the fabric that covered him. "You look like you took a few shots, buddy," Grant said. "I guess the shadow suit took the worst of it."

"Yeah," Kane said, nodding his heavy head. For some reason he still couldn't make his eyes open. "Everyone else okay?"

Grant didn't answer, just stood there looking at Kane's hunched form. There was something on Kane's face, a spiny protrusion that began at his left brow and wended down across his face, circling and encrusting his eye before swelling over his cheek. Whatever it was, it made Kane's mouth sneer, the left side of his top lip pulling up and away from his teeth.

"I said is everyone else okay?" Kane repeated, his words not quite forming with the placement of his lip.

"I think so," Grant began, "but we probably need to get you medical attention. You look li—"

Abruptly, Kane cut him off. "How's Baptiste?" he asked.

"I don't know," Grant admitted. "She ain't here, but the place got pretty wrecked. Rosie's checking what's left of the passageways now. We were all out of it. No one saw whether—"

"No," Kane mumbled, remembering as he spoke. "She bugged out, I saw her leave."

"Say again."

"Baptiste left," Kane explained. "Used the interphaser, took the kid with her. She was different, not thinking straight. I don't know…"

"You sure it was her?" Grant asked. The pair of them had had a few meetings with clones and doppelgangers over the years, so bumping into another was not beyond the realms of credibility.

"It was her all right," Kane rumbled. "When Maria pulled that stunt with the gem, I felt our…connection. The *anam-chara* bond. It was like a physical thing."

"Okay, man," Grant urged. "Just take it easy, we'll be out of here in a minute. Then we can get Reba—" Grant stopped, correcting himself as he recalled that the Cerberus physician was incommunicado along with most of their usual personnel. "We'll get someone to look at you," he finished lamely.

As Kane sat there on the ground, locked in his personal darkness, waiting for the team to regroup, he wondered just what had happened to Brigid Baptiste.

Standing a little way from the metal-flanged pit, Domi urged Grant over to her side with a wave of a milk-white hand. When Grant was close, Domi encouraged him to lean down so that she could whisper without Kane hearing. "What's happened to his face?" she asked.

Grant shook his head. "I don't know and I don't plan to speculate," he admitted.

"It looks like bone," Domi said, glancing across the cavern to where Kane was sitting. "Like his skull is trying to get free."

"He was in that gunk for a while," Grant reasoned, referring to the Chalice of Rebirth. "There's nanomachines in that goop, and it looks like someone's poisoned it. If Kane had a wound…" His words trailed off and he shrugged.

"You think he got infected?" Domi whispered.

"I think we'll wait for a medical opinion," was all Grant would say in reply, "and the sooner we get it, the sooner we'll know."

Domi nodded solemnly in agreement.

Three minutes later Rosalia returned, the blackened sword resheathed at her hip, the scruffy mongrel dog trotting along at her side looking none the worse for wear despite its ordeal.

One minute later, unable to climb out of the now sealed underground lair, the Cerberus team utilized the parallax point to leave via interphaser. The four of them disappeared in a burst of color as the interphaser opened up a gateway into the quantum ether, transporting them instantaneously to their intended destination.

Nobody noticed the fleck of ash drifting through the air of the cavern. Nobody saw it fall into the Chalice of Rebirth. And even if they had, they most likely would not have given it a second thought. Why should they?

BRIGID HAIGHT reappeared with the child Quavell in a fractured burst of multicolored light, arriving on the isle of Bensalem. Ullikummis stood in front of them, his magma eyes glowing faintly in the twilit darkness of his keep's throne room, trunklike arms folded across his huge chest. Brigid knew from looking at him that he had been standing just like that for hours, never bothering to move as he waited patiently beside the parallax point for her return. Beside him, two menacing stone dogs peered up from the ground, hulking animated statues with eyes like a man's.

Taking the blond girl's hand, Brigid led the way from the platform that served as a parallax point, walking her toward the stone giant who stood in the shadows of the room. The girl was scared, but Balam had taught her to remain self-possessed and so she did not cry or scream, just let out a tiny gasp as she walked closer to the monstrous rock figure, the two dog things eyeing her suspiciously.

"The child Ninlil," Brigid said, presenting Little Quav to her master.

Eight feet tall, Ullikummis stared down at the little girl who barely came up to his knee. The girl looked fearful of this looming presence in front of her yet she stood wide-eyed looking up at him, still meeting his gaze without flinching.

After a moment Ullikummis knelt in front of the girl, his body like a tumbling avalanche as he brought his head to approximately the level of hers. There, face-to-face, he studied the blond-haired girl, admiring her cerulean eyes, her feathery long hair that tumbled in wisps across her tiny shoulders. She looked nothing like he expected. Very slowly, the merest hint of a smile appeared on that rock-hewn face, making it all the more ugly and unreal in its appearance.

"Mother," Ullikummis said in a voice that sounded like two cliffs of eroded chalk finally giving up their battle with the elements and plunging into the ocean.

The girl looked up at him, fear etched on her face. She did not understand what the monster had said, could not possibly comprehend why he called her mother. In time she would learn.

Standing behind the hybrid girl, the leather-clad form of Brigid Haight smiled, too, pleased that the completion of her task had brought her master joy. She was his hand in darkness, his tool of hate, nothing more.

Gently, Ullikummis took the girl's tiny hand in his great stone mitt and together they strode across the rocky floor and off through the winding corridors of Bensalem Keep, making their way to the room that Ullikummis had set aside for the child who was his mother. "Young girl, one day you will be old," he explained as they exited the eerily characterless chamber that housed the parallax point.

Alone in the throne room, Brigid Haight listened to the thumping echo of Ullikummis's feet as he was lost to her in the shadows of the keep, reunited with his mother after four thousand years. They were two Annunaki together, Ullikummis and the child. Being reunited brought a sense of completion—they belonged together.

THE INTERPHASER brought the four-strong Cerberus field team back to the familiar gardens of Shizuka's winter retreat. Once there, Grant carried Kane back to the lodge while Domi and Rosalia followed, the dog jogging along at Rosalia's heels. The dark-haired woman was sullen, and she made it clear to Domi that she had no interest in talking as they made the short walk up to the lodge itself.

As they approached the building, Shizuka and Lakesh were waiting on the wooden balcony to greet them alongside several of Shizuka's faithful Tigers of Heaven. Domi had filed a brief report with Lakesh before they had returned, and an on-site physician named Kazuko was waiting to examine Kane the second that the field team arrived.

Lakesh himself looked concerned, but he retained a polite distance from Grant as the hulking ex-Mag was greeted by Shizuka with the briefest of hugs. Then Lakesh coughed politely and asked what had happened.

"Can't know for sure," Grant explained. "We were all out of it by the time Kane took on the wicked witch of the west. From what I can tell, he was unconscious by the time he landed himself in that previously hidden Chalice of Rebirth. What happened after that, I'm not sure but he came out looking like this."

Lakesh nodded. He saw Kane's head was masked with a bony growth that covered the left side of his face. His eye was entirely hidden beneath a bony ridge, and while his right eye could still open he had told them that he could no longer see anything.

In a quiet, well-lit room in the back of the huge lodge, Kazuko checked over Kane's condition, but the prognosis wasn't good. After a thorough examination, the doctor came out of the room and spoke to Lakesh and the others, leaving Kane himself to try to sleep.

"It is a form of ossification," the doctor explained, "and it appears to be spreading from a point somewhere close to Kane's left eye socket. I'll need to monitor its progress for a few days before I can say anything more definite than that."

"He'd been having trouble with his eyesight," Grant

confirmed irritably, "and he'd mentioned something about visions, but I didn't realize…"

Still wearing her torn dress, Domi reached up from where she sat on the wooden floor, placing her hand gently against Grant's arm. "You didn't know, Grant," she confirmed. "None of us did."

Sitting beside Grant on a soft couch, Shizuka added her own words of reassurance. "I have no doubt that you will do everything you can to help your friend, Grant," she said. "We all will."

"For now," Lakesh summarized, "all we can do is wait."

Before the elderly cyberneticist had finished, Rosalia turned from her position standing beside the door and left the room without a word, her dog trotting along obediently at her heels. The group of friends watched her go, and once she was out of earshot Domi spoke up.

"Yeesh, what's her problem?"

Grant looked thoughtfully down the corridor that Rosalia had exited by and he wondered what Kane would say. After a moment he stood, excusing himself from the group before hurrying after the dark-haired swordswoman.

"Be back in a minute," he assured them, which was probably something like what Kane would have said.

GRANT FOUND Rosalia standing by the external wall of the little herb garden, tossing a stick out onto the immaculate lawn for her dog to retrieve. The dog seemed to be enjoying itself, but Rosalia was clearly miserable.

"Everything okay?" Grant asked, immediately cursing himself for such a lack of subtlety.

Rosalia didn't look at him as she answered. "I'm fine."

Grant nodded, muttering her words back to himself under his breath. He turned back to the lodge where the door waited, still open as he had left it, leading into the main lounge of the impressive holiday home. But he didn't take a step. Instead he turned back once more and spoke to the outsider to their group without getting too close.

"Look, Rosie, I don't know why you're here. I don't think any of us really do," Grant said, "but Kane trusts you and that's plenty good enough for me. You did real good out there, saved my ass, maybe more than once. But then I probably saved yours, too—I didn't keep count. What I'm saying is, you're in this with us right now. If you're worried about Kane—that's cute. And if you're worried about what happens if Kane gets left on the bench, well, you don't need him to vouch for you no more. Okay?"

Grant watched as Rosalia's shoulders heaved up and down and then he heard the tremor in her voice as she spoke. "Stupid Magistrate men, always making speeches." To Grant, it sounded an awful lot like she was crying.

"You're welcome," Grant said as he made his way back to the lodge and his companions.

WHEN GRANT RETURNED to the lodge, he found Lakesh sitting with Domi catching up on the events that had happened around Luilekkerville. Domi was explaining about the birds that had seemed to guard the entrance to the subterranean grotto where they had ultimately encountered Maria Halloween and Brigid Baptiste.

"They sound an awful lot like the rocs of Arabic lore," Lakesh observed.

"It's what Rosie said, too," Grant chipped in as he took a seat opposite the conversing couple. "They seemed to be acting as guards and we encountered some other weird animals down there, too, crocodiles the size of dinosaurs. Any ideas where all this shit originated?"

"With a Chalice of Rebirth hidden in the cavern you encountered," Lakesh mused, "it's likely that its nanotech was being employed to enhance the genetic makeup of local fauna, maybe alter it, as well."

"I looked in the pit before we left," Grant said. "It wasn't just amber like the one that got used on Shizuka. There was other stuff in there, streaks of red and green and I don't know what else."

Lakesh nodded. "Your witch woman sounds like she may have had some esoteric knowledge of such things," he speculated. "A lot of what has been characterized as arcane knowledge over the centuries is in fact a rudimentary understanding—or misunderstanding—of the artifacts left by the Annunaki and the Tuatha de Danaan. If this woman had amassed knowledge of the supernatural arts over time, it's likely she came upon the chalice with some idea of how it functioned."

"You mean, she corrupted it," Domi said.

"Perhaps," Lakesh reasoned with infinite diplomacy, "or perhaps she discovered another use for it. The chalice is basically a medical repair facility, after all, and a lot of what we comprehend as disease is in fact the body's overproduction or overreaction to disease. Mucus, for example, is a necessary lubricant for the human body, yet once it becomes overproduced it can be irritating and even exacerbate a precondition, as in the case of the asthmatic.

"Which, I'm afraid, brings us to Kane's current dilemma," Lakesh continued heavily.

As Lakesh spoke, Rosalia reappeared at the doorway, her head held low as she slipped unobtrusively into the room. Grant nodded to her once in acknowledgment.

"One possibility is that, having fallen into the doctored Chalice of Rebirth," Lakesh outlined, "Kane's biology has been manipulated to some degree."

"He was complaining of the eye problem when we arrived," Grant reminded them.

"In which case, it's fair to say that the rejuvenation pit may have exacerbated that preexisting condition," Lakesh proposed. "Think of when you have an eye irritation, how the eye will weep and that you may awaken with hard sleep crusting the lashes. Though extreme, Kane's current reaction may be something similar."

When no one said anything more to that, Rosalia spoke up, changing the subject.

"What about the girl?" she asked. "What was her name, Quav?"

Lakesh's eyebrows raised in surprise. "Yes, you did mention Quavell. I'd quite forgotten in all the…excitement," he finished, hitting the last word apologetically.

"She was with Brigid," Domi elaborated. "Appeared at the same time via interphaser."

"And presumably disappeared the same way," Grant rumbled.

"But what would Brigid want with Little Quav,"

Domi pondered, "and why would Balam let her leave Agartha?"

"And why did she run?" Grant added.

The group went silent as those questions hung heavily in the air. There were no easy answers; it seemed to be such a riddle and the reappearance and subsequent disappearance of Brigid was perplexing.

"Perhaps he didn't," Grant suggested quietly. "Let her leave Agartha, I mean," he added when he realized everyone was looking at him, waiting for him to explain. "Maybe Brigid took her."

"But Little Quav's only value is in her genetic heritage," Lakesh said incredulously. "There's no possible reason for Brigid to remove her from Agartha."

"What's her heritage?" Rosalia asked, unaware of the full history the Cerberus people had with the infant.

"She's a hybrid," Lakesh explained, "which means she houses the genetic capabilities to evolve into an Annunaki—in her case, a specific member of the royal family called Ninlil, in fact. But for her to evolve requires an external trigger, and that trigger—so far as we know—can only come from a sentient spaceship called *Tiamat.*"

"Which is where?" Rosalia asked.

"Destroyed," Grant and Domi said in unison.

Rosalia thought about this for a moment before she spoke, her outsider's perspective allowing her to see and question things the Cerberus rebels hadn't perhaps considered. "If that's true," she said, "then why was the girl in hiding?"

"Because," Grant began, "the Annunaki have...a nasty habit of coming back to life."

"Then you've answered your own question," Rosalia said with a patronizing smile. After a moment she turned and made her way from the room, heading for the bathrooms of the winter retreat for a much needed shower.

"What did she mean by that?" Domi asked.

Lakesh spoke hesitantly, still working through the implications. "To us, Quav is just a little girl," he said, "but if *Tiamat* were still alive then that would change the whole game board. It's possible that the genetic download could be engaged and she might be turned into Ninlil, and thus ascend to her rightful place in the Annunaki pantheon."

"Is Ninlil a nasty—?" Domi stopped herself, snapping her fingers as if remembering. "Wait, of course she is. She's Annunaki, right?"

"But what possible benefit would that be to Brigid?" Grant asked.

"To Brigid Baptiste?" Lakesh mused. "None. And that's why it's so puzzling."

"I have another puzzle to add to the list," Domi said after a moment. "The people in Luilekkerville were celebrating the coming of Ullikummis like he was some great savior. They were talking about how love was the future, and how its strength was the strength of a rock. They were worshipping Ullikummis, but they didn't need the obedience stones anymore—these people were choosing the stone thing, like they really believed it. It was kinda scary."

Lakesh pondered this for a few seconds, considering the possibility of a growing congregation who would worship and follow Ullikummis, royal scion of the Annunaki.

"If Ullikummis no longer needs to recruit people by force, then there's no telling how large his potential army might become," Lakesh said, unable to hide the concern from his voice. "And if that *is* the case, we may very soon find the whole world turned against us."

Grant laughed cynically. "Yeah, what else is new."

"I suppose the real question," Lakesh declared, "is just how many people have now been converted to Ullikummis's church? There's no way of knowing, is there?"

* * * * *

The Executioner

Don Pendleton's

BLIND JUSTICE

**The landmark 400th episode of
The Executioner, starring Mack Bolan!**

An undercover Seattle cop is in hot water after
discovering that a U.S. senator and a Russian mob
boss are in business together. But with his fellow
officers on the senator's payroll, the detective has
no one to trust and nowhere to hide—until he runs
into Mack Bolan.

Available March wherever books are sold.

JAMES AXLER

DEATH LANDS®

Hell Road Warriors

Humanity's shattering battle for survival continues.

Canada hides a trove of Cold War-era secret government installations known as Diefenbunkers, filled with caches of weapons, wags and food. Ryan Cawdor and his companions agree to head west to retrieve four portable nuclear reactors — enough power to light up a ville for years. But they have death on their tail....

Available March wherever books are sold.